LOVE IS A FOUR LETTER WORD

CLAIRE CALMAN

Boldwood

This edition published in Great Britain in 2020 by Boldwood Books Ltd.

Copyright © Claire Calman, 2000

Cover Design by Hannah Lee

Cover photography: Shutterstock

A CIP catalogue record for this book is available from the British Library.

Paperback ISBN 978-1-80048-589-1

Large Print ISBN 978-1-80048-588-4

Ebook ISBN 978-1-80048-586-0

Kindle ISBN 978-1-80048-587-7

Audio CD ISBN 978-1-80048-866-3

MP3 CD ISBN 978-1-80048-865-6

Digital audio download ISBN 978-1-80048-862-5

Boldwood Books Ltd
23 Bowerdean Street
London SW6 3TN
www.boldwoodbooks.com

For my sister Stephanie, who told me to Get On With It

PROLOGUE

She sees herself fall in slow motion, the toe of her shoe catching on the edge of the paving-stone, her arm reaching out in front of her, her hand a pale shape like a leaf against a dark sky. The pavement swims towards her, its cracks the streets of a city seen from a skyscraper, the texture of the concrete slabs suddenly sharply in focus.

It is not a bad fall: a swelling on her left knee destined to become an outsize bramble-stain bruise, a stinging graze on the heel of her hand, a buggered pair of decent tights. Back at home, Bella balances half a bag of frozen broad beans on the knee and sips at a glass of Shiraz. She tells herself it is not a bad fall, but when she wakes the next morning it is as if a switch has been thrown, draining off all her energy in the night. She leans against the kitchen worktop to drink her coffee, not daring to sit down because she knows she will never get up again.

Overnight, London seems to have become a grotesque parody of a metropolis, no longer bustling and stimulating but loud and abrasive. Litter flies up from the gutters. Grit pricks her eyes. She feels fragile, a rabbit caught in the target-beam of headlights. Buses loom out of nowhere, bearing down on her. Cyclists swerve to avoid her, bellowing abuse. She tenses each muscle in her body when she crosses the road, imagines she can hear the thud-thudding of her heart. When someone bumps into her in the street, she thinks she will splinter into tiny fragments. In her mind, she sees her body shatter and the pieces shower through the air like the explosion of a firework, tinkling like glass as each one strikes the pavement. She imagines them coming to sweep her up so they could painstakingly reassemble her, but shards of her are left behind, unnoticed in the gutter, hidden by a litter bin or a lamp-post.

Her doctor is unsympathetic, sighing through his nostrils as she answers his questions. Months of overworking, he says. Prolonged stress. What else did she expect? Did she want to have a serious collapse? If so, she was certainly going the right way about it. No tablets, he says, no prescription. Time off. Rest. Rethink your life. That's it? she asks. That's it.

Her boss is unsurprised.

'You're no use to me half-dead,' he says. 'Sod off to the Caribbean for a month. Drink Mai-Tais till dawn and shag some waiters.'

The Caribbean? She is so exhausted she'd be lucky to make it down the road to the travel agent. Perhaps they could administer her Mai-Tais via a drip.

Visiting her good friends Viv and Nick in the Kentish city where they now live, she wanders at convalescent pace through the web of narrow streets, past lopsided houses and ancient flint walls. She focuses on one task at a time, as if she were a stroke victim learning afresh each skill she had previously taken for granted. Then, meandering down a quiet side street near the river, she sees the For Sale board.

Compared with the London flat she had rented with Patrick, no. 31 is a delight. Sunny. Spacious. With a proper garden rather than a sad, overshadowed strip of concrete. Yes, says Viv, a fresh start is just what Bella needs. Plenty of companies would jump at the chance to have someone with her experience.

She seems to enter a trance then, dealing with the solicitor, the building society. Writing job applications. Forms, paperwork become a welcome distraction, tangible things to focus on – things she can solve. You take a pen, fill in the spaces in neat block capitals. The questions are straightforward: Name. Address. Bank Details. Current Salary. You do it all properly and you get the result you were aiming for. It feels like magic.

She moves smoothly through the weeks on automatic pilot, gliding through her notice period at work, her smile efficiently in place, her projects on schedule. Now that she knows she is leaving, she cuts down on her hours, and fills her evening with paperwork and planning, even relishing each hitch and setback – the vendor's pedantry about the garden shed, the surveyor's discovery of damp – as something she can get her teeth into.

In her neat ring-binder, sectioned with coloured card dividers, she can find any particular piece of paper in an instant. The rings click closed with a satisfying clunk, containing her, keeping her life in order. She transfers her accounts, her doctor, her dentist, sends out exquisitely designed change-of-address cards. This is easy: making phone calls, folding A4 letters into three and sliding them into envelopes, measuring for curtains. And it fills her head. She needs it to hold her, as if each stage of Buying the House is a sharp staple grasping together the sections of an ancient cracked plate.

1

Now that she was here, this didn't seem like quite such a brilliant idea. Around her, on all sides stretched a cubist landscape of cardboard boxes. The removal men had thoughtfully set them down in such a way as to make traversing the room an epic expedition, necessitating the use of ropes, crampons and teams of huskies. And the heating had decided not to work. Of course. No doubt the vendor had extracted some vital organ from the boiler the moment they had exchanged contracts. He had taken the art of pettiness to new heights – or was it depths? – arguing over every fitting and fixture, frequently phoning Bella, his manner swinging between smarmy and covertly aggressive. He was sure she would like to buy his wrought-iron wall lights; they were practically new. No, she said, she wouldn't. The built-in shelves? She had assumed they were, well, built-in. What about the curtain tracks? The stair carpet? It still had plenty of wear in it, he insisted, hanging on in there like a dog unwilling to relinquish a bone. 'Mmm,' she agreed non-committally, deciding its durability was a disadvantage unless you wanted to design your decor around a theme of khaki ripple. He

was obviously attached to it, she pointed out, clearly he must take it
with him.

Now, sitting on the stairs, trying not to catch her jeans on the
exposed gripper strip, she stretched out one foot to flip open the lid
of the nearest box. Loo brush, bubble-wrapped mirror, squeaky
rubber crocodile. Oh-oh. She checked the label on the side: BTH.
Marvellous. That was supposed to be upstairs. In the bth. How
much clearer could she have made it? Evidently, she should have
written BOX FOR BATHROOM (THAT MEANS UPSTAIRS – THE
ROOM WITH THE BATH IN IT). Something else to add to The
List: lugging downstairs boxes upstairs and upstairs boxes
downstairs.

Her gaze fell on the puckered and peeling paintwork above the
skirting board. The only house in the street with psoriasis. The
damp. That ought to be top of the list – certainly above getting the
sash cords fixed or redecorating the bathroom or Polyfillaing the
crack in the study or painting a mural on the end wall of the garden
or... In her mind, The List stretched out before her, a rippling paper
path, unrolling itself to infinity.

There was a banging on the front door.

'Why didn't you use the bell, you old bag?'

'I did. It obviously doesn't work, slag-face.' Viv gave Bella a hug
and pushed a gold cardboard box into her hands.

'Just what I need. A cardboard box. I was running dangerously
low on them. How on earth did you guess?'

'It's cakes. Emergency rations. My God – are all the rooms as full
as this?' Viv waggled her head in disbelief, sending her precariously
pinned carroty hair lurching from side to side.

'I seem to have more stuff than I thought.' Bella shrugged.
'What's in them all?'

'I don't know. Books. Paints. Kitchen things. Families of refugees. You know, stuff.'

Viv opened a nearby box. 'Old exhibition catalogues?'

'I've been meaning to go through them and weed out the ones I don't want, but I haven't got around to it yet.'

'Is that the Kreuzer family motto: Dulce et decorum est procrastinati...?'

'Thank you for those few charming words. Make yourself useful, can't you? Help me look for the kettle. It's in a box marked KTCH, which stands for kitchen not kitsch before you make any smart-arse comments – it's probably up in the BTH.'

* * *

That first night in her new home, Bella left a light on as she always did – she'd had to dash out to the late-night corner shop to buy light bulbs because the vendor had removed every single one of them. She lay awake, looking at the slit of light under the bedroom door. *I ought to be feeling excited*, she told herself. *New house. New job. New city. I mustn't be so negative. So what if I've only got one week to sort out the house before I start at Scotton Design? So the house needs a few things seeing to? That's why it was so reasonable.* A counter voice cut in: *Are you completely clueless? As if you didn't have enough on your plate without turning your entire life upside down. Now you'll be living in mouldy chaos for ever and you don't even know anyone here except for Viv and Nick and you can't expect to see them all the time. They've got each other. They don't need you.*

As her eyelids drooped, she thought of Patrick. If he'd been here with her now, what would he be doing? *Snoring, probably*, she reminded herself sharply. He'd have liked the house, she decided, yawning and snuggling down under the duvet. That was the bugger about not having a chap around the place. He would have got the damp sorted. And the boxes. No, she thought, he wouldn't: Patrick would have stepped over the boxes, saying, 'We really must sort these out.' But at least he would have rubbed her cold feet to warm them up.

Bella bit her lip. *Enough with the self-pity, OK?* She considered the plus points: lovely house of her very own, with loads of potential especially now Mr Petty had stripped it of his beloved wall lights and nauseating carpets; near Viv so her phone bill would plummet because they wouldn't have to have their epic long-distance calls any more; no longer having to hold her breath every time her colleague Val (known as Valitosis) came within exhalation range; interesting new job that should be less stressful. Yes, she comforted herself, less stress, that was the main thing. No more having her face stuffed into someone else's armpit on the tube. No more spending a fortune on taxis to get home safely late at night. No more dingy flat where she had to have the lights on even in the daytime. No more thoughts of Patrick confronting her every time she opened the front door to a flatful of silence. She made herself do her Pollyanna voice – Golly gosh, wasn't she just the luckiest girl in the whole wide world, a fresh start. Gee, it sure was exciting. She could hardly wait.

2

Right. Pens, briefcase. Shoes polished. Lipstick. Hair. Oh, bollocks. It wasn't supposed to do that. It made her look like a sheepdog that had been lolloping through the undergrowth. She stuck out her tongue and panted to complete the effect. Perhaps her hair would be better pinned up? She scooped it up off her neck and made what she hoped was an elegant face in the mirror. Tremendous – now she resembled a coiffured poodle. She had a hat somewhere. Out There, in the Box Zone, there was definitely a fetching little item of headgear. The question was: which box? She kicked the nearest one as if it might make a hat-containing-type noise. A look at her watch. Now was not the time to start hunting for hats. And what would she do with it anyway? She could hardly keep it on all day. Perhaps she could claim to be Muslim. Or having chemotherapy. She stood at the kitchen sink and drank a glass of water to settle her stomach. Good grief, this was worse than going on a date or preparing for her first day at school. You're thirty-three for God's sake, she told herself. They're not going to pick on you or try to nick your pencil case.

* * *

Mummy stands talking to Mr Bowndes, the headmaster. She lays a hand on his arm and tilts her head back as she laughs. Bella looks down at her own feet, at her new shoes. They are navy blue with shiny silver buckles and straps that are still too stiff to do up herself. It is September but she is wearing pristine white ankle socks with neat blue anchors around the cuffs. The other girls, she sees, have knee-length grey socks. Autumn socks.

Through her new blue felt hat she feels a pat on her head. She looks up. 'So nice to see a pupil properly dressed with the correct school hat,' says Mr Bowndes, leaning towards Mummy, 'So few parents bother now.'

He laughs as if he is making a joke, but Bella supposes it must be a grown-up joke because she does not know what is funny.

'But it's so *charming,* I think, no?' Mummy does that thing with her voice, almost as if she is going to start singing, and taps the brim of Bella's hat with one long finger.

Standing still in her hat, Bella imagines she is a navy blue mushroom. She wishes she were in the woods, her feet sunk in velvet moss, her toenails growing, stretching, becoming roots in the earth. Rabbits would stop and talk to her and tickle her with their noses. She would listen to the leaves as they rustled in the wind.

Mr Bowndes waves bye-bye to her mother then deposits Bella with an older girl who shepherds her to the correct classroom.

She is the only one wearing a hat.

* * *

It took her longer to find Scotton Design than she had expected. This was probably because she was coming at it from the other way round, she decided. Still, there seemed to be a Brigadoon-like quality to the place. Surely it had been down that turning just past the shoe shop? Hang on a tick – last time, she'd come from the station, so that meant she should have turned left back there, not right. Or did it? She stood still for a moment, trying to ignore the flutter of panic rising in her stomach. A passer-by sighed loudly as he detoured around her, impatient at yet another gawping tourist blocking the pavement. The tower of the cathedral loomed large to her left – ah-hah, cathedral on left, so – yes, past greasy chip shop and Waterstone's.

Renewing old London habits, she veered automatically into a café as she neared the office, to pick up a cappuccino and a Danish. Excess froth splurged out of the steam hole in the lid, sidling lava-like towards her fingers.

She was still licking her fingers as she entered the reception area to be greeted by her new boss.

'Bella! You're here! Great!' Seline checked her watch. 'New client meeting at 2! But I'm out most of the morning so I'll have to brief you in two mins! OK!'

'Fine!' Bella lifted her voice, attempting to interject exclamation marks to match Seline's tone. Had she really been like this at her two interviews? 'Of course!' She looked around for somewhere to set down her cascading coffee. Tomorrow, she'd be sure to get herself a quadruple espresso so she could boost her energy levels and not sound like the dormouse from *Alice in Wonderland* by comparison.

'Gail! Do the honours, will you!'

'Here – let me take those.' Gail disentangled Bella from her cup, her coat, her briefcase. 'Pay no attention to Seline. She's just trying to impress 'cause you're t' swanky art director from t' big city. There's the loo, by the way – kitchen – coffee-maker – tea bags in there. Now come and meet the other inmates...'

* * *

'Shall we go to the tapas place again?' said Viv on the phone the next day. 'But I always go there – is it too pathetic?'

'Why spend ages traipsing around town hunting for somewhere new just to prove you're an exciting, adventurous person who doesn't always go to the same two restaurants when you already know that you aren't adventurous and they are clearly the two best places to go? Count yourself lucky you've not got much choice.'

'Neither have you. You live here too now, remember?'

'Yes, but I've retained some semblance of urban sophistication, whereas you probably think focaccia is a Romanian folk-dance.'

For now at least, Bella genuinely preferred this provincial paucity of choice. In London, she had felt like a hero from Greek legend faced with an impossible dilemma: Patrick used to narrow it down in stages – first, by continent, then country. 'Right, Europe. Italian, French, Greek?' Then to the quest for the elusive Holy Trinity of decent food, friendly service and good atmosphere, juggling combinations until it was almost too late to be worth going. 'The Conca d'Oro has that nice waitress but the veg was soggy last time.'

'Le Beaujolais? Good chips but can you handle the look of condescending superiority when you ask for vinegar?'

* * *

'Sorry, sorry, sorry.' Viv swept into the tapas bar twenty minutes late. 'There was a complete *crisis* at work. The entire network crashed because some total arsehole plugged in a hair-dryer and overloaded the electrics.' Viv loved a good crisis. They ordered a couple of beers, and debated over whether the *pinchos morunos* or the *pollo al ajillo* was a better bet.

'What do you think?' Viv indicated the waiter with her eyebrows. 'Bit tasty?'

Bella wrinkled her nose.

'You're *so* fussy. I thought you liked Latin men?'

'He's probably from Bromley,' Bella said. 'I know, I know. I'll never get anyone at this rate. You sound just like my mother.'

'Did I say that? Of course you'll find someone else. No need to panic – not for ages and ages.'

'What's that?' Bella cocked her head as if listening for something. 'What?'

'Tick. Tick. My biological clock. Surely you can hear it? My mother can hear it over fifty miles away apparently. I don't care. I've decided not to worry about having sprogs. I'm just going to get some on time-share for two weeks a year.'

'How are the parents anyway?' Viv said, speaking through the lime wedge that she had decorked from her beer bottle and clamped between her lips like a comic mouth. 'Have they been to view the new Kreuzer estate yet?'

'Fending them off as long as possible. *Alessandra* asked after you, as always, last time we spoke.' Bella coloured her voice with theatrical timbre as she said her mother's name. 'I can just see her peering at the damp – "Oh is that a *deliberate* paint effect, Bella darling?"'

'What you need,' said Viv, 'is an action plan. To meet men.'

'I never turn down invitations, no matter how dull they sound.' Thanks,' said Viv. 'That's the last time I ask you out.'

'Not you, stupid.' Bella took a swig of her beer straight from the bottle. 'I told you, I'm not bothered. I like being on my own.'

'Liar.'

'Pig. I do. Why shouldn't I? Just because you've found Mr Perfect, you think anyone single must be some pathetic half-person.'

Viv shook her head.

'Even Nick's mum would hardly describe him as perfect. What about the new job? What's the official rating?' A vestige from when they used to hunt in a pack. The other two, Kath and Sinead, had long since defected by committing the cardinal sin: getting married. And since Viv had been living with Nick, Bella was the sole remaining singleton.

'0.5. Two married, one gay, and one too wet to risk leaving in the same room as a packet of crackers.'

'Not even a whiff of a man lately?'

'I can't even remember what one looks like. They're the ones with the stubble and the big egos, right? I went out a couple of times with that account exec. from the ad agency, Tim, remember? But he was deathly. Wittered on about his shares portfolio and what I should be buying and selling. Bleugh. I'm better off without. I hate all that couply stuff anyway.'

'Which stuff?'

'You know. All that having joint opinions about everything: "*We* think this and *we* do that. *We* consider *Citizen Kane* to be overrated and *we* prefer Szechuan cuisine to Cantonese..." Their personalities go all amoebaed into one like a matching pen and pencil set.'

'That's such crap. We're not like that.'

'See? *We're* not...? Whatever happened to *I*?'

'Anyway.' Viv sighed and signalled to the waiter for another two beers. 'There's lots of good bits: love, companionship, sex for a start.'

'Sex? What's that? Is that the thing that happens somewhere between the first snog and the slamming of the front door? Ah, yes, I had some of that once...'

'So, have you not—' Viv nodded euphemistically, 'since—?'

'No. No-one since Patrick. I have been designated a shag-free zone. It's official.'

No-one since Patrick. She could remember the last time. It was Christmas. Boxing Day. They'd just got back to the flat after a slow and drizzly drive home from visiting his parents in Norfolk.

* * *

The flat is cold and unwelcoming, the fridge pathetically unChristmassy, bare except for a half-used tube of tomato purée, a sad lemon and two bottles of wine.

'I think I'll slope off to bed,' she says, half-suppressing a yawn. 'So tired!'

'Good idea. I'll come too.'

She undresses slowly, pulling off her things distractedly, tugging her still-buttoned cuffs over her hands because she can't be bothered to undo them. Reaches for her big black T-shirt under her pillow, her fluffy bedsocks. Pads through to the bathroom to brush her teeth.

'You reading tonight?' asks Patrick.

Her Christmas books are still in a carrier bag in the hall. She shakes her head. A click as he switches off the light.

She feels his hand snake over her side, under her T-shirt, cupping her tummy from behind.

'You're nice and warm.'

She turns over to kiss him goodnight. ''Night,' she says.

She feels his tongue push tentatively between her lips; starts to murmur that she's really too sleepy, it's been a long day. He strokes her hair, speaks softly, telling her he loves her, how soft her skin feels, how sexy she is.

Her body starts to respond automatically to his touch, his hand moving between her thighs; she feels herself growing wet, hears his low sigh as his fingers find her.

* * *

Boxing Day, the year before the one just gone, she remembered. That's when it was.

'Now he's rather nice. Over there – don't look.' Viv's voice shifted to a stage whisper.

'Fine. I'm not looking.'

'No. Look now, quick.'

Bella craned her head round to see the unwitting quarry, pretending to be looking at the Spanish poster advertising a bull-fight on the wall above. Her voice dropped to a whisper.

'Viv, he's *with* someone. See that other person at the same table with the earrings and the polka-dot blouse. She didn't come as a side order with the meal, you know. Here's some bread and a woman for the evening.'

Viv waved her away dismissively.

'She could be his cousin, come for a visit.'

'She could be the Dalai Lama in disguise, but let's look at the most likely option first, shall we? Two people: one male, one female, in a restaurant, in the evening. Sounds suspiciously like a couple having a relationship to me. You ought to know. That's what normal people do. I read it in one of the Sunday supplements.'

* * *

They walked as far as the cathedral together before their routes took them separate ways. How stunning it was lit up at night – and not a tourist in sight to appreciate it. By day, it was a magnet for Japanese groups following their tour guide bearing a rolled umbrella aloft like a drum majorette, and troupes of French school-children sporting identical blue caps and matching plastic pouches round their necks advertising: 'My passport and all my money. Steal me.'

Bella walked across the bridge. The river glinted darkly below. A few boats bobbed gently, clunking woodenly against each other. It looked mysterious and exciting, the kind of night when your partner might turn to you and say, 'Let's go to Rome for the weekend – now!' Did anyone really have a relationship like that? Viv frequently complained that she and Nick never managed to get away. And even when Bella had been with someone, they had never done spontaneous things like jetting off to the Continent on the spur of the moment or having sex on the kitchen floor or in the bath. Once, in a fit of horniness, she and Sean, her boyfriend before Patrick, had tugged down each other's jeans and attempted to do it on the stairs. But the jeans were in the way and there seemed to be far too many knees involved in the proceedings, and after two minutes the step digging into her lower back was all she could think about. They'd had to stop and trip upstairs to his bedroom, their legs pinioned by their half-mast jeans, by which time much of their fiery passion had fizzled into a damp squib.

It was just one of those pointless ideas they use to fill up the pages of women's magazines: 'Love-life lost its magic? Spice it up: initiate sex at unexpected moments and in surprising places.' But they were always special magazine-world clichés about romance and sex, stuff like 'Tuck little love notes into your partner's pockets for him to discover during the day' and 'Surprise your man by whispering to him that you're not wearing any panties when you're out together.' He'd just think you were going prematurely senile. What if you told him while you were tootling around Tesco's hunting for decent olives? That would certainly be a surprise. Would he really be so overcome with excitement that he'd lean you back over the long-life milk? Or take you over a freezer filled with coffee Vien-nettas and Arctic Rolls? Wouldn't that be awfully cold on your bottom? Would other shoppers ignore you – how English – and perhaps try to reach past your thigh, saying, 'Excuse me, dear, could I just get to the mandarin cheesecake? See, I've my sister-in-law coming at the weekend.'

A young couple wove towards her, stopping every few feet to kiss, veering erratically in their path like drunken crabs; an older pair, in their fifties she guessed, passed by holding hands. When she was first with Patrick, she had usually felt glad at the sight of other couples laughing and kissing and canoodling. There seemed to be a secret bond between them all. Sometimes, four pairs of eyes would meet and smile: 'We know how good life is, don't we?'

Now, it just made Bella depressed. God, how smug couples were. If she were ever stupid enough to be in a couple again – that sounded dreadful: in a couple, like *in* prison, in detention, *in* a mess – she would shun smugness. How can you be so ungenerous about other people's happiness? she reproached herself. She lengthened her stride and resolved to be more positive. Things were fine. Time for herself so she could concentrate on her house. She could slump about all weekend in slobby clothes. Go out with lots of different men. No need to keep tidying the towels because he couldn't grasp the concept of folding. No need to buy that ridiculous, expensive, three-fruit marmalade just because he liked it.

But I grew to like that marmalade too, she reminded herself. And I don't seem to be going out with lots of men, do I? That was true, she admitted. But she could if she wanted to; it was the prin-ciple that mattered.

* * *

Lying in bed that night, Bella thought about Viv and Nick. Strange how seamlessly Viv had gone from being Viv to being Viv and Nick, as if he had always been there. He was unmistakably a fixture, built in to Viv's life, and Viv to his. Wouldn't be Bella's choice, of course. Hair had evidently been on strict rations when Nick reached the head of the queue. He had soft, malleable features that looked as if you could squish them out of position and they might stay that way, like plasticine. And his devotion to his car, a pale blue Karmann Ghia, was a bit sad, especially since it was overfond of the hard shoulder, tending to break down on any journey over twenty miles. Still, he and Viv obviously loved each other to pieces. She could certainly think of worse matches. Her own parents for a start, her father so mild, so eager to please, her mother... well, at least she wasn't like her.

Perhaps Viv was at that same moment thinking about Bella. Was she lying there in bed, snuggled up to Nick, saying to him: 'Poor Bella seems to have thrown in the towel. No sex for more than a year. Probably never find anyone half as nice as Patrick again. Still, should be over him by now.'

Bella could hear it cycling round and round in her head. *Should be over him by now, should be over him by now...*

Beneath the two words *'YOGHURT – IDEAS??'* on her notepad, a sketch of Bella's new boss was taking shape nicely. The gap between her neck and her shirt collar, the glasses propped on top of her head apparently watching the ceiling. As if it were a thing apart, Bella watched the line of her pencil recreate the angle where Seline's chin jutted forward in eagerness, a chicken heading for corn.

'Bella?' Seline raised her eyebrows at her.

Bella clunked her coffee mug down on top of the sketch and tried to look thoughtful, as if weighing up all the various options before giving her opinion. Could they possibly still be talking about the yoghurt campaign or had they moved on to the corporate design deal for the country-house hotel? She felt like a schoolkid, about to be told off for not paying attention. *Bella Kreuzer! Are you daydreaming again?*

'Erm...' she volunteered, trying to peer sideways at Anthony's pad to read the note he was scribbling for her.

'Lifestyle Yoghurt?' Seline prompted. 'Any more thoughts on the redesign? The focus groups research suggests it looks too healthy. The client wants a new look.'

'Yes, I've been thinking.' Bella nodded wisely, every inch the creative director, keen to consider yoghurt-carton design very seriously indeed. 'I certainly think we could strengthen the idea that these yoghurts are fun and sensual, too. The customer – consumer – wants to feel that she can be healthy yet self-indulgent and just a bit sinful at the same time. I'll do some roughs tomorrow, with a sexier typeface.'

'Great!' Seline clicked her pen against her teeth, pleased. 'Anyone else?'

The inside of Bella's lower lip was sore where she had been biting it. She had only been in the job for a fortnight and already she was finding it hard to keep a straight face; it was as bad as when she'd been in advertising or women's magazines. How was she supposed to maintain a sensible, grown-up expression when people started talking about yoghurt or detergent or a new paint range as if it were a cure for cancer or a way to bring about world peace?

Seline, who ran Scotton Design (or Scrotum Design as Anthony liked to call it), was in many respects a perfectly sane human being and, as she frequently claimed, 'as fond of a joke as the next person' – which would be true if the next person were also a stranger to the concept of irony. But she often acted as if the sky would fall in if the lettering on a packet of panty-liners didn't convey dryness, freshness, a carefree attitude, a healthy sex life, and a busy, affluent lifestyle. And that was just the lettering. Who needed panty-liners anyway? That's what knickers were for. Soon they'd be marketing liners to keep your panty-liners fresh and dry.

Bella told herself she shouldn't knock it. On a good day, she prided herself on her ability to know exactly which typeface looked more carefree than any other. Besides, it kept her off the streets, and someone had to pay for all that damp treatment – and the extractor fan, and replacing those two sash-cords, and the buggery doorbell, and she could do with a freezer, too... On cue, The List of Things to be Done appeared in her head, winding itself around her, binding her like an Egyptian mummy. She closed her eyes at the thought and comforted herself with the knowledge that she could go and see Viv soon if she could escape without Seline heading her off at the pass.

* * *

'Bella! What a surprise.' Nick came into the kitchen and started filling the kettle. 'It seems like only yesterday that we saw you. Ah. It *was* yesterday. So, how've you been in the last twenty-four hours?'

'I'm going, I'm going. It's her fault. She made me come.' Bella pointed at Viv.

'I did. It was me.' Viv held Nick around his waist. 'But she's doing it for you. She's showing me how to make her posh fish pie so I can do it for your parents at the weekend.'

'Correction. I am in fact making the fish pie for the freezer while Viv stands there and nods and says "Oh, I think I see. Show me how to peel just one more potato and then I'll have a go".'

'Cup of tea, anyone? No? You found the wine then?' Nick topped up their glasses.

'Then you take the olives...'

Nick's hand shot out and grabbed one.

'And you give them to Nick because Dad doesn't like them.'

'...And lay them on one side to pass to Nick.'

Nick went and stretched out on the sofa.

'I'm out of earshot now if you two want to talk about men and sex and girlie stuff.'

'Shoes, Nick!' called Viv from the kitchen.

There was a discreet rustling, as of the sound of a newspaper being tucked under feet.

'Nick, imagine you're a proper man for a minute.'

'Cheers, Bella.'

'Oh, shush. You know what I mean. Viv says I should ask you how to attract a bloke.'

'Since when did you start taking Viv's advice? I didn't think you wanted one.'

'That's just what I said. Viv doesn't believe me. I wouldn't mind some sex though before I forget how to do it.'

Viv joined in.

'Come on. She's lovely. She should have queues of chaps banging on her door.'

'No. People always say they want your honest advice and then they get pissed off with you.'

'I promise not to, Nick. Scout's honour.' Bella held up her hand in a three-fingered salute.

'When were you ever a scout?' hissed Viv. Bella waved her away.

He shook his head and kept on reading a magazine while he nibbled gerbil-like on a mint Matchmaker.

Viv made little kissing noises at him. Bella joined in on the other side.

Nick sighed.

'At your own risk then. Of course, it's only my opinion and I realize I'm not a *proper* man or anything, but if you really just want a fling, then get your legs out, woman. Wear a short skirt and laugh at our jokes. That should do it.'

'Is that the best you can do?' Viv flicked his magazine.

'What? What? I've read this bloody sentence twelve times now. Kindly bugger off.' He rested his magazine over his face.

'Nick, we promise to bugger off in a minute.' Bella slowly lifted one corner of his magazine-tent and peered underneath. 'And we'll make you a coffee and be sure to laugh at your jokes – when you make one – but do I, you know, look all right?'

'Jeez. What are you like? As I said, skirts are good. Aside from that –' Nick started counting off on his fingers '—one, you wear too many dark things. It's depressing. Two, do something about your hair – it's great but half the time no-one can see your face, which seems a bit of a waste. Can't you pin it back or up or something? Three, you want to burn that terrible jacket. Don't you own anything else? It's miles too big – you look like you're hoping no-one will notice you.'

'Nick!' Viv warned.

'What? What? What have I done now?'

'Nothing. It's fine.' Bella reached across him for a Matchmaker. 'It's Patrick's.'

'Oh. Sorry.'

''s no biggie. Carry on.'

'Plus you could try smiling from time to time. Men like that. It makes us feel wanted.'

'Like this?' Bella adopted an enormous toothy grin and skipped energetically around the room. 'Isn't life fab! Pollyanna was a chronic depressive compared to me!'

'So, I suppose it wouldn't be a waste to cover *my* face with hair then?' said Viv.

'I knew this would happen. I hate both of you.' Nick heaved himself up from the sofa. 'If anyone wants me, I'll be pretending to be a proper man, reading my car magazine in the bog.'

* * *

There were two messages on her answerphone when she got home: one from the damp man, saying he couldn't do the damp until the weather was better – perhaps he was hoping that every extra day of rain would make it worse and he'd be able to hack off another foot of plaster and whack up the bill; and one from her father, Gerald: 'Just calling to say hello. See how it's all going. Well, I dare say you're managing fine. Give us a ring sometime. Lots of love, Dads.' He always finished like that on the answerphone, as if he were writing a letter.

She wasn't in the mood to speak to anyone, there was nothing on TV, and – having lugged her folio with her notes and sketches in back home – she didn't feel inspired by the prospect of trying to make yoghurt sexy, so she ran herself a deep bath with lavender oil instead. Her candles were reduced to sad stubs, having dripped down their twiddly fake verdigris holders into a Gothic encrustation, and there were spatters of wax on the tiles at one end of the bath. She sat on the edge of the bath while the water was running in, idly picking off bits of wax and flicking them into the loo, then spent fifteen minutes looking in boxes for more candles. She ran her fingers through her hair as if she were posing for a shampoo ad until her fingers got tangled, then she wafted slowly around the room hunting for a hair clip.

'I'm too sensitive to expose myself to the glare of artificial light,' she said out loud. 'Where are the rose petals for my bathwater? My trained eunuchs to paint my toenails and squeeze my spots?'

The candlelit bathing had started with Patrick, but then it was the sort of thing you fell into quite legitimately when you were a couple – along with soaping each other's backs, mounding soapsuds into exaggerated body parts, and volunteering to have the end with the taps. Right on cue, the image of Patrick as she had last seen him appeared in her mind.

She grabbed her loofah mitt and started scrubbing over-vigorously at her skin. Was this really supposed to have an effect on cellulite? Or did it just make you red and sore so that the cellulite was less noticeable? She peered at her thighs in the flickering light.

As well as making it hard to see her cellulite, reason enough surely, the candles were in fact highly functional. Once activated by turning on the light, the extractor fan would continue its deranged mosquito whine for almost an hour even after the light had been turned off. Bella planned to get it fixed at some point, any day now almost certainly, once the damp had been done, but The List had reached such epic proportions that she felt unequal to the task of tackling even a single item on it, so for now she left the door open and the landing light on when she went to the loo – and she had baths by candlelight.

She lay in the bath, lapped by the clean scent of lavender and the flicker of the candles. The events of the day whizzed around her mind, prosaic yet insistent. Was Seline annoyed with her? She should have asked Anthony about next week's presentation. How long would the damp treatment take? And how messy would it be? She might even have to move out for a few days. If only someone else would come along and solve everything. Bella sank lower in the bath, soaked her flannel and draped it over her face. She closed her eyes and imagined she could see herself from above, wondering what it would be like to float up from her body, feel her mind, her thoughts detaching themselves, pulling at her flesh as they dragged away like a sticking plaster. Rain pattered hard against the window, fingers tapping a tattoo against the glass.

She willed herself to hear *his* tread, the twisting of the doorknob.

Behind her closed eyelids, she could see the candles in her mind, their flames sending skittering shadows on the walls, dancing patterns of light over her glistening thighs, her breasts. The door swings open and *he* looks at her questioningly. She smiles her assent and he comes towards her and kneels down next to the bath. His flop of hair falls forward and he runs his hand through it to push it back. Silence. He does not need to speak, but his eyes gleam with longing. At first, he just looks at her, his gaze tracing her shape, then he pushes back his sleeves and reaches down to her—

Downstairs, the phone rang and her answerphone clicked in.

'Hello. Dad again. Do you fancy coming for a visit at the week-end? Be lovely to see you. Mum says you're welcome to bring anyone, you know. If you want to. If there's someone. Well. Or just your good self of course. More than enough. Lots of love. Oh, and we've still got your house-warming present.'

Bella rolled her eyes at an invisible audience. Still, she hadn't visited the House of Fun for quite a while. She couldn't fend it off for ever. The water was getting too cold, hovering at the same temperature as her skin so that she was hardly aware of it as water around her. Another minute or two and it would start to feel cool; she'd have to top up or get out. Out, Bella decided, or she'd look as alluring as a pickled walnut. It wasn't too late to ring Dad back. Perhaps she would go; it might be fine. She could do with a change of scene anyway, have a walk with Dad and the dog, a break from staring at the still-packed boxes. She shivered and shook herself, automatically tapping each foot against the side to shed excess water, a relic from childhood baths and protecting the carpet. *Do try not to drip absolutely everywhere, Bella darling. If it gets wet, it'll start to shrink.*

4

'Ev'ry time we say goodbye, I die a little...' Bella sang along with Ella Fitzgerald while sucking on a sherbert lemon, cursed at a driver surging onto the roundabout in front of her. '...why a little, why the gods above me...' She should have left at lunchtime to miss the Friday exodus. Since Bella had moved, it was barely more than a fifty-mile journey to her parents' place, a wisteria-covered house in a pretty-pretty village in Sussex, but it was turning out to be a slow drive, much of it cross-country on minor roads. If only she hadn't got stuck on the receiving end of one of Seline's interminable monologues about the various ailments of her cats. In the end, she had backed out of the door, shaking her head in sympathy: 'How awful. Falling out in handfuls? Crusty scabs? Poor thing.' They were always suffering from some disgusting condition, which would be related to everyone in the office, one at a time, so that all through the day she could overhear the same fragments – 'Ooh, suppositories? Really?' – as if played on a continuous tape loop. Why on earth didn't Seline just shoot them and get some new, unscabby ones? She peered at the signs. Second, third exit; that's the one. '...think so little of me, they allow you to go...'

* * *

It was properly dark now and the red tail lights of the cars in front bored hypnotically into her eyes against the deepening blue-black of the road and sky. Night driving seemed so full of promise, the road stretching out before her as if it could take her anywhere she wanted to go, her path plotted by a trail of lights like an unnamed constellation crossing the sky. Suddenly, the sign she had just passed filtered through to her consciousness. Her turn-off was coming up: A259 Rye, Hastings. She abandoned her attempt to overtake a Fiat that was even older than her red Peugeot, and nudged back into place to be ready for the turning. A reproving flash from the car behind. Concentrate, woman! If only she didn't feel so tired all the time.

There was an old truck stop a couple of miles along this road, she seemed to recall, a relic of an era of bikers in black leather who roared their engines to impress girls in zip-up boots and miniskirts. By some miracle it had not yet been closed down or transformed into an Unhappy Eater or Loathsome Chef with smooth plastic seats, smooth plastic fried eggs and unsmooth, authentic bad service, heralded by badges proclaiming 'Hi, I'm NIKKI. It's my pleasure to serve you,' their enthusiasm as convincing as a squeezed-lemon-faced aunt in a purple party hat. Why didn't they just tell it like it is – 'Yeah? I'm Charmain. I'll bring it when I can be bothered.'

Bright lights, the sound of eggs spluttering into hot oil, the smell of all-day breakfasts. The few men at the tables looked up from their papers or their mugs of tea when Bella entered. She wished she'd stopped long enough to change out of her work clothes. The clacking of her heels seemed grotesquely amplified by the lino floor as she crossed to the counter to order, drumming out a message in Morse: *Look at me, look at me.* She buttoned up her

tailored jacket, to compensate for her new skirt. The crisp hori-
zontal of its hem framed her exposed knees. She fought the urge to
tug it down.

'Pay when you're done, love,' the waitress behind the counter
said. 'Here, hang on a tick for your tea. I'm just making fresh. I'll
bring your sandwich over in a minute.' She emptied the teapot,
spooned in some fresh tea. Steam billowed around her hands,
clouding the shine of the metal teapot, the gold of her wedding
band, as water rushed from the urn.

'All right, Jim?' she turned to a chunkily attractive man who had
come up to pay. 'Where you off to this time, gorgeous?'

'Only Southampton. Better give me a roll for the road though,
eh?'

'Give you a roll anytime, Jim.'

'Now, now, lady present. Take no notice,' he said, turning to
Bella. He had on a white T-shirt underneath his soft cotton checked
shirt, the way American men often wear them. She could see the
tendons flex in his tanned neck. He pushed back his sleeve to the
elbow, absently rubbing at the dark hairs on his forearm.

'All right?' He nodded, smiling.

Bella looked down, suddenly aware that her gaze had lingered
on him too long. Her eyes dropped to his hands. The nails were cut
close, the fingers full of easy strength.

'Fine, thanks.'

'You sure now? Need a ride or anything? You look a bit lost.'

'No. Really.' Bella snapped him a poised but distant smile. 'I
have my car.' She folded her arms in front of her, then felt silly to be
so pointedly defensive. 'Thank you.'

'No bother.' He stepped back a pace, then smiled and raised his
hand –

Sorry. I'll keep my distance – before turning again to the waitress
at the till.

· · ·

The bacon was thick and salty, between chunky slices of hot buttered toast. Bella tore into her sandwich and slurped her tea in an I'm-all-right-Jack, independent sort of way. Lady, indeed.

Standing at the counter waiting to pay, she saw that they had those solid slabs of bread pudding, the indigestible sort that her dad liked so much, a world away from the vanilla- and cinnamon-spiced faultless desserts her mother made. She ordered two slabs.

'I'll just take for those then, love. Jim paid for your tea and sandwich.' Bella looked at the woman blankly.

'Said he hated to see a damsel in distress. I think he took a fancy to you,' she sighed. 'Lucky you. I wouldn't mind a ride with him myself.' She laughed and Bella smiled, bawdy conspirators.

For the rest of the journey, she found thoughts of her knight-in-checked-shirt returning insistently. She imagined saying yes, she did need a ride, then climbing high up into the lorry cab.

He would stand below, watching as her skirt rode up, revealing the backs of her thighs as she clambered in. Sitting next to him in the lorry, high, high above the road, with the night close in around them, she'd turn to absorb his profile silhouetted against the star-pricked sky, breathe in the smell of male skin, fresh sweat, cotton.

Here, in the warm bubble of the cab, the vibration of the engine thrumming through the soles of her feet, she feels safe. No need to talk, to spoil the heavy hum with the thin clatter of words. There is just him and her and the road ahead. The thickness of his body next to her seems like some rock or standing stone, solid and unyielding. She wants to feel his hands, his fingers warm on the back of her neck, the shock of his rough chin against her cheek. To be held in silence.

Then, she reaches out and her fingers trace a path over the faded denim of his jeans, feeling the cloth stretched taut across his leg. He turns to face her, to see her eyes, her assent. Puts on his hazard lights, pulls over onto the hard shoulder.

Now he leads her round to the back, stretching for her hand in the orange flick-flick of the lights. He lifts her up effortlessly into the back of the lorry, his hands firm and confident around her waist. She steps back and leans against a stack of boxes, waiting. His shape in the darkness moving towards her. A hand on her hair. His mouth. Hands. Hitching up her skirt. The smell of anticipation. A sharp intake of breath at his touch, warm against the cool skin of her thigh. His voice, murmuring low in her hair, her neck. His hands. His—

A car flashed her, coming the other way. She was frozen in the glare for a moment, then realized and dipped her headlights. You sad spinster, you, she told herself, fantasizing about lorry drivers. What next? Dreams about builders saying, 'I hear you've got some excess moisture that wants seeing to'? Electricians offering their services: 'I'll just turn you on now'? Delivery men asking, 'Where shall I put it, love?' Good grief. *For God's sake, go and have a proper fling, woman.* It was all very well having a gap after Patrick, but this was getting beyond a joke. She was probably technically a virgin again by now, all sealed over the way pierced ears went if you didn't wear earrings in them.

It was always strange returning to the parental home, immersing herself in that peculiar mixture of pleasure and frustration. There was delight in the house itself: the gleam of well-polished furniture, its quiet colour schemes, its tidiness and orderliness – so different from the flat she had shared with Patrick, and from her new house with its brilliant cushions and exotic rugs, the pictures, still packed in boxes, that would line the walls, the trailing house plants that already spilled from the shelves; there was enjoyment of her mother's cooking, one thing they shared, and of her father's easy good humour, his guilelessness, his pleasure in seeing her.

Irritation was never in short supply either, however. The way her parents always expected her to go and say hello to the neighbours she didn't like, even though she was sure they were as baffled by the need for this periodic politeness as she was; the way they used wineglasses that must have been hand-blown in Lilliput so that she felt she was filling up her glass almost every minute, her hand reaching for the bottle noted by silent eyes; the way Dad was so infuriatingly slow and fair all the time, always seeing everyone's point of view; and, most of all, her mother's unruffled efficiency, her air of stoic disappointment.

Was anyone ever really a grown-up when they were with their parents, she wondered. You might think you were, but it was surely a sad piece of self-delusion. Perhaps you'd be discussing life or books or politics with them like any bunch of civilized adults of equal standing, then you'd utter one little opinion that was slightly provocative and your father would give that gentle, indulgent laugh, that little nod and smile that said 'You will have your funny ideas, but we'll humour you because you're only young and you don't know any better.' Or your mother would purse her lips, carefully not quite concealing her disapproval: 'It's a shame you have that opinion. Perhaps you'll grow out of it with time. Still, I suppose I've only myself to blame as I raised you.'

Going back home, Bella felt the inevitable yet unspoken questions hanging in the air:

Have you got another boyfriend yet? shone out at her from the ivory silk lampshade in the hall. *Are you making enough of an effort?* peeked at her from behind the velvet curtains. *You're running out of time,* glinted at her from the silver salt-cellar. *How much longer must we wait?* whispered the soft carpets under her feet.

Alessandra, Bella's mother, was more subtle, of course, with a diploma in Reproach by Implication so that even the most innocuous topic of conversation could become a minefield, hidden dangers lurking beneath every cautious tread. Her silences seemed multifaceted, glittering with doubt, shame and splintered expectations.

'Do you remember Sarah Forbes, from the year below you?' she had asked on Bella's previous visit. 'Who used to live in that house off Church Street with the fake bay window? Just married a lovely young man. She had such a pretty headdress for the wedding – and it drew attention away from her nose.'

The subtext was elaborate, but crystal clear: *She's a year younger and she didn't have your advantages, but even she's managed to get married. To somebody decent. And she's not even nice-looking. You should do better than her.*

Bella had sidestepped the shots neatly and returned fire.

'How lovely. I'll send her a card. Will she keep on her job at the shop, do you think?'

She may as well get married. She's not exactly firing on all cylinders on the career front. Can't you at least be proud of my talents and achievements?

'Oh, I shouldn't think she'd need to do that, Belladarling. Her husband's a lawyer; a junior partner in a very reputable firm apparently.' Alessandra smiled serenely. 'He's doing very well. Still, men can afford to concentrate on their careers, can't they? They don't have the same pressures as we women.' Impressive: an attack on two fronts.

She's hooked someone not just with money, but a professional with good prospects.

Men don't have a time bomb nestling in their reproductive organs, so it's fine for them to be ambitious and successful. Can't you hear that clock ticking?

Feebly, Bella had lobbed back a boulder, a heavy and clumsy

last shot. 'A lawyer, eh? Oh, never mind. Couldn't she find someone with a respectable profession? You know that old joke: What do you call a hundred lawyers chained together at the bottom of the ocean? – A good start.' Pathetic. A damp squib.

It didn't even merit a countermeasure. Alessandra had sighed softly, unimpressed, and patted the back of her hair, smoothing her already perfect chignon.

'Perhaps you wouldn't mind making some coffee, Bella dear?' A furrowed-brow glance at Bella's crumpled shirt. 'I must just go upstairs.' She had got up and said, over her shoulder, 'There are home-made *fiorentine* in the blue tin.'

The *coup de grâce.*

If you can't manage to find a man and give us grandchildren, you can at least be useful by making some coffee. Perhaps if you could be bothered to make your own biscuits, like I do, you would have a man.

And the way she pronounced foreign words so over-perfectly, as if she were a newsreader. Especially Italian, although Alessandra had actually been born in Manchester, her parents having come to England several years before. The way she said 'Bella' – with that preposterous lingering on the double 'L', the way an Italian waiter would as he poked his outsize pepper-phallus under your nose: 'Black pepper, *bella* signorina?'

'I don't want a fucking man anyway,' Bella wanted to tell her, to see her automatic flinch. As if her mother would believe that. What kind of woman could possibly want to be on her own? A nun? Alessandra's face would wear that baffled look, frowning at her daughter as if she were an alien species. Perhaps she *would* become a nun. Imagined her mother's expression as she informed her of the solemn decision: 'Mother, I'm joining a convent. You'll never see me again.' That mixture of what might pass for feelings shadowing those tiger eyes: incomprehension, shame, the guilty glint of – what? – relief? She'd rather be an anchorite, a hermit. Who knows, in her austere cell she might even take up painting again, devoting herself to the glory of colour and shape in solitude, the world outside no more than fibres for her to spin into images. Alone, the patterns of her thoughts would be clear and vibrant, shocking the virgin paper with their boldness, her brush caressing and seductive. She snorted at herself: Saint Bella of the Divine Brushstrokes.

It was late when she arrived and her mother had already gone to bed. Bella peeked into the utility room to say hello to Hund, the dog, but he was asleep in his basket, curled into an old childhood blanket. Her father had waited up, however, and was sitting in the kitchen reading a glossy women's magazine. He hugged her fondly and put on the kettle.

'Guess what I've got, Dads?' Bella put the slabs of bread pudding onto a pair of bone-china plates.

'What a treat – don't tell your mother. Is this true?' Gerald asked, stabbing his finger at a page in the magazine. 'It says 64 per cent of women are more likely to fall in love with a man if they see him cry.'

'I doubt it. Didn't you know, they make up 72 per cent of those statistics or they get them from asking five people in the office. Still, I suppose most women do want a sensitive man.' She poured out the tea. 'Not a wimp, of course, but someone in touch with their feelings and all that bollocks.'

Gerald snorted, laughing into his cup. 'How delicately put.'

He broke off a wodge of the bread pudding and looked at her over his steel-rimmed glasses.

'Met anyone, um, interesting recently? – he asked in his interfer-ing-old-parent way.'

'It's OK, Dads. I don't mind when you do it. 'Fraid not. You can keep your morning coat in mothballs for the foreseeable future. Might as well flog it, in fact – I can't see it happening.'

'Well, you know we love you whatever you do. We just want you to be happy.'

'Yeah, yeah. Dutiful parental speech duly acknowledged. But you want grandchildren. You all do. My friends say the same. It's just a phase – you'll get over it.'

Gerald smiled.

'But what'll we do with the Winnie-the-Pooh breakfast set we've been saving? We've got twelve rolls of cute bunny-wabbit wallpaper in the loft.'

'Oh, shut up,' she said affectionately. 'I've brought you your favourite bread pudding. What more do you want?'

Bella slept in her old room. It was very different now, rather more restful, she mentally conceded. Alessandra had had it redecorated the week after Bella left to go to art school in London, covering with tasteful tones of subdued peach the ambitious mural of a Rousseau-style jungle painted over one wall. *Of course, you're welcome to do another if you like, Bella darling, perhaps something a little more* simpatico, *hmm? A spray of lilies could be very pretty on the wardrobe door.* It had been getting very tatty anyway and she wouldn't have been bothered to retouch the whole wall. The room had been altered at least twice since then, although it wasn't even used very often. The bed was in the same position, though, next to the window, snug between the wall and the side of the wardrobe. Lying in it now, Bella felt she wanted to be tucked in tight and read to. She pulled up the quilt over her chin and turned off the light.

* * *

She is lying in bed, whispering to Fernando, her toy frog. His fluffiness is flat in patches, where he has been cuddled to excess. The little side lamp is on, giving out a soft, warm glow because

Fernando is afraid of the dark. The light has a pink headscarf tied around the shade, to make it less bright.

Bella can hear Mummy talking to Poppy on the landing. Poppy comes and babysits sometimes. Bella likes Poppy. She has frizzy hair with coloured threads woven into bits of it, chocolate raisins in her enormous patchwork bag, and once she let Bella stay up and watch the Saturday-night thriller, although she wasn't supposed to.

Out on the landing, Mummy is saying:

'—and don't let her keep getting up. She often says she thinks there's something under the bed, but don't allow any nonsense.'

'Rightio,' says Poppy. 'Have fun.'

The bedroom door opens and Mummy comes in.

'We're off now, darling. Don't be a bother to Poppy now, will you?' She comes over and leans down to kiss Bella goodnight. Mummy smells wonderful – of perfume, and silk, and sparkly earrings, and evening – and Bella breathes her all in and reaches up to put her arms around her.

'Now don't muss me, Bella. I've just done my hair. Goodnight, darling. Sleep tight.'

Daddy comes in behind her. 'Just come to say night-night.'

He treads softly, although she is still awake, and sits down on the bed. He scoops his arms under her and squeezes her tight. She can feel the smooth, soft stuff of his tie against her cheek, the rough cloth of his jacket against her nose.

'Will you check, Daddy? Please?'

He gets down on his hands and knees to look under the bed.

'All clear,' he says, getting up and blowing her a kiss from the door. 'See you later, alligator.'

'In a while, crocodile,' she replies.

5

'No rush to get up,' Gerald said, as he poked his head round the door with a cup of tea. 'Your mother's had to go into town to have her hair done, so you're a free woman.'

'Nice of her to put out flags and form a welcoming committee.'

'Fancy some breakfast?'

On her customary stroll around the village, she bought a couple of postcards of endearingly awful watercolour views of the high street and the church, and wandered along to The Whistling Kettle to write her cards and have a coffee.

'Mum's back,' said Gerald, on her return. 'Don't forget to mention her hair, eh?'

Bella tugged at a pucker in her shirt and knocked on her parents' bedroom door.

'Mmm?'

She opened the door a little way and craned her head around it. 'It's only me. Just come to say hello.'

'Oh, *hello*, Bella darling.' Alessandra glanced up at her from the dressing table. 'Why are you hovering there? Come in, come in.

Lovely to see you.' Bella dipped to kiss her mother's proffered cheek.

'The hair's great. Very elegant. Colour's nice, too.'

Alessandra scanned Bella's face as if to check her expression, then turned her head this way and that in the mirror.

'I think I'd have made a better job of it myself. Anyway, how *are* you, darling?' Alessandra covered her eyes with one hand to shield them from a cloud of hairspray. She smoothed down a wisp escaping from her French pleat. The salon-smell filled Bella's nose, sending her back to long hours spent waiting at the hairdresser's as a child, swinging her legs, reading her book or drawing pictures in her special grown-up sketch pad that Daddy had given her.

'Fine. Yup. I'm fine.'

Alessandra's threefold reflection peered up at her expectantly from the triple mirror.

'We haven't seen you for ages,' said the full face from the central frame. 'You really must come more often.'

'I'd love to, but—' Bella shrugged. 'There was the move. There's still loads to do, and you know how busy it gets with work and all.'

'Well, of course, we can't compete with the excitement of the rat race,' said the right profile, briskly dusting its cheek with translucent powder.

'The house is looking lovely. As always. Is that a new vase in the hall?' The reflection nodded and glanced at her sidelong.

'Your father misses you terribly,' said the left profile. 'You should really try and think of him sometimes.'

'I *do.*' Bella hooked her thumbs in the belt loops of her jeans and focused on the toe of her left boot. How nice the worn leather looked against the soft green pile of the carpet, like a piece of fallen bark on a floor of springy moss. Perhaps she should go painting in the woods? Sneak out, as if meeting a secret lover. An image of dark trees came to her, the shadows beneath sliced by shafts of sunlight.

Ah, Bella dear, dabbling with your paints again? I am glad. So nice for a woman to have an enjoyable hobby...

Alessandra's mouth formed a rictus-smile as she applied her lipstick. 'What do you think, hmm? It's new. Amber Spice.'

'Lovely.' Bella nodded at the reflection. 'Brings out the colour of your eyes, too.' Alessandra's glittering eyes, flecked like tortoise-shell, brightened in the mirror.

'Do you really think so?' She smiled, her feathers smoothed. 'Let's go down and have some coffee.' The reflection blotted its lips, turning to left and right. 'I've made some new *biscotti*. You must try and guess what's in them.'

Bella inhaled the salt air and looked out across the sea. It was a clear, bright day, but windy, whisking the water into froth-topped waves. She loved the beach on a day like this, cold enough to keep the Thermos brigade cocooned in their cars, watching the ocean with undisguised suspicion. Although she now lived not far from the sea herself, she had a fondness for this particular stretch of coastline, the beach of her childhood ten miles from her parents' house. Dad had evidently wanted to come, too, but she'd just scooped up her car keys and swept out as if she were distracted. But then her mother wouldn't have wanted to be left out and it would have turned into a sad parody of a family outing. There'd be all that hunting for a spot sheltered from the wind and the fussing about her hair and it just wouldn't have been the same.

Two windsurfers bounced over the waves, dipping and soaring, their dazzling pink and green sails like the wings of exotic birds. The tide was out and, down by the water's edge, a small girl shov-elled sand inexpertly into a bucket. Her white hat was pulled down so low that Bella thought she must only be able to see directly downwards. She looked intent on empire-building, but her cardigan sleeves kept getting in the way and she was too young to have mastered the art of rolling them up properly. Her mother sat nearby, reading a magazine and taking swigs from a can of Coke.

Bella chucked another pebble hard towards a small piece of driftwood further along the beach. It skittered along the shingle. A man with a yapping Jack Russell scowled at her, as if she had been aiming at his dog.

'Nearly,' she told herself. 'One more go, then back to the House of Fun.'

* * *

Daddy takes her onto the beach and starts to help her off with her shoes and socks.

'Fancy a paddle, ding-dong?' He sometimes calls her that for fun, because of Bell, short for Bella, but Mummy says it is silly and not right – Bella is a beautiful name. It means beautiful and she should know because she chose it and she's Italian.

'Me do it.'

He takes off his own shoes and socks and rolls up his trousers so they are all bunched around his knees. The sea is cold and she squeals as it rushes up over her ankles. Through the water, her feet look as if they do not belong to her, as if she had just found them while searching for shells. They are pale and soft and the sun makes little bright lines on them through the waves. When she steps out of the water, the shingle seems twice as hard and sharp on her soles.

'Ow, ow, ow!'

Daddy scoops her up and holds her high above his head, up with the big white gulls that he says cry out for all the sailors and fishermen lost at sea. She is not sure how they can get lost because there are no roads and you do not need a map. You only need to look around and there is the beach. Then he swings her suddenly upside down and the world is shingle and sea and sky then sky and sea and shingle again. She screams with delight.

'Daddy, Daddy, put me *down*.'

She lets him put her socks back on because her feet are still damp and they are hard to do properly. He gets them all crooked so the heels are round at the side, then he buckles her red shoes too tight and the left one pinches her foot a little, but she doesn't say.

He takes her for cherryade and 'Welsh rabbit' in a café which has bright strips of colour hanging in the doorway, slapping softly in the breeze. All she wants is for this day to be forever: the gulls sailing above her, the sweet pink bubbles of the cherryade, the scrunch of the shingle, the salty taste of the sea when she licks her fingers, and Daddy doing up her shoes, looking down at the buckles as he fastens them, then up at her as she sits perched on the breakwater.

'All right then, ding-dong. Off we trot. Mummy will be waiting.'

* * *

Alessandra was fussing with her hair. 'Beautiful,' said Gerald. 'As always.'

She waved at him dismissively with a gesture of her long, tapering fingers.

'Why do we bother spending so much time and money making ourselves look lovely for you men?' She turned to Bella, including her, silently noting her faded jeans and hair pulled back into a hasty ponytail, then turned away again. 'When you can't even seem to tell the difference?'

She walked towards the kitchen.

'Amuse yourselves, and keep out from under my feet, both of you. I'm just going to prepare a few bits for dinner. Nothing special as it's just us.'

'Nothing special' turned out to be individual asparagus and gruyère tartlets followed by a layered terrine of smoked chicken and spinach with salad.

'Any news?' asked Alessandra to the air in general once they were safely on the home stretch of dinner, warm pears poached in port served with crème fraîche.

Are you seeing anyone? Bella sensed the silent question crawl across the starched linen tablecloth, edging its way around a china bowl of tight apricot rosebuds. *Are you even trying?* crept in its wake.

'Nothing major,' said Bella, concentrating on scooping up a wayward piece of pear, while redirecting the conversation with the practised ease of a politician. 'The house needs some work to eradicate the damp.' Held out her hand at waist height. 'The plaster's got to be hacked off up to here.'

'Sounds expensive,' Gerald said. 'Do you need any help?'

'Have you—' Alessandra began.

'Thanks, but I'm fine money-wise... and Seline seems to be very happy with me so far, probably because I've brought some juicy clients with me ready to be squeezed. She said if all goes well, we might discuss setting up as a partnership next year.'

'But that's wonderful. Shall we drink a toast?'

'Of course it's good that they appreciate your talents, but isn't that rather risky?' asked Alessandra. 'Wouldn't you be liable if the company went bankrupt?'

Bella took a drink of her wine.

'Well, of course, it's always good to look on the bright side,' she said, starting to get up from the table. 'Shall I make some coffee?'

'Perhaps I'd better make it, Bella dear. The percolator's being rather temperamental.'

'It has my sympathy,' Bella said under her breath.

* * *

In the garden on Sunday morning, Gerald took Bella for the traditional guided tour. They stood together by his vegetable patch, pointing, assessing, as if judging it for a medal at a horticultural show.

'It won't be at its best for a while yet, of course. I'm planning to grow some squash this year. Your mother says they make good soup.'

'Oh? Don't they make an *excellente* soup?'

'Behave yourself, daughter dear.'

Every time Bella mentioned or admired anything, Gerald would weave along the narrow paths between the beds with surprising grace, saying, 'Have some, have some. Here, let me dig some up.'

It was depressing, she hadn't done anything yet with her small plot, while Dad was doing such wonders with his large garden.

'I'm wondering whether I should have it redesigned – make it easier to manage somehow?' she said. 'It's getting out of hand already.'

'Very sensible. I'll have a look if you like, or get someone who actually knows what they're doing.'

'Of course, I've no idea what's fashionable any more,' Alessandra said, plucking a blouse from her walk-in wardrobe to offer Bella. 'But this has always been useful.'

And it has to be better than that awful shirt.

'It's gorgeous,' Bella said, stroking the slippery satin sleeve against her cheek. 'Are you sure you don't want it?'

'We don't go out as much as we used to. I've far more evening clothes than I can use.'

If I were your age, I'd be out dancing very night, fending off strings of suitors.

Bella held up a silk chiffon top and looked at herself in the mirror. It was delicious, red and rich as cherries.

'The colour's wonderful with your hair. I'll never understand

why young people seem to wear so much black all the time. Take it.'
Alessandra pulled out a matching skirt from the rail. 'Here – I can't
get into it any more. All part of the joys of ageing.' She patted her
still slender hips.

You won't be young for ever.

'And you could do with some decent things. With your looks, it's
such a waste not to make the most of yourself.'

Why don't you try harder? You won't catch a man if you don't.

With the blouse and skirt on, Bella felt different – unfamiliarly
elegant, graceful, grown-up. The skirt swirled softly about her legs
as she walked up and down the bedroom. The voluminous sleeves
of the top were translucent, semi-revealing, more alluring than bare
flesh.

'That's really very glamorous on you,' said Alessandra, assessing. 'Lovely for a special occasion. Or if someone takes you out to
dinner?'

'Women don't get taken out to dinner any more.' Bella ignored
the implied question. 'We all pay our own way nowadays, I think
you'll find.'

'Oh. Well, yes. I just meant...' Alessandra gave a small laugh. 'It
needs high heels, of course,' looking down at Bella's weekend boots.

Don't you want anyone to notice you?

'I do have some smart shoes, you know – just because I don't—'

'No. Well, of course, we can't expect you to waste your best
things on us.' She turned and left the room.

Alone in her parents' bedroom, Bella faced herself in the mirror.
Her reflection looked back, coolly appraising. The cherry top and
skirt seemed suddenly ridiculous, absurdly glamorous, too obviously not her own – like a little girl all got up in her mummy's high
heels and feather boa. Who would be fooled by it into thinking she
was really beautiful? They would know she was a fraud, a cuckoo in
the nest, trying to acquire something she could never have. She

tugged at the zip, jamming it in the fabric before pulling it free, and reached for her jeans.

'Don't forget your house-warming present,' Gerald said as she was marshalling her things by the front door. 'Have you space on the back seat?'

'Gerald-dear, can you manage it, please?'

She didn't need to unwrap it to see what it was. There were two bits: one large and heavy piece that was evidently some kind of lamp base, and one awkward-looking shade. Even without seeing it, Bella could tell it wouldn't look right in her house. It was too large and, knowing her mother, too grand. Chances were the base would have exotic birds painted on it or tasteful flowers. It was bound to have been expensive. She could have had some decent new towels for the money. Or a couple of seriously good saucepans.

'Gosh, how wonderful,' she said. 'How exciting to have a proper present.'

'Aren't you going to open it?' Alessandra stood poised behind it proprietorially. It was evidently of her choosing.

'But it looks so well protected as it is. I'd better transport it wrapped, I think. Then I can have it to look forward to when I get home.'

'Of course.' Alessandra smoothed back a wisp of hair and folded her arms. 'Well, safe journey then.' She hovered forward, printed a bird-like kiss on Bella's cheek.

Gerald handed her an envelope once she was in the car.

'Not a big fat cheque, I'm afraid. Something for the garden.'

'Looks a bit flat for a cherry tree.'

'Be off with you.' He bent down to kiss her goodbye. 'The receipt for the other present's in there too, in case you want to exchange it for whatever we should have got you in the first place. Feel free to invite us to your house-warming. If you're not too embarrassed by your crumbly old parents. We'll come early and lend a hand.'

'Don't be daft, Dads.'

No chance, she thought. She could imagine it now.

Her sitting room. Friends standing and talking, doing the buffet balancing act with plates and glasses and napkins. Carefully manoeuvring themselves around the still-stacked boxes. The Arrival of the Parents, like the Entrance of Cleopatra into Rome, with much fussing and removing of scarves and gloves and coats and saying they'd left such-and-such behind then realizing they hadn't, and where might one find the...? Her father worrying about the car, fretting like an old man, surely something could be done about the parking problem? And Alessandra sweeping into the kitchen, eyes flicking over the photograph of Bella and Patrick still in place on the pinboard, and saying how absolutely *sweet* the kitchen is – how convenient to have everything so close to hand – how much easier to manage – and gesturing at the drapes where they pooled deliberately onto the floor – of course, there was always so much to do in a new house, wasn't there – never enough time for hemming curtains and all those dreary little jobs – oh and bare boards with rugs in the bedroom – Bella should have said – they'd have been quite happy to help out with the cost of a carpet – more than happy – or was that the thing to have nowadays? It was so easy to lose touch with what was *in*.

Come early and lend a hand? Thanks, but no thanks.

Bella gave a peremptory toot as she drove out of the gate. In the rear-view mirror she saw her father's arm raised high, as if signalling from a desert island to a distant ship, her mother's hand tentatively lifted, stretching out for something she couldn't hope to reach.

6

'Why not do an evening class – that way, you'll meet people and learn something at the same time!' Bella had been leafing through a women's magazine in the loo at work. The advice was always the same; whenever someone wrote in saying they wanted to meet people, the answer was predictably of the get-out-and-join-clubs variety. But did you ever meet likely men at an evening class? Bella sounded out Viv and Nick later while at their place for supper. Nick decreed it a rational approach (Viv: 'Rational? Oh, well, that's the main thing, of course,') and asked what subject she planned to take: carpentry or car maintenance? Bella had rather fancied stained glass or patchwork; she whimpered at Viv, who would have none of it.

'Look, do you bloody want to meet men or don't you? Go to patchwork classes if you want, but don't come running to me afterwards whingeing that the best bet in the class is a forty-seven-year-old midwife because at least she's got hair on her chin.'

'That'd do. I want to meet more *people,* otherwise I feel like I'm just a visitor here.'

They sat round the dining-table eating garlic and ginger prawns

with stir-fried noodles, trying not to laugh at Nick and his attempts
to use chopsticks. He dropped a prawn for the third time as he was
trying to raise it to his lips.

'The suspense is killing me, Nick. Have a fork.' Viv half-turned
towards Bella and gnashed her teeth silently. 'He does this every
time.'

'No, no. I'm getting the hang of it now.' The prawn teetered
dangerously as three pairs of eyes watched its unsteady course from
bowl to mouth.

'You won't get a gold star anyway, you know.' Bella's chopsticks
threatened to snatch the prawn away deftly.

The prawn fell with a soft plumpf into its nest of noodles. Nick
went into the kitchen and started clattering about.

'There's no point anyway. Even if I met someone, I never think I
know how to *do* relationships. I can do the going out to dinner bit
and the having lots of sex bit, then I get lost. There must be some
secret formula that I don't know about,' said Bella. 'Can't you give
me your top ten tips or something? You seem to have it sussed.'

'Viv, have you hidden the forks with the blue handles?' from the
kitchen. 'I don't like the other ones for Chinese.'

'Yeah, that's right. We're completely perfect.' Viv shook her head
and bellowed back. 'In the *second* drawer – where they *usually* are.'

'No magic formula?'

'What, like my Scottish granny's drop scones? If there is, no-
one told me and, God knows, no-one bothered to tell Nick. I
mean, Nick thinks mutual support means leaning on each other
after a heavy session at the Tickled Trout. I haven't a clue. Yes, I
have. I s'pose talking's the main thing – when you want to and
when you don't want to so that neither of you sits around
seething for weeks over some piddly little problem that suddenly
explodes into door-slamming, crockery-hurling and suitcase-pack-
ing. Oh, yeah – and a little love doesn't go amiss. Gets you

through the—' she raised her voice '—ALL TOO FREQUENT CRAPPY BITS.'

Bella stuck out her lower lip. 'Is that it then, guv?'

'I still can't see them.' A plaintive note had crept into Nick's voice. 'No. You need huge dollops of luck as well.' Viv got up and marched through to the kitchen. 'Not *that* second drawer, *this* second drawer. And,' she continued, 'you need to be able to wade through all the pigs and creeps and mummy's boys to find yourself a nice, only averagely neurotic male who can't even find a fork in his own kitchen but who is at least prepared to have a proper go at all this stuff, too.'

'I might as well end it all now.' Bella stabbed at her stomach with her chopstick.

'Wait till next week. Then it's Nick's turn to do the floor.'

* * *

Leafing through the booklet of adult education courses from the library while she was supposed to be working, Bella thought she could do with lessons just to make sense of the brochure. Was there some logical reason for the range of subjects, prices, and locations to be encrypted in quite such a complex way? She was tempted to leave it till September. Maybe she'd have more energy for deciphering it after the summer and she could start afresh with the new academic year. But, knowing her, she would have forgotten all about it by then. For her, the saying 'Why procrastinate today when you can do it tomorrow and have it to look forward to?' was not a joke but a perfectly valid philosophy of life. She should definitely do it NOW. Her sole achievement in the last two days seemed to be making a lemon cake, hardly top priority, and hemming her bedroom curtains. She had even cheated by adding 'Hem bedroom curtains' retrospectively to the epic List, soon to be available as a ten-volume boxed set, just so she could relish the rare satisfaction of being able to cross something off.

She waded back through the brochure again – perhaps she should do it by location? Just choose the one she could be bothered to get to and pick a subject at random. Or choose blind? She shut her eyes, flicked open the brochure and stabbed the page. Learning to Draw and Paint. Most amusing. Probably the only subject on offer that she didn't need because she could already do it. Well, used to be able to do it. Her early dreams of being a painter seemed like an embarrassing first crush, a piece of folly best forgotten.

There ought to be some kind of evening class that you could take for all the really tricky stuff. What was the point of worrying about Intermediate Spreadsheets or Creative Machine Embroidery when you really needed Having a Relationship – Complete Beginners or Getting Your Act Together, Level I? Surely Advanced Cake Decorating was, well, the icing on the cake? You had to have a cake first and that meant getting all the ingredients in the right proportions and then mixing them so they all melded together

properly. The analogy was beginning to become entwined in itself and was also tugging her mind towards thoughts of lunch.

She picked up her bag and nipped out to the sandwich shop. The classes would have to guide you through slowly, of course, so that you progressed gradually from, say, Lesson 1: The First Phone Call to Lesson 2: The First Dinner, then Removing Clothing Without Fumbling, Zen and the Art of Putting on a Condom, Meeting His Parents, Dealing with Sulks (Novices), and Walking Out: How To Say I Need More Space When You Really Want To Say Piss Off.

* * *

Car Maintenance/Complete Beginners was due to start on Tuesday evening at half-six. Bella dashed home after work to pick up her car. It wouldn't start. Ha-ha, ha-ha. Very droll, she thought, slapping the dashboard. How cheering to witness that God obviously did have a sense of irony after all. And, of course, she panicked, and kept revving it, and gave it too much gas and everything else she knew she wasn't supposed to do, and the engine flooded. She tried giving it the nice cop/nasty cop treatment, alternating between 'Come on, you're a great little car, you'd like a little outing wouldn't you? Let's go,' while lunging in her seat to demonstrate the concept of forward motion, and 'You bastard – one last chance then I'm trading you in for a scooter.'

She turned off the engine and sat there for a few minutes. Marvellous. Another element in her life that didn't work. The evening-class thing was a stupid idea anyway, she'd obviously never meet anyone like this; she probably had mildew between her legs by now. Why couldn't she simply accept the fact that she was a sad, pathetic spinster who would never have a man or children, and throw herself into helping starving refugees or victims of unpleasant wallpaper by going round the world on a tricycle or doing a sponsored walk to Llandudno in flip-flops?

One last try. It started. Of course. Glanced at her watch – it might still be worth it; she could still enrol at least. By the time she got there, and found a parking space, the lesson was half-gone. She found the room and, wisely as it turned out, peered through a pane in the door before plunging in.

A group of about a dozen people were clustered around what she assumed must be a car engine. They suddenly parted to let a fiftyish man in blue overalls get to the centre. As they moved aside, they turned in Bella's direction. All except two of them were women. The two that weren't huddled close together and looked very awkward; one had ginger hair that stuck up all over his head as if he'd just had a shock; the other had such bad acne, you could have used his face to map out constellations; neither could have been a minute over seventeen. She pressed herself back against the wall like a B-movie spy. A narrow escape. Hell, who wanted to learn about engines anyway? That was what mechanics were for.

It seemed a bit of a waste, however, now that she was there. The noticeboard's list of classes for that evening offered Be Your Own Accountant (who could resist?); Italian/Intermediate (possibly interesting, but she hadn't yet progressed much past *grazie* and *spaghetti al pesto* and Alessandra would be bound to go on about it and correct her pronunciation); Polish Folk-Dancing (checked watch: class nearly finished); and Life Drawing/All levels (starting in 30 seconds). Probably not many men, but she would enjoy herself anyway, and she needn't tell anyone; she hadn't sat in an actual class since she'd been at art school but she had loved that complete absorption in the task. When she drew, she was entirely focused, her concentration lasered into looking, really seeing, and interpreting her three-dimensional vision into two dimensions. She hurtled along the corridors, trying to find the right room. Why did these places always have peculiar names or numbers for rooms? The one she wanted was called WG4, but there didn't seem to be a WG1, 2 or 3.

She finally tracked it down in an annexe and leapt into the room in the middle of the tutor's introductory blurb. He said they must all call him JT and ask as many questions as they liked. Despite the fact that the tutor insisted on calling himself by initials, he seemed to be OK. 'Erm...?' Bella found herself saying to avoid using JT, which sounded like a cleaning product or a megalomaniac boss who thought he was being chummy with his staff. How could anyone say 'Call me JT' and not sound embarrassed? 'Erm' suggested they all start with a quick fifteen-minute study before moving on to a longer pose.

The model disrobed and moved into a standing position, leaning forward with his leg on a chair. There, she was getting to be with a naked man after all, and without any of that awful awkwardness. No having to laugh at laborious puns, no discovering he thought foreplay meant ten minutes of energetic rummaging in her pubes, no cystitis, no having to introduce him to her mother. Marvellous.

Bella rootled in her bag for the stubby end of a pencil. How odd it was, she thought; as soon as you really started to look, to draw, you no longer saw a naked person. The model became simply a skeleton overlaid with flesh, a collection of volumes and planes, areas of light and shadow. If only she could reduce people to this simplicity the rest of the time: the angle of a leg, the curve of a shoulder, the weight of hand on hip. It wasn't that drawing was easy – far from it; how would she manage to convey that foreshortened foot, for a start, without it appearing deformed? And do his dangly bits without making them look like chicken giblets? But if you really looked, you did start to learn, you did get better at making sense of it. You could make some personal interpretation that was akin to the reality. Yet you could live on the planet for a thousand years – well, thirty-three, but she bet it didn't get any easier – and still find other people, and yourself, a total mystery. She dismissed the thought as fruitless, focused her attention on the model and lost herself in drawing.

When it was time for the model's break, Bella noticed the room around her, the other people in the class, as if she had awoken from a trance, forms coming into focus. Blinked as if the lights had been switched on suddenly. Found it hard to speak for a moment or two, her head still filled with pictures, shapes. Saw the words as symbols in her mind first before she could translate them into sounds, the letters only abstract lines and curves for a second as if they were pictures rather than meaningful language. Drawing *was* rather like being in love, she decided, the completeness of it, no need for anything else.

She was aware of a presence at her left shoulder. JT, checking her progress. He nodded, approving.

'I take it you're not exactly a beginner,' he said.

7

Sunday. The day designed for the sole purpose of reminding all single people on the planet just how sad and lonely they really were. It wasn't as if she had a shortage of things to do. There was the small matter of the boxes, for a start. It was weeks now since she'd moved in and she was still surrounded by her cardboard cityscape. But what was the point of unpacking everything when it would all have to be repacked when she got around to having the damp done? She couldn't descend on Viv and Nick again. Viv kept saying it was fine, but the other evening Nick had remarked that they needn't bother having any children now because they had Bella: no need to worry about getting her into a decent school – no need to fund her through college – no arguments about her staying out late or hogging the phone for hours. Fantastic, he'd said, why hadn't anyone else thought of it? Why put yourself through all those years of anxiety and heartache when you could just adopt a thirty-three-year-old who could cook and everything? Hilarious. My, how she'd laughed.

She got out her list. 'Sort out house', it said. 'Sort out garden'. They both seemed a bit epic for a Sunday morning. 'Damp'. She underlined it firmly to give herself the feeling that she was somehow hastening its progress. Added 'Chase Mr Bowman again' as a sub-entry beneath it. 'Crack in wall/studio'. That was obviously more of a DIY project, more of a get-someone-else-in-to-sort-it-out sort of thing. 'Shower curtain', the list continued. 'Blind for bathroom'. Ah, that was more like it. She could manage a little light selecting of shower curtains. Habitat wasn't open till noon. Plenty of time to whizz round and have a quick tidy-up. After a spot of breakfast.

A breakfast tray was assembled with cornflakes and cold milk, tea, a toasted muffin; she whapped a tape of *The Philadelphia Story* into the video and settled back into the sofa.

That was the trouble with the world today: there were no men like Cary Grant any more. Or she'd have quite happily settled for James Stewart. It was coming up to the moment when – the night before she's going to marry another man – he kisses Katharine Hepburn before they head off for a drunken moonlit swim.

'It can't be anything like love, can it?' he whispered into her hair.

'No, no, it mustn't be, it can't!' Hepburn breathed, leaning against a tree, her face bathed in moonlight.

'Would it be... inconvenient?' drawled Stewart. 'Terribly!'

And she even managed to look beautiful when she was drunk.

Bella clicked off the television and leant her head back against the cushions. What if she never found another man, never mind Mr Perfect, just anyone at all? She'd become one of those single women who fuss over their cats as if they were babies and go on group holidays to Thailand to learn about batik. After a while, friends would give up all hope of ever matching her up with someone and would think of her with pity, while telling her how much they envied her her freedom – how wonderful to be able to do her own thing all the time – she could jet off to New York without having to cross-check diaries six months in advance – no need to spend her entire life in I-hoovered-so-you-wash-up negotiations – no squabbling about who took out the rubbish last time – no being questioned about why she had spent quite so much money on a linen jacket and didn't she already have a jacket anyway, did she really *need* another one? – no endless debates about whether it would be betraying their socialist principles to send the children to private school, not that they wouldn't prefer a state school *of course,* but Lottie was just so bright and she'd never get enough attention in those outsize classes, it wouldn't be fair – how wonderful it must be to be able to stretch out in bed, never waking cold and coverless at three in the morning and have to wrestle a small corner of duvet from the snoring pig next to her.

Good grief, it was nearly noon now. She must, must, must do something constructive. Go sketching or something. JT had said they should all be drawing every day – '... an indispensable routine, like brushing your teeth.' Her gaze fell on a small section of peeling wall above the skirting, awaiting the attentions of the damp man (she imagined him as having some mild but unpalatable complaint, possibly of a fungal nature). Then on the boxes again. Perhaps she could pass them off as an intentional part of the décor; it might become fashionable: Designer Clutter. Sunday supplements would devote pages to artfully arranged boxes of junk, their contents spilling onto the floor in close-up grainy photographs displaying the essence of blasé chic. She was reminded about the quest for a shower curtain. Surely, if she owned one, she would become one of those dynamic morning people who leap out of bed at six a.m. to shower then eat yoghurt in the lotus position, rather than loitering in the bath for over an hour reading and fantasizing. She would go to Habitat now, right this very minute, then come back and take a good hard look at the garden.

Patrick had hated Habitat, loathed it as he loathed any kind of shopping that didn't involve the acquisition of food, claiming colour-blindness, taste-blindness, any impairment he could think of to be excused – 'You go, Bel. You're good at that sort of thing. It all looks the same to me.' She had been genuinely baffled, as if he'd claimed not to be able to tell the difference between fruit cake and prawn cocktail. How could someone not mind what their surroundings looked like? Surely, a house was like a wonderful, three-dimensional painting to be composed: the juxtaposition of colours, the contrasting of textures, the fall of light, the *frisson* of a controlled clash. 'A quilt's a quilt,' said Patrick. 'If I'm underneath it and asleep, why should I care what it looks like?' Bella bit her lip; why did she always miss him most when she was remembering something annoying about him?

If Bella had thought about it properly, she'd have realized that Habitat was no sensible place for a single person to go at the weekend. Now she knew the dark and horrible truth: Habitat was the core, the pit of woe at the centre of Sunday Hell. She had never seen so many couples; they must be growing them in pods in the basement. They were Clone Couples with quarry-tiled kitchens, shiny espresso machines, terracotta bread crocks and 'wacky' fish-shaped soap dishes. They had loose-weave, crumpled curtains and loose-weave, crumpled jackets and loose-weave, crumpled children. It was all part of the master plot to make you fulfil your role as a consumer (whatever did happen to the good old customer?) correctly and spend, spend, spend. In supermarkets, they put sweets and chocolate by the till at grabbable height so that your hand will reach out and take a triple pack of walnut whips of its own accord; in home-furnishings stores, they extrude perfect, ready-made families onto the shop floor so that you, the Sad Single, will be inspired by these visions of familial bliss. You start to feel warm, broody, generous; if only you buy a set of rustic peasant coffee mugs, a Mediterranean juice jug and a checked tablecloth with matching napkins, surely you too will acquire a co-ordinating Perfect Husband and Children set and resulting Perfect Life.

She couldn't so much as circumnavigate a sofa without falling over a buggy or having a small, dungareed person trundle straight into her knees; often, said small person would try to carry on like a wind-up toy, proof she was sure that they were fuelled by some sinister unseen power source. And what were all those toys for? It was supposed to be a furniture shop. She didn't want to be looking at corduroy camels or jolly sacks o' bricks or cute baby seals with please-don't-club-me-mister big dark eyes. She caught herself actually starting to walk towards the till holding a small fluffy pig – *for herself*. She was just giving it a little piggy voice in her head, with excited squeals – 'Ee, ee, are you taking me home?' – when she looked down and saw it in her hand. A soft toy. She was as appalled as if she'd suddenly realized that she'd walked out without paying. It was the thin end of the wedge. Next stop: forty cutesy, squidgy creatures with *sweet* names all piled up on the pillows. Then she'd end up having late-night conversations with them and keeping photos of them in her wallet. At her previous job, she had worked with someone who had brought a teddy bear into the studio and held out its paw for her to shake – a woman who otherwise looked perfectly sane and normal. No thank you. She would not turn into Soft Toy Woman. How could you – how could anyone have cuddly toys on a *double* bed? Wasn't there something just the teensiest bit weird about it? A tad Lolita-ish? Paedophiles' delight?

She phoned Viv to report the incident and turn herself in. 'But you didn't actually buy one, right?'

'No, but I hovered dangerously on the brink. And, and, and – even after I realized how close I had come, I thought maybe I could still get it and keep it *under* the pillow – as if that didn't count. Shoot me now, before it's too late.'

Viv's voice dropped to a whisper as she confided that Nick had a toy. 'He hasn't!'

'He has. God, I shouldn't be telling you this. Breathe a word and you're a dead woman. It's a little fluffy dog, but it's OK because he's had it since he was small. It's called Max.'

'It's not *called* anything. It's fur fabric and fluff.'

'Don't be so intolerant. It's really quite sweet. He makes it bounce on my tummy and do somersaults.'

'Perverts!' Viv might as well have said they wore traffic-warden uniforms in bed or liked to wee on each other. 'If there was one other cynical old bitch in the world I thought I could rely on – no, don't try to defend yourselves, you're only making it worse. This is a sad, sad day.'

Bella resolved to restrict future visits to the Danger Zone to late-night closing day, which was when professional, single women who wore smart, coordinating items with proper lapels and waistbands rather than big, shapeless sacky things over leggings went to look at lamp bases in the evening because they had no-one to eat dinner with.

Annoyingly, the prospect of sorting out her studio looked just as daunting that afternoon as it had every other day. What about the garden? That was marginally more appealing. She went to see the current state of play from behind the safety of the French windows. She leant her forehead against the cool of the glass and squished her nose flat like a child wanting to be let out to play. No doubt about it, it was getting worse.

When she'd first viewed the house, the garden had seemed merely rather dull: a tired patch of lawn, some straggly, nondescript shrubs, a few tangly climbers. How could things have got out of hand so quickly? It was becoming increasingly difficult even to see to the other end. This wouldn't have bothered her if she'd had an acre or more; presumably, it must be one of the penalties of being wealthy – not being able to see the boundaries of the grounds, feeling tired by the time you'd reached the end of the corridor. But this was of modest dimensions, barely enough room to swing a snail. It was embarrassing. She must exert some sort of control while she could still get out there. Soon the triffids would be nosing up to the French windows, their tendrils skittering across the glass; the ivy would wind itself around the house like a boa constrictor, tightening its grip, sealing her in. She'd be like Sleeping Beauty, circled by a barrier of briars, waiting for her true prince, the only man brave enough to battle through.

Where on earth should she start? She'd need a machete, a compass and a Boys' Own Survival Guide out there. Have to tie a length of string to the doorhandle so she could find her way back to the house. Perhaps Viv would give her a hand. But she and Nick already had their hands full trying to repaint their bedroom. The lawn looked as sad as uncombed hair scraped across a bald patch. It desperately needed mowing – all she needed was a mower. And that enormous monster bush needed hacking back – if only she had a pair of secateurs. She retrieved her list from the kitchen drawer. 'Garden centre', she added. 'Get tools'.

The garden centre was busy; there were people buying sheds and hefting sacks of compost into car boots and tying trellis panels to their roof-racks, a hive of industry. Even watching them made Bella feel tired. Retired couples bent lovingly over shrubs and rose bushes, as curious and nurturing about a prospective purchase as over a new grandchild. Bella passed a woman of about sixty wearing jeans and a multicoloured waistcoat. 'Now, you're a nice little fellow,' the woman was saying to a variegated holly as Bella went by. 'That's what I'll be like,' thought Bella, 'Wearing clothes thirty years too young for me and chatting to plants. I bet she's got cats.'

Perhaps she should simplify the whole garden – just have lawn and a small tree and a couple of tubs. Then the small tree would become a large tree and overshadow the whole garden so she couldn't even see out, like buying a sweet little mongrel puppy only to watch it grow and grow until you realized it had been born of a great Dane and sired by a buffalo.

She would definitely have to sort out the garden properly before it was worth spending much on plants, she realized, because there was nowhere to

plant them in its current state. In the meantime, she chose a few small pots of herbs to cheer herself up. While paying, she noticed a sign by the till advertising the services of a garden designer: 'Time to turn over a new leaf? If your garden's more of a jinx than a joy, don't stay indoors and cry. Whether your taste tends towards the traditional or the avant-garde, simple or stupendous, I'll help you create your ideal garden and turn your dreams into reality – at a reasonable cost.' It offered a free initial consultation, without obligation. She noted down the name and phone number.

Planting out her herbs to avoid the greater evil of doing her laundry, Bella resolved to phone the garden man immediately. It was Sunday, so he probably wouldn't be there, was probably yet another person out having a wonderful day in the bosom of his family, carrying his youngest on his shoulders, taking the older one to kick a ball around at the park. Exchanging smug smiles with his slender wife as she stirred the gravy, the children grinning impishly as they tucked in heartily to a mound of Brussels sprouts. The Sunday lunches of her own childhood had been rather different. Her mother's frown as she subdued a rogue lump in the gravy, concentrating as she added a dose of red wine to the pan. The heavy cutlery, awkward in Bella's childish hands, the fine china, immaculate tablecloth. Her own quiet face, pale moon in a cloud of dark hair. Her father's rich voice, talking, soothing, bridging the silences, playing a game of make-believe, Happy Families.

She shook the thought away and rummaged in her handbag for the phone number she had noted down. At least she could leave a message, and it meant she could cross off something from The List. His answerphone said to leave a message for 'Will Henderson or Henderson Garden Design'.

'I need a man with a machete and a vat of weedkiller,' she said, 'oh, yes, and a new garden.'

She went and extracted her list from the drawer again. Damn. Added 'Call garden designer' to the bottom, then crossed it off firmly and went upstairs, feeling positive enough to face her studio.

The crack in her studio wall was longer than she had remembered. It was the kind of crack to be tutted at, the kind to make you say, 'Something should be done about that' as if you were an authority on such matters.

Bella did both of these things, then stood back to squint at it through half-closed eyelids. It seemed a shame to fill it in with boring old Polyfilla; plus there was the minor fact that she didn't have any. She nodded to herself, as if she had come to a decision, then began to delve into the boxes, foraging for her paints.

8

'No, no, no, no, and no.'

'I'll take that as a no then?' Bella said.

Something gave her the feeling that Viv wasn't mad keen on the idea of going to a poetry reading.

Viv claimed to be allergic to poetry ever since an unfortunate experience at school when she had fallen asleep – her chin suddenly hitting the desk with a loud thunk – while the unfortunately named Mrs Doring was reading them 'The Lady of Shalott', raising up on her toes to emphasize the poetic meter as if she were mounted on a bouncy spring.

'But it's not *poetry* poetry, Viv, not wandered-lonely-as-a-cloud wafty stuff. She's really funny. Some of it's rude. You'd love it.'

'Can't be done, babe. Friday's our takeaway and video night.'

'But this is Culture,' Bella said. 'You remember Culture. You had some once, about four years ago.'

Viv remained immovable. All couples have a regular evening together when they sit glued to a movie, chomping their way through chicken chow mein and beef in black bean sauce or

Special Set Meal No. 2; it was a Universal Law, like gravity or e=mc2, not to be questioned. Patrick, poking through a drawer, 'Where's the wonky list gone again, Bel?' The menu of the Wong Kei. 'Why do you need it? We always have the same thing: 5, 8, 27, 41, 63, 66. Free prawn crackers.' Jeez, she could still remember the numbers, a code inscribed in her memory like the combination of a safe. How long before she could forget them?

'You're very sad. Anyone would think you were joined at the hip. No, no, don't try to protest. I'm going to get you two matching anoraks next Christmas. Orange, with *cheeky* foldaway hoods.'

'You should go anyway,' Viv said. 'There might be some nice men there.'

'Right. What kind of man goes to a poetry reading?'

'You're beyond help. Well, don't blame me if you never find—' she made a melodramatic bad-horror-movie noise '—The One.'

The One. The magical, perfect fantasy Mr Right that every woman knows is Out There, somewhere, struggling on through his lonely existence, because he hasn't yet found Her, his fantasy woman, his The One. Rationally, Bella reminded herself that life didn't work like that; of course there would be many hundreds, maybe even thousands, of men in the world that would be a good match for any one woman. Most you would never meet but that should still leave you with many, many opportunities to have a perfectly nice life with a perfectly nice somebody. But what if there really were only The One, the ideal person who was supposed to be with you? You might miss your bus one morning and he could be on it, single and ready to meet you and you would never even know how close you had been. Or you might glimpse him across a room, your eyes would meet for a moment and you'd wonder 'What if?' Someone else might have got to him first, be stifling *your* person in a dead-end, loveless marriage. Even now, this very minute, your very own Mr Right could be cavorting with another woman, the unfaithful bastard, ignoring the niggling thought fluttering in his mind like a moth, struggling to be noticed, that something vital was missing from his life. If you did ever chance to find each other, The One would, of course, recognize your true loveliness and be blind to your sticking-out stomach and chubby arms.

She would go on her own. Why not? She was an independent woman, an elective spinster as she had once heard someone say. How much better it was to have a diversity of interests, to be going to a poetry reading rather than sitting slumped on the sofa watching telly, your biggest concern whether to stick with the familiar, No. 63 Chicken with Chinese Mushrooms, or live dangerously and go for No. 67 Chicken and Cashew Nuts.

Most of the seats were already taken by the time Bella arrived at the poetry reading, having extricated herself with difficulty from a conversation with Seline about the prospect of going into partnership as things were going so well. Bella hoped to defer the moment of actually Making a Decision for as long as possible. Or longer. She didn't know what she wanted, other than not to have to decide. She helped herself to a glass of wine and covertly peered over the rim in quest of any lone, attractive men. It would be considerate if they could carry a small sign or wear a lapel badge: 'Available' or 'Married but looking for a leg-over' or 'In relationship but keeping my options open'.

There was quite a crowd. The last time she'd gone to a poetry reading, there had been only two other people aside from herself and what she concluded must be the poet's family and immediate hangers-on. She'd felt obliged to exaggerate her appreciation to compensate for the lack of audience and spent the whole time nodding and brow-furrowing in an elaborate mime of gosh-how-profound-how-sensitively-attuned-I-feel-so-deeply-privileged-to-hear-these-soul-enriching-words. The poet's entourage had openly stared at her at the end of each poem to check that her reaction was sufficiently intense. Why was she trying to meet their expectations? she'd wondered. Wasn't it the poet who was supposed to be doing the performing?

She settled by a table piled with Nell Calder's books, and looked around for somewhere to rest her glass. There was an empty corner on a table nearby – she reached for it at exactly the same moment as someone else. Their glasses clashed.

'Oh, sorry,' they said in unison.

'Er, cheers then.' The man smiled, looking directly into her eyes. Nice face, but how rude, she thought. Unnerved, she looked away quickly. She didn't want to give him the wrong idea. His hair could do with a bit of a brush. It was strangely springy, sticking up at odd angles here and there. She peered at him sideways. He caught her at it and smiled.

There was an amplified whoompf and whine as the microphone was wrestled from its stand at the front.

'Oh, hello, signs of action, I think,' said the springy-haired man at her side, stretching to see over a woman wearing a peculiar patchwork hat with a ludicrously high crown.

'Do you think she's got planning permission for that hat?' he whispered to Bella, indicating the woman with a nod. 'This is a conservation area.' Mid-swallow, Bella laughed, spraying her wine with a snort. Oh, terrific. Well, it was one way to attract attention.

Embarrassed, she looked away. Nell Calder was being introduced.

Applause.

'This one was inspired by my ex-husband,' said the poet. 'It's called "Can I have custody of the egg-timer?"'

Conscious of Springy Hair's presence by her side, Bella made a

sweeping I'm-just-looking-for-my-friend cast of the room, trying to
see round the woman in front. Suddenly, across the room, half-
hidden by a woman holding her glass in front of her, Bella caught a
glimpse of a man. Dark, floppy hair. The edge of a face with horn-
rimmed glasses. Patrick? A jolt. Dry mouth. Thudding heart. Even
now. Craning her head to see, the memory caught her unawares,
flooding over her in a wash, leaving her pale and breathless.

* * *

She catches herself looking round the room for him. Perhaps he is
in the kitchen, rootling about in the fridge for a corner of cheese, or
in the loo absorbed in a copy of the *National Geographic*. Of course
he isn't here. She *does* know that. And yet. These people – his sister,
Sophie, who suddenly looks so slight and frail as if the lightest
breeze would carry her off, her right hand clasping her left arm
behind her back, holding herself; James, one of Patrick's oldest
friends, uncomfortable and aware of his paunch in a too-tight
borrowed suit; Rose, Patrick's mother, immaculately turned out as
for a wedding, solicitously anticipating with lighthouse eyes the
needs of every guest – 'A drop more dry sherry? Another smoked
salmon canapé? Everyone's been marvellous, really. I've hardly had
to do a thing. Do let me get you something. Just a little bite?'; his
father, Joseph, held together by his crisply tailored suit, dark as
wrought iron, staring down into his heavy glass at the ice boulders
floating and colliding in their enclosed lake of

Scotch – he looks as if he would gladly join them, slide into that
welcoming liquid and feel it flow round him, through him, in him,
pushing out the warm blood that obstinately completes another
tireless circuit of his body, swooshing through him, steeling his
arteries with its icy anaesthetic, clasping him sweetly until he is
numb and feels no more.

And there, a small clutch of Patrick's colleagues, balancing side plates and cocktail napkins and glasses, taking embarrassed bites of too-good, tempting titbits; his brother, Alan, nodding in earnest agreement with Aunt Patsy, scooping up the coins in his trouser pocket, chinking them in his grasp, then jangling them loose again: scoop, chink, jangle – finding what comfort he can by being in control at least of these compliant coins.

But, of course, *he* isn't here. Bella knows it, and yet still it seems as if these people who were closest to him – people who had helped him take his first stumbling steps, compared scabby knees with him in the playground, coughed over a first stolen cigarette with him, worked with him, argued with him, laughed with him, kissed him, loved him – they seem between them to make a shape, a Patrick-shaped space, so that really she feels he must be here. Surely they would only all be here because of him?

'Try and eat something, Bella, hmm?' A platter of soft asparagus stems, swaddled like delicate newborns in thinly rolled brown bread (no crusts, of course – 'These little extra efforts do make all the difference I find'), hovers under her nose. Bella takes one and obediently moves it towards her mouth. She could do this. She could function like a normal person. Her teeth mechanically march up and down, doing their drill. She presses her lips with her napkin – blue, mid-blue, almost the same colour as that old shirt of Patrick's, the one with the collar so worn she'd tried to get him to cut it up for shoe-cloths, the one that now lies unwashed beneath her pillow waiting for her, waiting for her to press her face into its crumpled cloth, breathe its soft blueness, button it around her.

Ting, ting. A strange sound, metal on glass. A knife tapped against a wineglass, edge on, like a child chopping off the head of a boiled egg; a sound effect to punctuate every wedding, every anniversary, to herald every speech, a sound of celebration. Someone is saying something. Yes, faces are all turning in one

direction. Bella tilts her face in mimicry, one more sunflower
unthinkingly following the sun.

Alan, Patrick's brother, is speaking:

'...all for coming, many from a great distance. I have – we have
all – been immensely pleased. Touched. To see so many of you
here. So many friends. Family. I – well.'

He clears his throat, presses his lips firmly together, sealing in
the words.

'Anyway,' he smiles tightly, 'I know Patrick wouldn't have wanted
us all to be mooning about with faces as long as a wet weekend, and
he would have hated to see good liquor go to waste, so please, raise
your glasses. To Patrick.'

'To Patrick,' they echo.

Alan raises his glass again, the ice tinkling softly like a half-
heard bell blown by a distant breeze.

'May his memory live on,' he says. 'May his memory live on.'

No, she thinks, she won't settle for a neat collection of memories, tidily bound up like a photograph album. She wants to run
back to the cemetery, kick off her too-stylish, horribly perfect
shoes, flicking each piece of smug black suede in a reckless trajec-
tory high, high over the wall into the woodland beyond. She would
fall to her knees, then, and scrabble at the earth, push the sticky
clods aside with her hands, haul at the damp soil, and wrench
open the lid of that gleaming box. She would reach in and shake
him and shout, 'Stop it, Patrick. Stop it! It's not funny. Don't do
this.'

She could see his face crinkling suddenly with laughter, his
finger pushing his glasses further up his nose, giggling uncontrollably. 'That was brilliant,' he'd say. 'I really had you all there. You'll
never know how hard it was to keep quiet all that time. When the
vicar went on about how I'd always been a considerate, honest man,
I had to bite my cheek to stop myself spurting into laughter. Oh,

come on, Bel, it *was* funny – admit it. Great hat, by the way. Is it new?'

And she would have to laugh then, too, and whack him playfully for scaring her so, and then they'd talk about it, sharing the best bits again, doing impressions, comparing the outfits, commenting on who turned up late, which part was most moving, who wept the most conspicuously, who merely dabbed the corner of one eye politely with a handkerchief, laughing together.

But it isn't a joke. And she knows then that she won't go back to the cemetery. Can't go back. Won't plunge her arms down deep into the spongy soil. As long as she didn't look, then it could still be just a box down there, no more than a long chest of polished oak lying empty in the silent earth – and Patrick could be anywhere: at home, pottering about 'doing things that need to be done around the house' as he would say, which mostly seemed to involve looking at appliances or objects in need of repair, saying 'hmm' a lot and then sitting down with a coffee and a crossword puzzle; at work, being sensible and efficient, writing reports or out on a site somewhere, assessing, noticing details, making notes; engaged in a meaningful relationship with his beloved computer; or sprawling on the sofa, a newspaper over his face, snorting with that peculiar half-whistling noise as he breathed out until she nudged him or tweaked his nose to get him to stop.

Someone is hugging her. She squeezes the navy-suited body back softly, politely, unaware of who it is yet grateful for its solid warmth. A hand pats her consolingly on the shoulder, a master rewarding his faithful dog for carrying out a trick well. And it was a trick. Sip your sherry, nibble a canapé, proffer your cheek to be kissed, shed a silent tear or two. No screaming; no wailing; no ugly, wrenching sobs dragging her whole ribcage; no face bizarrely painted with black mascara trails, streaked by tears that seemed as if they would never run dry; no sitting curled up on the floor, head tucked tight to her knees, clutching herself, holding herself together in case she falls apart in sharp, brittle fragments, or subsides slowly, sliding across the floor in a pool of tears and pain. No. She could accomplish this trick very well indeed. She smiles and kisses the cheek, wondering how soon she can leave.

9

'...Isabel, isn't it?' A hand was waving in her face, claiming her attention. Recoiling slightly, Bella craned again to see the man. His face turned: a longer nose, thinner mouth. Quite different. Not Patrick at all. No. Of course not. She shook the thought away and turned to concentrate on the person standing rather too close in front of her. It was the woman in unlawful possession of an offensive patchwork hat.

'No,' said Bella, automatically. 'It's Bella.' Who was this woman? Under the brim, her face did look sort of familiar, but Bella couldn't quite place it.

'Well, that's short for Isabella anyway, isn't it?' The woman glared at her almost accusingly.

'Not in my case. It's just Bella.' She smiled. 'I'm so sorry – I'm terrible with names—'

'Ginger Badell. We met at Scotton Design just the other week. I create concepts for Benson Foods.' The woman clutched at a tall, thin man hovering in a nervous orbit around her and steered him by his elbow towards Bella. 'And this is Roger, my *amore*.' She looked to either side of Bella, and pulled the stringy *amore* closer as if worried that Bella might suddenly make a grab for him and slurp him into a passionate embrace.

They chatted politely for a few minutes, while Bella tried to glance round unobtrusively for Springy Hair. Had he gone?

'So nice to see you again.' said Bella, backing away. 'I must just grab this chance to buy a signed copy – do excuse me.'

There were three other people in front of her waiting to have their books signed. Bella looked around the room while she waited. Springy Hair had obviously left. She would have thought he might say goodbye. Not that she'd been interested; he must have been a bit weird, the way he'd looked at her. He was probably a stalker. Probably hadn't fancied her anyway. Probably was just being friendly out of pity. Must be on his way home now back to his wife. And his four children. And their dog. Bloody hell. Even that bonkers Ginger woman with the world's worst taste in millinery had a man. Well, just about, although he seemed to have about as much testosterone as a mouldy flannel. And she said concepts instead of ideas and *amore* with a sickening coy look and was far too intense. And, worst of all, she probably looked down on Bella, pitied her because she was obviously alone.

She reached the head of the queue.

'What shall I put?' The poet sat with pen poised. 'Is it for anyone special?'

'Hah!' The man behind her gave a start. Oops, she hadn't meant to be quite so emphatic. She ahem-ed as if she'd only been trying to clear her throat. 'I should be so lucky,' she said.

* * *

When Bella got back home that evening, there was no message from the damp man. How dare he? She had become accustomed to his regular messages with ever more intriguing excuses about why he couldn't come yet, but she was definitely, no question, the next job up; she was in his little book, so there were no two ways about it. How like a man. Just when you were getting used to being let down by one in a particular way, he switched to some new form of irritation. She had come to expect the little flashing light on her answerphone that indicated another exciting episode in the life and work of Mr Bowman. Her favourite so far was that the lodger had left without giving notice. Quite why this should prevent Mr Bowman from hacking off her plaster, she was unsure, but he was adamant on the matter.

There was, however, another one from that Henderson person, the garden designer; they had been playing answerphone tag for days. Perhaps he would like to join Mr Bowman on the list of people who were supposed to be helping her Sort Out Her Life but inexplicably never turned up. He might like to come and overturn half of her garden and leave her with a nice big heap of soil and rubble. Then it would complement the sitting-room with its attractive collection of boxes. Maybe she should just offer to sleep with Mr Bowman – might that move her up his list of priorities? She suspected otherwise; no doubt he would say, 'Well, I'm sure that would be most acceptable Mrs (he couldn't quite bring himself to say Ms, but she was evidently much too old to be a Miss, so she must be Mrs) Krer... er (he typically ahem-ed his way politely through her surname rather than risk embarrassing himself by actually trying to say it), but I've got to service two other ladies first and they been waitin' longer 'n you.'

Will Henderson's message said his man with a machete was still chomping at the bit, but that they didn't seem to be having much luck getting each other, her life was obviously one non-stop glamorous social whirl. Perhaps he would pop round on Saturday morning, around 10ish, but if not OK, could she phone and leave another message. Actually, could she phone anyway because she hadn't given him her address.

Streuth, she might as well programme his number into the phone's memory. Certainly she would, if she ever found the manual and managed to suss out how to programme the memory, she would do that.

* * *

She phoned in the morning, from work.

'Hello again. Bella Kreuzer here again. Just calling—'

'Hello?' The phone was picked up.

'Mr Henderson? In the flesh? You do exist, then. You've completely thrown me now. I was getting on so well with your answerphone. Best relationship I've ever had.'

'Shall I hang up and leave you two alone together?'

She gave him her address, agreed that Saturday morning would be fine. 'And please can I beg you not to cut anything back before then,' he said. 'It's so easy to lose something wonderful because it doesn't look like much and you might not recognize it.'

'I promise. Scout's honour.'

Friday. Best day of the week. In the afternoon someone would slip out for cakes and, if Seline was out of the office, a couple of bottles of wine. They'd dabble at bits of work while reading out highlights from *Hello!* and playing 'Choices' – 'Would you rather live in an MFI showroom for three months *with* people coming round and watching you all day OR sleep with the man in the sand-wich shop?'

'Which – not the one with the teeth?'

'Yup, *and* you have to snog him.'

Bella sketched in her layout pad, toying with grandiose schemes for her garden – a Victorian summer house on wheels, topiary

pyramids, Moorish channels of water criss-crossing like a
Mondrian grid, enormous craggy rocks with a full-scale waterfall, a
swing hanging from a massive cedar tree, suspended on ropes
entwined with roses and ivy. Could you transplant two-hundred-
year-old trees, she wondered? Perhaps not.

Seline suddenly swept into the office unexpectedly. There was a
muffled clinking as bottles were hustled under desks, computer
games swiftly replaced by Quark layouts.

'Has anyone seen my copy of *Hello?'* she said.

* * *

Saturday morning. The doorbell rang. Was it really that late or was
this Henderson character early? She ran down the stairs, buttoning
up her jeans. Shoes? Never mind.

'Springy Hair!' She tried to turn it into a cough. The funny man
from the poetry reading.

'It's *you,'* said Springy Hair. 'What did you say?'

'Nothing, nothing. Just a tickle in my throat.' She cleared it
loudly. Very alluring. Why not just hawk phlegm all over him?
'What are you doing here?'

'I've come to blowtorch your garden. Will Henderson.' He
smiled. 'Hello. I'm glad I've bumped into you again.' He apologized
for having dashed off after the reading without saying goodbye.
He'd been embarrassed when he saw her talking to the woman
with the hat after he'd been so rude about it.

'Hey, psychedelic toes.' He nodded at her shimmering blue nail
polish. 'Or is that a rare disease I shouldn't mention?'

Good grief. Blue toenails, as if she were a teenager. She cast
about for a pair of shoes.

'So, have you just moved in then?' He waved at the multi-storey
box park in her sitting-room. She explained that there was no point

unpacking everything because there was still the DAMP to be done.

'I see it in capital letters in my head now because I've been meaning to have it done for so long. Mr Bowman's more elusive than the Scarlet Pimpernel.'

'Bowman, eh. Hmm-mm.'

'What? What?'

'No, he's very good. You're not in a hurry though, are you?'

She explained that she'd already been waiting for over two months, then launched into a tirade about Mr Bowman and his imaginative range of excuses, he never came when he promised, now he wasn't even bothering to ring to say he wasn't coming. Was he a local legend, Bella asked, was that why Will had heard of him?

'No. He's my brother-in-law.'

'Yeah, right. Very droll.' At school, certain kids always made that joke; if you passed a man wearing a bad toupee on your way to the library (holding a sticky-handed boy with the tips of your fingers) and you hissed 'Wig!' at your neighbour, he would say, 'That's my uncle actually,' and pretend to be offended. It was a fashion, a phase, like jacks or saying 'Vanies' or putting cartoon-character stickers on the inside of your desk lid.

'No. He really is. Sort of. Well he's my brother-in-law, in-law. My sister's husband's brother. What does that make him?'

'It still makes him a very annoying person who hasn't done my damp, I'm afraid.'

They went out to the garden. He nodded in places, humming, clucking his tongue in others, making a running commentary to himself – 'mellow brick wall, dum-de-dum, courses of flint – hmm-mm, concrete pavers – dodgy lawn – few decent shrubs – good clematis dum-de-dum – Russian vine, oops – brambles – perennial weeds – clear this bit – transplant that–' He plunged between bushes, got down on his hands and knees to peer under things, stuck his hand into the soil, crumbling it between his fingers.

She saw him make scribbly sketches, numerous notes, tiny diagrams. He would come back and measure properly if she wanted to go ahead, he said.

'OK if I ask you a few questions?' Will put down his mug and took out a notebook from one of the bulging pockets of his jacket.

'Sounds ominous. It wasn't me, Officer. I wasn't even there. Ask anyone.'

'Remain calm.' He looked up from his notebook. 'Trouble is, the reason people end up with a garden that doesn't suit them is they plunge straight in without thinking about what they really want.'

Bella shifted in her seat and sat on her hands to stop herself fiddling. 'I feel as if I'm in an exam.'

'You are.' Will rolled up his sleeves. 'If you get too many wrong, my fee goes up.'

'Ready? Right, question 1. What do you want to do in this garden?'

'Can't we start with an easier one?'

'No we can't. Judging from the state of it, can I assume you're not a veteran plant-collector? So do you want somewhere for eating out? A bolt-hole from the rat race? Place to sunbathe in privacy? All of the above?'

'What was the middle one again? I don't know, I don't know. But privacy's a must. I want a secluded corner somewhere with lots of traily things hanging down. I hate feeling people are looking at me. Does that sound terribly paranoid?'

'It must make life pretty awkward.' Will jotted something down in his notebook.

'What? Being paranoid?'

He shrugged as if it were obvious.

'No – just – well, I imagine you get looked at quite a lot.' He raised his eyes from what he was writing.

'Next question?'

Bella looked down into her mug of coffee, then started to watch his hands to avoid his penetrating gaze. Why did he have to look at her like that? It was quite rude really. Now he had made her feel self-conscious. He was obviously only saying it to wind her up anyway. No-one could find her attractive the way she looked this morning in these grotty old jeans and baggy jumper. Her hair was loose and she hadn't even bothered with lipstick, never mind the whole routine that she needed to feel even half-presentable.

'Any kids?'

'Nope. What's that got to do with it anyway?'

'Play space. You might want a sandpit. Swing. Whatever. Any on the horizon?'

'The Vatican will declare me a modern miracle if there are.'

'You're not keen on kids then?'

'Is this really part of the questionnaire?'

'Not really. I'm just nosy.' That look again.

Bella laughed. At least he was honest.

'It's not that I don't like them. I just—' she shrugged. 'I – anyway, I'm — more coffee?'

Bella spent some time fiddling with the lid of the kettle, loudly opening and closing cupboards to look for biscuits.

'Don't bother. Really.' Will got up to go. 'I've been here way too long already. So, think about exactly what you want in the garden, any must-haves and so on. Make a list.'

'Right. List-making, I'm good at that. Will you really design it to suit my every need?'

'Not at all. I'll nod and say, "I see. No problem," a lot, then ignore you and do whatever I thought of in the first place.'

Will held out his business card.

'Call me. Here – let me give you a few in case you want to pass one on.' Bella smiled. 'You had too many printed, didn't you?'

'Well, it's ever so cheap if you have a thousand done.'

'A thousand? Grief. Give me a stack. I can do shopping lists on the back.'

'They're quite good for sticking under wobbly table legs in restaurants too.'

There were no spare drawing pins on her kitchen pinboard, so Bella tucked one of his cards behind the corner of a photograph. The one of her and Patrick. Her finger rested for a moment on the pin, feeling its cold hardness solid beneath the fleshy pad of her fingertip.

She had been cooking when she heard the news.

* * *

Bella is stirring her sauce, giggling at Viv's description of some pompous pillock she has had to endure at her all-day conference.

'So she offered him this piece of Brie and he said, "Actually, I'm a *Stilton* man myself," and laughed, expecting us to acknowledge him as a great wit. Jill and I couldn't look at each other. And he was wearing a blazer, with those shiny buttons with little anchors on them.'

'A blazer, eh? Hangin's too good for the likes of 'im.' The telephone rings.

'Get that, will you? I have to keep whisking – this is looking a bit blobby. It's probably Patrick. Running late. Can we save him some supper? Blah, blah. Tell him we've got baked bananas – that'll speed him up.'

'Good evening, Kreuzer and Hughes residence.' Viv's over-corrected receptionist voice is spot on.

'Yes, yes, she is. She's just here.'

Viv hands her the phone, saying it is Patrick's father. 'Hello, Joe? How are you? Patrick's not back yet. He—' She is silent.

There is only the ticking of the kitchen clock.

Viv stops whisking and looks up. Bella's face is a mask, pale and blank. 'Mm-mm. Still here. I'm OK. Where are you? Hang on.' She casts about for a pen. 'OK. Where do I come to?'

Her writing scrawls unevenly across the bottom of a shopping list on the back of an envelope. Looking at the loops and lines of ink as they appear on the paper, she knows she will remember this moment for ever: standing in this kitchen, seeing the name of the hospital as she writes next to words that suddenly seem pointless, incomprehensible – butter, potatoes, green veg., coffee – NOT decaff, disp. razors for P. Wasn't potato a peculiar word when you thought about it? Had she really been in such a hurry that she had put disp. razors? The look on Viv's face, the way the whisk falls from her hand into the sauce. How loud the kitchen clock is. Why is it so loud?

Bella's eyes rove across the cork pinboard and its patchwork of cards, lists and messages: Taj Mahal Take Away. Call for Free Home Delivery. Friday Night Tandoori Special. A picture of herself on the beach at Arisaig, from a holiday they'd had together driving up the west coast of Scotland. A preposterously cute photo of Lawrence, Patrick's nephew, dressed as a nativity shepherd, wearing a tea towel on his head. A lone jet earring, optimistically waiting for its companion to be found. An old note: *B. Don't forget, not back till 10. Please save some nosh or I'll manage with toast (sob...). Big snogs. P.* A blurry picture taken on automatic timer of them both in bed wearing red felt antlers last Christmas.

She is shaking. This is probably normal, she tells herself. She feels as if she is outside her own body, watching her hand clutching the phone like a lifebelt, looking at her bare feet on the floor. She cannot feel the floor properly beneath her; presses her soles hard into the cork tiles, making contact with the ground. She is nodding, saying yes, yes, she is on her way, she will be there as soon as she can.

'It's Patrick isn't it?' Viv says.

'There's been an accident. On a site.' It sounds like a line from a poor movie. She wishes she could rewind the tape and say something more meaningful, more poignant, *better*.

'Is he...?'

Patrick is alive but unconscious, suffering from severe head injuries and internal haemorrhaging.

'Shoes?' Bella is saying. 'I need some shoes.'

Her legs start shaking compulsively as she sits and tries to lace up her boots, her knees pumping up and down like pistons. Viv kneels by her feet and ties the laces, holds Bella steady by her shoulders.

'You can't drive like this,' Viv says. 'I'll take you.'

* * *

'...or the weekend?' Will was saying. 'Mmm?'

'Sorry if I'm boring you. It's just that now's a good time to get your garden under way, so call me soon. Yes? Am I being too pushy?'

'No. Yes. You're right.'

'I am pushy?'

'No. About coming back. Soon. Next weekend? Or perhaps that's not—'

'Fine. It's fine. See you then, then. Never sounds right, that, does it?'

'Which?'

'Then then.'

'Have you thought of having treatment? They're working wonders with laser surgery these days. Burn whole lobes of your brain right off.'

'Thank you. I'll bear it in mind. I'm going now, but don't forget.'

'I won't.' She nodded decisively. *Forget what?* she wondered.

10

'Croissants,' said Will, waving a paper bag under her nose as she opened the door. 'As I've made you get up early.'

'Nonsense. Been up for hours. Done my ten-mile morning run. Hundred press-ups. Hoovered the house. Licked the windows clean. Retiled the roof.'

They took their croissants and mugs of tea out to the garden, stood talking as they leant with their backs against the French windows, pleasantly warm from the spring sun. What kind of plants did she like, he wanted to know.

She closed her eyes to picture it, to see it fresh and alive in her head: grasses, she said – feathery heads waving in the wind, catching the light – different textures, felty foliage and shiny stems and those plants with the downy, pleated leaves that held the rain-drops like glass beads – drifts of colour – scented things, big blowsy roses and lavender and jasmine – herbs, lemon balm, plants for cooking – dramatic, spiky jobs, maybe a yucca, something that could be lit up at night, throwing its shadow on the wall.

They talked of shapes, proportions, styles, materials. He sketched ideas, paced up and down, swirling his arms like a manic conductor, showing her, squatting to model the position of an urn, standing tall like a tree for her to assess the effect from the house. Discussed the budget – 'Don't go mad, I'm not the Sultan of Brunei.'

'No marble patio, then? No cavorting gold nymphs in the fountain?' He asked her even more questions, how much time would she spend looking after the garden? 'Be honest,' he said. Was she lazy? What else did she do with her time?

'Is this OK? My mother calls me the Spanish Inquisition.'

'Hah! My mother makes the Spanish Inquisition look like a church outing.'

Would he like a bite to eat, only odds and ends from the fridge, she said, embarrassed that she had taken up so much of his time again, but perhaps he would have a proper hot roast lunch waiting for him at home?

'No chance.'

'Help yourself.' She set out dishes on the kitchen worktop. 'This is sort of a grazing lunch. Just pick at whatever you fancy.'

'What a treat. Like a midnight feast – I love picking.'

'Me too.'

'Me three.'

Bella looked at him. 'I used to say that when I was little.'

Will insisted it was a banquet compared with the contents of his own fridge.

Cold chicken with basil dressing, home-made coleslaw, hot ciabatta bread, runny Brie. She shrugged.

''s just leftovers. Don't you eat properly?'

'I *do*. Why do women always imagine that men don't cook? I can do a good roast chicken. A stew sort of a thing.' He seemed to be thinking. 'Chops!' he said triumphantly. 'Pasta with sauce.'

'Homemade or jar?'

He scowled. 'Ah! *And* I do a mean stir-fry.'

'All men say they can do stir-fries. Didn't you see that documentary? Apparently, the Y chromosome is linked with the ability only to cook over a high heat – that's why men like barbecues.'

Back outside, Will drew her to the far end of the garden. He stood behind her, pointing back at the house over her shoulder. She could feel the warmth of his breath in her hair. Imagined for a moment she could hear him swallow, hear the air swell his lungs, the double beat of his heart.

'There. See? What I suggested before about the patio? With wide steps.' She moved away, scraped her fingers through her hair.

'Fine. Now, what about this awful lawn?' Will stamped on it.

'Get rid of it. It's in a chronic state. We can returf, of course, if you want, but I wouldn't bother. It's not a good use of space here. Just think—' He gestured in a broad arc, a wizard weaving a spell. 'No mowing. No edging. More space for interesting plants...'

'Won't it look too hard? Like a car park?'

'Not unless you specifically want Tarmac. I was thinking of a sweep of shingle, so we can plant directly into the soil below – ornamental grasses, herbs, whatever. Or big, clunky grey cobbles, with water...'

'Like a beach? I'd love that. My dad used to take me when I was little. I still go to the seaside when I feel crappy.'

'Same here. Oh – look at that—' He strode off and plunged into the border between two overgrown bushes.

Bella stared at the ground, remaking it as her own private beach in her head, a stretched-out curve, water lapping at the stones, the wetness bringing their colours to life, the surf frothing at her feet.

* * *

She leaves the post-funeral 'do' as soon as she decently can, sooner really. Slips silently around the room to say goodbye to the cornerstones of Patrick's family: Joseph, who hugs her so tight she can barely breathe. 'Keep in touch, won't you? Come to see us.' Rose kisses her cheek. 'You've been such a comfort.' Sophie, suddenly looking like a child, her eyes large and shadowy. 'Can I come and stay, Bel?' Alan just gives her a big squeeze. He cannot speak.

She drives to the coast. Patrick had taken her there a few times, when they'd gone to stay with his parents. Now she needs the sea air in her lungs, the sting of salt in her nostrils, the wind to blow away the surface of her skin, leaving her purged, raw but renewed.

Turning into the road that leads to the beach, she is surprised as always by the sudden emptiness at the end of the road where it curves sharply round. If she carried straight on, she would hurl out above the shingle, sailing into the big sky, soaring like a great metallic gull for one beautiful, arching moment, then falling down into the waves, diving deep, sinking to settle on the seabed. There, fish would nibble at her flesh, weave dances between her bones. Crabs would clatter, sea-muffled, over her ribs. Her hair would wave like seaweed. Barnacles would colonize her, make her their city, and she would be part of another world, her salty tears unnoticed in the sea.

The car slows and she concentrates on turning left into the cul-de-sac, past the 'Unsuitable for motors' sign, to park. Pulls her old, crushed mac from its permanent home in the boot of the car. She scrunches down onto the shingle, her black suede court shoes sinking into the pebbles. Slips them off and walks a few steps further. Streuth, these stones are hard; she wishes she'd brought some other shoes. Still, it's not normally what you think of when you go to a funeral: 'Have I got everything? Tissues? Black hat? Beach shoes?'

The wind flicks her hair across her face, into her mouth, and she huddles closer to the breakwater for shelter. How weathered it is; the wood is smooth to the touch, sanded by the waves and – well, sand, she supposes. She leans her head against it and squints along its length. The narrow gaps between the boards have tiny pebbles lodged in them, but whether by a determined child or by the force of the sea, she cannot tell. She wiggles her toes down into the shingle, incongruous against her sheer black tights.

'Fuck, fuck, fuck,' she says, under her breath. 'Bugger, bugger, bugger.' How could he do this to me? That's just so typical of Patrick, it really is. He's so bloody perverse. Always has to go his own way. Only he would go and get himself killed in such a ridiculous fashion and with such bad timing. There is a kind of pleasure, a comfort in this facetiousness. Better to be pissed off with him, better to rail against his annoying habits than to allow her mind a stretch of silence, where the darkness lies in wait, curled up patiently, ready for the moment when she would let it in. If she could hold out long enough, perhaps it would just slink off, bored with waiting? But she knows; she knows it is there. It would slither around her ankles, coiling and uncoiling itself until she let down her guard. Then it would wind itself about her, sliding over her, heavy and cold as stone, pulling her down into a well of dark. She would never be able to climb up again. No. She had peeked over the edge and the fear of it had clawed at her stomach. She would not do it. Could not.

'Bloody Patrick.' She shoves the shingle down sharply with her foot.

* * *

'...OK with that then?' Will stood close, looking down at her. He seemed to be expecting something.

'Mmm?'

'Welcome back. Are you happy for me to take out those shrubs? They're eating up space.'

'Won't it feel very exposed?'

'Trust me. There'll be plenty of seclusion. We can put a pergola across that corner, with a purple vine and some spring clematis. Oh, I know—' He ran to the end of the garden and Bella found herself following. 'Say just here – a secret hideaway seat with a living willow roof. Just wide enough for you and whoever to sit—'

'Yes.' She turned away from his gaze. 'I'd love that. But without the whoever. A single seat's fine.' Pretended not to hear him behind her as she walked towards the house.

'Are you sure?'

'Oh, is it your birthday? How old are you?' Will nodded towards the ornate lamp from Bella's parents, still half-shrouded in tissue. 'If you don't mind me asking?'

'Yes I do mind, and no it isn't anyway. House-warming present from the parents. I haven't got round to exchanging it yet. Vile, isn't it?'

He shrugged. 'Not at all. Just a bit stately-homeish. Not quite you, I'd have said.'

'Oh? Are you an expert already then?'

'Yes – I have teams of detectives working round the clock, faxing me hourly updates on you.'

'And what do they say?'

'That'sclassified.Besides,theyhaven'tgotroundtolampshade preferences yet.'

She shook her head, suppressing a smile. 'That reminds me, I've got to phone the old dears. Weekend duty call.'

'Ah. You're a close family then?'

* * *

'Come on, Dads.' Bella silently willed her father to answer the phone. 'Oh. Hi. It's me.'

'Bella dear! How nice!' Her mother's voice sounded tinged with veiled panic. Bella pictured her in the hallway, twiddling with her silk scarf, looking around desperately for Gerald. 'Well. How are... things?'

Are you going to be single for ever?

'All well with the house?'

We don't seem to have been invited for a visit yet.

'We got your card. I'm glad you liked the lamp. I wasn't sure, you know, whether it was quite... Anyway.'

You're impossible to please.

'It's very elegant.' Come on. Go and get Dad, can't you. 'I've started drawing again.' Bugger. She hadn't meant to reveal that. Now her mother would give one of those indulgent laughs, Bella playing at being artistic. How amusing.

'That's marvellous, dear. I am pleased. It always seemed such a waste when you let it go. You should make use of your talent.'

What a shame that you never stick with anything. God, she never lost an opportunity to have a dig. 'How's Dad?'

'I'll just get him for you.' Relief whistled down the phone line in two directions. 'Gerald! It's Bella on the phone.'

Will appeared and made a 'T' sign with one hand laid at right angles on top of the other. A question.

'Yes please.' She nodded.

'Yes please, what?' Her father's voice came on the phone. 'Hiya, Dads. How's tricks? Just getting the staff to wait on me.'

'As it should be, of course. Is Viv there? Say hello from us.'

'No. I followed your advice—'

'Makes a change.' Gerald laughed.

'Oh, shut up. I've got someone in to sort out the garden.'

'Good. Does he know his stuff?'

'Hang on, I'll ask him. Will?' She called through to the kitchen. 'My dad wants to know if you know your stuff.'

Will's head appeared round the side of the doorframe.

'Tell him I learned it all from a garden-design-by-numbers kit when I was eleven.'

'Did you hear that, Dads?'

'He sounds all right. Is he single?'

'Oh, *Daddy*! I've no idea. You're worse than Viv.'

'Well, is he?'

'How should I know? Probably not. What's it to me anyhow?'

Will's head reappeared in the doorway, this time at knee height. 'Biscuits?' he said. 'I must have biscuits if I'm to be creative.'

'I was wondering about having a mural on the end wall.' Bella indicated the far end of the garden.

Will said, sure, she could have what she liked, but it could be expensive. His artistic skills didn't extend that far so he'd have to subcontract it. Bella explained she was planning to do it herself.

'Your *face*.' She laughed. 'It's such an open book. I can see you thinking, "Oh no, a client who thinks she can paint. She's going to mess up the whole garden with some terrible scene of Tuscan olive groves."'

'Not far off. I thought you'd favour a Gothic folly actually, covered in creepers. Some wild romantic fantasy.'

'Touché. You're pretty close.' She described what she planned: a *trompe l'oeil* crumbling archway, framed by a real climbing rose perhaps, revealing a tantalizing glimpse of a sunlit secret garden beyond, with a path curving off into shadows. He didn't mean to be rude, he said, but it sounded like quite a tricky feat to bring off.

'I can always paint it out if it looks hideous.'

'Or train the rose right over it.'

'Are you this rude to all your clients?'

'Only the ones on a tight budget. Add another couple of grand and I can be a real smoothie: "A mural! What an inspired idea! And you'll paint it yourself? How delightful! That will give it your own *unique* stamp."'

'Doesn't suit you. I'd rather have the rudeness, thanks.'

'Erm, your downstairs loo seems to have been invaded by boxes. Where are they all coming from?' Will asked.

'I had to clear some space in my studio. Surely you can manage the stairs?'

He explained that many clients didn't like the gardener to use the upstairs one. Some of them wouldn't even let him in the house. In the past, he'd gone for a pee behind a bush in the garden because these people had made it all too clear they weren't expecting him to cross the threshold. He always took a flask because he could never count on even being offered a cup of tea.

Bella was outraged. Didn't it make him angry? He shrugged.

'Some people are like that. It's no good getting yourself worked up about every little thing that annoys you. You'd never get through the day.'

'But I love ranting about things that annoy me. It's practically my favourite pastime.'

'Hmm? What's your favourite then?'

His words were accompanied by that look again. That peculiar, assessing look as if getting her measure, as if he were trying to see inside her head.

'Arguing.'

'Besides,' he said, 'I got my own back. I slapped on another grand to the bill. They could have built a whole separate trades-men's loo for the money.'

'The bathroom's round to the right.' Bella pointed up the stairs. 'Oh, hang on.' She followed him upstairs. 'I think I used up the soap.'

He watched her foraging in boxes.

'There's definitely some in one of these. Hang on, hang on.' She caught sight of his expression. 'Do you find it amusing that I can't find anything in my own house?'

'I do. Why don't you just blitz all the boxes in one go and unpack everything so you know where it is?'

'Because of the DAMP!'

'Ah, now I know why you're letting me use your posh loo. You want me to have a quiet word with my brother-in-law-in-law, don't you?'

Bella opened the door to her studio to look for another box. There was definitely some soap somewhere.

'But this is fantastic!' Will was standing in the doorway, looking at the almost-completed mural on the wall with the crack. 'You realize I feel like a total prat now? Why didn't you say you were a professional?'

'But I'm not really. You know I'm only a so-called creative director, which is fancy-schmancy for designer. I only paint for me. You can't earn a living at it.'

The crack had been incorporated into a painting of an old, peeling wall including a half-open window. On the window sill there stood a small stoneware pot. Part of the wall was brightly lit, as if illuminated by the fake window, the part beneath the sill in deep shadow.

'I bet you could earn a crust doing murals.' He pointed at the window. 'I thought the pot was real. And this bit of tree that you can see through the window. It's a winter-flowering cherry, isn't it? Maybe *Prunus* x *subhirtella* "Autumnalis."'

'Show-off. I haven't a clue. It's whatever that is out there, in the neighbours' garden. It was in bloom when I first moved in.'

'This is bloody good, you know. I bet you I could get you a couple of commissions if you're up for it.'

'You mean I'd be a proper artist?' Bella clasped her hands together. 'Oh, I've dreamed of this for so long! Slaving away in my humble garret over a hot paintbrush. Going without cream doughnuts in order to buy paint. At last my genius has been recognized!'

'Do you do this about everything?'

'Sorry, sir. Can't help it, sir.'

'You're doing it again.' Will shook his head. 'I'll tell you one thing though—'

'Should I get my notebook?'

'Can you shut up for a second? If you always joke about something that's really important to you, you're selling yourself short.'

'What makes you think painting's important to me?'

He said nothing. He leant against the door-frame and just looked at her.

She felt herself flush as if he had accidentally caught sight of her naked.

'So what if it is?' She crossed her arms and bit her lip. 'Still got to eat, haven't I?'

'Of course. But if you don't take your work seriously, you can bet your bollocks no-one else will either.'

Bella laughed. 'Bet your bollocks? Good grief. Where on earth did you get that from? Haven't got any bollocks. I'm a person of the female persuasion, in case you hadn't noticed.'

Will went into the bathroom and closed the door.

'Your metaphorical bollocks,' he called from the other side. 'Which you certainly have got.' She could hear him weeing, which felt very intimate. Bella started to go downstairs. 'And, yes, I had noticed,' she heard his voice from above.

Over a number of phone calls, a few faxes, and many cups of tea in the following fortnight, the garden plan was finalized and a modest budget agreed. Some of the construction work – the patio, the pergola – was to be carried out by Will's subcontractor Douglas. Will explained that he could keep the costs down if Bella helped with the clearing and planting, and it would speed it up. 'My other projects are all civic stuff at the moment, so we could do most of it at the weekends if you'd prefer it,' he said. 'Then you can help and

oversee it and change your mind completely and say you'd envis-
aged something rather more Versailles-ish and please could we
move the garden a little to the left.'

'You sure you're happy?' Will said. 'You can do any amount of
fiddling with the details later but we've got to get the foundations
right at the beginning or it'll never work.'

'So,' said Bella, 'the acid test: do you share your brother-in-law-
in-law's belief that work is more of an interesting concept to be
discussed rather than something to be actually done, or can you
make a start soon?'

He could. He would. He was raring to go, he said. It was up
to her.

'So what's he like then?' Viv leaned back in her chair at the tapas bar.

'Oh, hello, this is a bit of all right.' Bella turned round the wine bottle to examine the label. 'Who?'

'Your garden man. Is he a rugged man of the soil? Tough, but secretly sensitive underneath?'

'Not as such. I think Will and sensitive are not words that would naturally fall in the same sentence.'

'Still, you seem to be spending a lot of time in his company. I miss you.

And Nick's hankering for your prawn thing again.'

'Glad you both appreciate me for my lovable qualities and not just my magical way with a piece of ginger root.'

'So, when are you next seeing him?'

'I am not "seeing him" at all. He is coming to start *work* on Saturday morning.'

'Bet you get up early to put on your make-up. Tastiness quotient?'

'What are you like? You're obsessed. You're supposed to be past all this.'

'I have to have some vicarious pleasure, don't I? Don't you feel sorry for us dreary couples, stuck in our routines, the highlight of our week a Chinese and a video on Friday night? Anyway, you must have thought about it.'

'Why must I? I'm not the one who's obsessed. I told you, I haven't got the energy to have a relationship. All that going out and doing things. Being pleasant. It's too complicated anyway. Your lives get all interwoven, then afterwards you have to try and disentangle the mess. Don't look at me like that.'

'Like what? There isn't always an afterwards, babe.'

'There is with me. The relationship's just the bit that happens before I get to the afterwards.'

Viv sighed. 'So, is he tasty or what?'

'He's not really the kind you have mad passionate fantasies about. Not handsome, but quite attractive. Cuddly. His eyes are nice. He's sort of solid-looking, like a tree, as if you could lean on him. And he has this little scar – here.' She raised her hand to her eyebrow.

'Not that you've spent any time looking at him at all.'

Bella wrinkled her nose. 'His hair's a bit peculiar, springy, bits of it stick up oddly.'

'Golly. Wild hair. How awful.' Viv's eyes widened, taking in Bella's sprawling curls.

'Very droll. I'll have you know I've got fourteen asylum-seekers nesting in here – would you have me comb them out onto the street?' Bella knocked back the remainder of her wine. 'Anyway, he's certainly no dashing Mr Rochester. He's just an ordinary bloke.'

'Do I get any wine at all? Don't write him off though, babe. Remember, Mr Rochester did have a bonkers wife locked in the attic. There's a lot to be said for an ordinary bloke.'

* * *

When Bella had first moved in, the weekends dragged terribly. She floated from the shops to Viv's back to home, drifting from room to room, ineffectually shifting things from one place to another, tackling the occasional task as if it were an epic obstacle requiring mammoth reserves of energy – the making of a velvet cushion-cover, the stitching of a curtain hem. Now, the weekend seemed to retreat before her, like Christmas when she was a child, impossibly far off. The week at work stretched out, a predictable cycle of meetings, designing, staring glassy-eyed at her computer, and chatter, nipping out for cappuccinos – I *think you mean* cappuccini, *Bella darling*. She found herself drawing more often. Her layout pad filled with sketches of her colleagues in a gallery of postures, her pen moving at speed over the paper, capturing the way they stood, sat, leaned, stretched and worked.

On Thursday, she trawled through hundreds of transparencies, her eyes blurry from squinting through a magnifying lens, her back aching from hunching over the light-box. Almost every hour, she went and dawdled in the office kitchen, wiping the surfaces and cleaning the coffee jug and chucking out the dodgy milk, anything to kill time.

Viv phoned.

'Are you all right? You sound terrible.'

'This just feels like a very, very long week. Finding it a struggle to feign enthusiasm about Buck's-fizz-flavoured yoghurt.'

'You're kidding?'

'No, I'm just not in the mood for it, you know.' Bella was already wishing she'd asked Anthony to get her two Crunchies on the chocolate run.

'No – Buck's-fizz yoghurt. Were you joking or is that a real thing?' Viv invited Bella to a party on Saturday.

'Nick's cousin Julian has just breezed in from Rio and we're trying to show him that we have an exciting life, too—'

'But you don't.'

'You know that, we know that. He doesn't. Nick says he can't bear Julian being all smug because we're so settled and couply and boring. Say you'll come. You're not doing anything else, are you?'

'Charming. I could be. Masked ball. Movie première. Romantic weekend in Hull.'

'So you're free then?'

'Unbelievably, yes.'

Bella offered to turn up early, to lend a hand. 'And can I bring anything?'

'Anything but Buck's-fizz yoghurt.'

* * *

Saturday. At last.

'No croissants?' Bella peered at Will from behind her front door.

'I knew I'd spoiled you too early on.'

'Oh, well, you're here now. Come in anyway.'

She passed him a plate. And a croissant. Tried to stop herself from grinning like a fool, biting her lip. Annoyed with herself for being pleased to see him. Surprised. Bustled into the kitchen, speaking to him over her shoulder, avoiding his gaze. *Don't be too keen.*

'Went out early and got them. Hardly slept anyway, so thought I might as well get up.'

'Oh? Why's that?'

'Oh, you know...' She turned the tap on full, concentrated on scrubbing the sink.

Plastic sheeting topped with dust sheets was spread all the way from the front door to the French windows; everything – bricks, rubble, shingle, plants – would have to go through the house because it was midterrace.

They set to work, clearing the brambles, moving plants to protect them from the debris.

'Don't overdo it,' he said. 'You'll do your back in if you're not used to this kind of work.'

'I suppose you think I'm just a fragile female?'

'Why are you so defensive? It's nothing to do with what sex you are. It's what you're used to that matters. You can't spend all week sitting at a desk and then leap straight into heavy physical work.' He leant his garden fork against the wall. 'Time for a break anyway.'

'This is going to be so beautiful.' He gestured with a sweep of his arm as if already he could see it completed. 'But it is going to get worse before it gets better, so be warned.'

Douglas arrived at lunch-time, to lift the turf from the lawn and prepare the sub-base for the patio. He was a quiet man and merely nodded hello to Bella.

'Very shy,' Will whispered. 'Frightened of attractive women.' Will marked out on the ground where the pergola would go.

'And this is where your little bower will be. See? You'll be invisible even from a few feet away once the plants are in.'

'Perfect,' she said.

Bella seemed to have been staring into the black hole of her wardrobe for a very long time. Perhaps if she stood there long enough, some gloriously expensive, chic little crêpe-de-Chine number would find its way onto one of her hangers. She could really do with some new clothes. It was basically down to three options: black silky trousers with brown wrapover top or cream silk shirt, short red skirt with sexy black top which helped divert attention away from the fact that her stomach stuck out, or purple dress that was too clingy and made her feel clammy under the arms.

Her gaze fell on the cherry-red two-piece that Alessandra had given her. The fabric was glorious. She took it out and held it up against herself. It was beautiful; too good for her really. She didn't feel smart enough to do it justice. Besides, it was probably way too dressy for the party. No. Back to her three options: the trousers were the most comfortable, but she was in the mood to give her legs their annual outing. The purple, then. At least it was a change from black. What the hell, she'd just use loads of deodorant and hold her stomach in. It was a good dress to flirt in. It made her feel more forward, more daring.

She was definitely spending far too much time thinking about sex. Probably because she wasn't having any. She still had an unopened packet of condoms in her bedside drawer. 'You should always be prepared,' Viv had said. 'Keep some in your bag, too.' As if she might suddenly be overcome with lust in the greengrocer's and wrestle some unsuspecting shop assistant to the floor as he was trying to arrange the cauliflowers. Viv evidently imagined she had bouts of spontaneity, although there was little enough evidence for it. Even if she was just nipping out for a pint of milk and a loaf of bread, she wrote a list. She was beginning to regret that she'd splashed out and bought a packet of twelve condoms rather than three. At this rate, she'd be lucky to get through it before its expiry date; good grief, at this rate, the packet could constitute a lifetime's supply.

'I'll be off then.' Will called up the stairs.

'OK. Hang on a sec. I'll be right down...' She thundered down the stairs.

'Ah, do I hear the patter of a tiny buffalo stampede? Are you—' He stopped.

'What? What's the matter?'

'Nothing. Sorry. Haven't seen you in all your finery before. Didn't recognize you without mud on your face.'

'Er – do I – look all right? It's not too –?'

'Too what?'

'Well, too clingy. See—' she turned side on, 'my stomach sticks out.'

'My God! You're right. People will be whispering in corners about it. Perhaps you could hire a small marquee to wear instead.'

'We are not amused. Just answer – does it make me look fat or not?'

'No. You answer a question. Do you seriously imagine people will be looking at your stomach in that dress?'

'Was that no, I don't look fat or no, you're not answering the question?'

'Unbelievable.' Will shook his head. 'Is there some weird mass hysteria that only affects women? Why does every female on the planet think she's fat?'

'So is that a yes, then?'

'Mind-boggling. Have fun, Moby Dick.' He turned to go. 'I'm off to fight my way round Tesco's.'

* * *

Odd. She was sure she had a couple of bottles of wine left. The mice must have drunk them. Now she'd have to go via the supermarket on the way to the party.

It was surprisingly crowded. Who on earth would choose to shop on a Saturday evening, she wondered? Maybe they were all swinging singles out looking for action. She was always reading that supermarkets were a great place to meet people. Was that so you could see in advance whether you had compatible tastes? Never mind whether you had any interests in common or similar politics, values, ideologies. Did he buy gravy granules, chicken nuggets or Quorn burgers – that was what you really needed to know. She started peering into people's trolleys; what she wanted was someone with fresh pasta, decent wine and plenty of chocolate, who kissed sexily and could make her laugh. Was it so much to ask?

A voice came over the tannoy: 'Make your way to the fish counter for smoked haddock fillets – on special offer today only...' Bella looked up. Perhaps she would make a kedgeree. Suddenly, there, at the far end of her aisle, she thought she saw Will, apparently absorbed in his shopping list. Ha-ha – she'd go up and tease him about looking for love among the baked beans. She could sneak up behind him and pinch his bum. No. She could say something suggestive. No. She could pretend to be a normal person and say hello in a friendly manner. Yes. She would do that.

As she moved towards him, Will abandoned his trolley for a moment and disappeared around the corner. She wondered what kind of things he bought, bet it was frozen lasagne, beer and probably something unexpected – Battenberg cake maybe. A look into his trolley. Apples. Bananas. Frozen lasagne – hah! Tins of things. Nothing exciting. Two large plastic packets: Newborn Ultra-Dry, they said. Unisex. Soft and Snug. A large blue plastic bottle: Johnson's Baby Bath.

She recoiled as if she had been bitten. Backed away into a gangly youth in a bow tie who was rearranging the shelves.

'Sorry,' she said. 'Sorry.' Turning, clutching her basket, swinging it into a woman. 'Sorry, sorry.' Heading for the wine, the till, the exit.

12

'Ah-ha!' said Viv when she opened the door. 'The sexy purple. Are you out to entrap someone in particular or is it just a lure for any unsuspecting male who happens to be passing?'

'It's either part of a cunning plot to overthrow the Government and change civilization as we know it or a sad and desperate attempt to inveigle some feebleminded myopic man with excess testosterone into chatting me up. You choose. So you don't think it shows off my stomach too much?'

'I see there's been no unexpected rise in self-esteem on the stock market then.' Viv waved her in.

Bella raised one eyebrow. 'Call yourself a hostess?' she said. 'I've been here forty-five seconds and not been offered so much as a Twiglet. Have you got anything decent to drink or shall we have what I brought?'

Viv slavered garlic and herb butter onto slit baguettes while Bella tipped pistachios and olives into dishes.

'Getting enough to eat there, are you?' said Viv as Bella cracked open yet another pistachio nut with her teeth. 'Are you all right, babe? You look a bit peaky.'

'I'm fine. Give me a top-up, will you?'

'Steady on. You've got a whole evening to get through. What's up?'

'Nothing. Everything. It sounds stupid.'

'What'sstupid?' Nickbreezed intothe kitchen. 'Ah, do I spy pistachios?' He scooped out a handful from the dish.

'I just saw Will in the supermarket with a trolley full of nappies.'

'What a bastard!' Nick shook his head. 'What? I thought that's what I'm supposed to say. Thought I'd get it in before you did. Who's Will anyway?'

'Bella's garden man. I said you bloody liked him. Well, he's obviously not worthy of you, then.'

'I feel such a fool. Ever since I met him, there seemed to be this thing between us –'

Nick raised his eyebrows suggestively.

'Go away,' said Bella and Viv at the same time.

'This unspoken assumption that we like each other. I bet he flirts with all his clients just to butter them up. He's probably turning to his wife and cooing over their baby – and laughing about me and my stupid boxes and my stupid mural – and I hate him now only not as much as I hate me and I wish I'd never met him. It's really all my fault because I allowed myself to like him which was stupid, stupid, stupid. And I can't even send him away because he's started and there's soil everywhere and if he doesn't finish the garden, it'll look like a total tip and the house already looks like a warehouse. More wine, please.'

'Oh, babe. I'm sorry. We'll find you someone nice, won't we, Nick?'

'Me? What are you looking at me for? You're always saying my friends are clueless.'

Bella dug into the pistachios again. 'Forget it. It's a lost cause. I don't care any more. I'm going to be celibate for ever and devote myself to art.'

'Like Sister Wendy?'

'Yes. But with a better orthodontist.'

'Right, that's your lot.' Viv plucked the dish of nuts out of her grasp and put it in the sitting-room. 'By the time you two've finished, we'll have to put them out in an eggcup.'

Nick loosened his tie, rolled up his sleeves and waggled his fingers, as if limbering up to perform a little something by Chopin on a concert grand.

'If someone,' he nodded at Bella, 'would care to chop the tomatoes for the salad, I will prepare...' He paused for effect. 'The dressing.'

'Oh, darling,' Viv pouted and opened her eyes wide in mock awe. 'May we really stay and watch?'

He washed his hands and held them up straight, surgeon-like, from the elbows.

'You may,' he said. 'Towel?'

The Making of the French Dressing – Nick's sole culinary skill – was a five-act epic drama starring Nick, ably supported by a pestle and mortar, fat cloves of garlic, two types of mustard, some extremely overpriced olive oil from one particular Tuscan olive grove, and other rare unguents that Nick liked to hide from view 'to preserve the mystique'.

Bella washed and chopped the tomatoes, while Nick embarked on Act One: The Crushing of the Garlic with the Sea Salt.

'It's a joy and an education to watch you, Nick,' Bella said. 'Have you thought of giving master-classes?'

'Mock if you will,' said Nick, 'but I have yet to see you leave so much as a caterpillar on your plate when I serve up a salad.'

'True, O Great One, but it's such a waste for so small an audience. Why don't you wait till the guests arrive, then we could judge your performance and give you marks.' Bella raised her hands in turn as if lifting score placards: 'Technical merit, 5.6. Artistic impression, 5.9.'

* * *

The doorbell rang. Nick was still on Act Three: The Mixing of the Two Mustards with the Garlic, and Viv was 'elbow-deep in bloody lollo rosso', so Bella went to the door.

It was Sara and Adam, a couple whom Bella had already met, and Nick's cousin Julian, who had been sent out for more paper napkins but had tried three different shops with no success and arrived back at the same time. Bella offered them drinks and tried not to look at Julian too much.

More people started arriving and Bella got hooked up in an argument two couples were having about nursery schools. When she ventured an opinion, all four of them turned as one and gave her that look; one woman voiced the predictable statement on their behalf: 'Of course, when you have children of your own, you'll feel differently.' How could she argue with that? She felt about six years old, being admonished for yet another piece of naughtiness or folly, her mother giving her that patronizing look – *When you grow up ... When you're older... Then you can do what you like.* Hah! When would that magic day ever come? She was tempted to embarrass the couples, to tell them that, tragically, she could never have children because... because she had some horrible disease, she had donated her womb to science, her Fallopian tubes had been mangled by a mad surgeon, her ovaries refused to release any eggs without written authorization.

From across the other side of the room, Julian caught her eye, raised his glass, and beckoned her with his head. God he was tasty.

Bella hastily excused herself from the cul-de-sac argument – 'Must just... old friend... excuse me' – and tried not to appear to be rushing over towards him.

She should definitely have stopped drinking at that stage because she'd already had more than she was used to. At some point in the evening, she noticed a burst of too-loud laughter and was inwardly curling her lip in smug disapproval when she realized that it was her own; but she didn't seem to care any more. For once, she wanted to forget about being sensible and play the wanton woman, to act the bimbo, flirt outrageously and simply enjoy the obvious effect it had on men. So she found herself laying her hand on Julian's arm and gazing at him with rapt attention while she asked him to tell her all about his travels. He returned her eye contact with frank interest and happily talked about himself.

It was well after one a.m. when the last guest had finally been folded into a taxi, and Viv had ushered her into their spare bedroom.

'Don't argue. You're in no condition to go anywhere,' she scolded affectionately. 'Julian's volunteered to have the sofa bed, so you're in here, though I think he'd have been more than happy to squeeze in here with you judging from the way he's been eyeing you all evening.'

Viv started to make up the bed. Bella pulled pathetically at one side of the sheet but subsided into giggles when she tried to remember how to do proper hospital corners.

'Will you stop it?' said Viv, suppressing a spurt of laughter herself. 'You're supposed to be the sensible one.'

'He could have this little corner here.' Bella keeled slowly over onto the bed while it was still only half made. 'I promise not to touch him. Or only a little bit. Do you think he fancies me then?'

'Shift off. If he'd stood any closer he'd have been in that dress with you. But I wouldn't bother if I were you – he's off to Washington in a few days. Anyway, he may be quite hunky, but he's not all that interesting really and he's got an ego the size of the EU butter mountain.'

'Nice shoulders.' Bella smacked her lips in appreciation. Viv sighed and pulled the quilt over her. 'Night-night,' she said. 'No rush to get up in the morning.'

'Just ask Room Service to send him along,' Bella mumbled into the pillow. 'I'll look after him. He'll be quite safe with me.'

13

'You said you'd show me around town.' Julian's voice on the phone was confident, expecting assent. 'I'm only here for a few days and I've got to shoot up to Coventry tomorrow. How about Friday, after work? I'd love to discover all those secret places the tourists never see.'

I bet you would, Bella thought, hearing herself accept with a flirtatious laugh. Why bother with innuendo when you could be blatantly suggestive? God, she had been so drunk at the party. She hadn't done that for, what, two years? It was after she'd had that pregnancy scare.

* * *

She is nearly two weeks late. At a large, anonymous Boots, she buys a do-it-yourself test kit; sitting on the bus, she runs her finger along the prophetic box in her bag as if it already knows the answer. Women are often late when under stress, she reminds herself. That must be it. When she steps inside her front door, she makes an effort to be casual, flicking on the kettle and idly scanning the newspaper rather than running straight to the bathroom, as if being unbothered could influence the result.

Awkwardly, she tries to pee into the minuscule phial, getting wee all over her shaking hand. The result should be almost instant, but still she lives through each second, waiting to see if the little blue line would appear in the white square, meaning 'Rejoice, a babe shall be born' or, as in her case, 'Oh fuck'.

The square remains white and the relief is overwhelming, as if someone has thrown open all the windows letting in a heady flood of fresh air. But by now Patrick has already talked himself into the idea that she is definitely pregnant. She had noticed him limbering up for the Proud Father role. Caught him holding the foot of a tiny blue fluffy all-in-one while they were supposed to be looking for a dressing gown for his dad in Marks & Spencer's. He'd taken to peering into estate agents' windows at absurdly large houses they couldn't possibly afford.

That tiny blank square seems to strike him like a physical blow. His skin looks grey, his eyes dark with disappointment and loss. She holds him tight, hugging him to her as if he were a needy baby himself, kissing his hair again and again. Later, they go out for dinner and drink two bottles of spectacularly expensive wine, followed by numerous drams of malt Scotch at home, each with their own reason to be numbly intoxicated. Bella relishes each sip, feeling the relief swirl round her mouth, seeping into her nostrils on a tide of smoky peat and dry oak.

The next morning, both of them feel ill and Patrick makes some lame comment about knowing what morning sickness must be like and how it was all good preparation. Bella silently makes the coffee and avoids his gaze. He does not mention it again.

* * *

Friday morning was bright and sunny, definite skirt weather. Shaving her legs in the shower, Bella told herself it was just because of the skirt. She certainly had no intention of letting Julian run his warm male hands all over her silky-smooth calves, no siree. Similarly unconcerned about which underwear to put on, Bella foraged through her top drawer then scooped up the contents and chucked them onto the bed. Her decent cream-lace set and her sexy dark red bra and pants were in the linen basket. She should have done a load of washing yesterday; too late now – not enough time for it to dry. What if Julian were to come back afterwards for coffee or something? She didn't think she could pass off lines of hung-out socks and pants as welcoming bunting.

She picked through the garments, holding them aloft between finger and thumb as if sifting through a rubbish tip. Three pairs of ageing, greyish, allegedly white cotton briefs; a Valentine's Day pair emblazoned with a red heart on the front and the legend 'I'm Yours'. – I *don't think so.* She dropped them back into the drawer. A pale pink pair with too-loose elastic. Peach 'control panel front' pants that came up to her waist and pressed against her bladder so she had to go to the loo every twenty minutes. Black lacy knickers that were so skimpy that knickers seemed too big a word for them; they were constructed from so little material that they made her hips and bum feel unusually large by comparison and they had a just-clinging-by-a-thread sensation that was far from relaxing. Besides, they had been a present from Patrick. She stuffed them back into the drawer.

She could nip to the shops at lunchtime and pick up a plain pair of cotton pants to change into at the office. This was ridiculous, she reproved herself, no-one would be looking at her knickers; this was a stroll around the city and perhaps a spot of supper – theoretically, no underwear assessment would be involved. Still, she really could do with some new tights and things anyway, and it wouldn't take long.

As she was dashing out the door to go to work, the phone rang. She let the answerphone click in but hovered by the door to hear who it was. It was Will.

'Oh, hello you. I'm glad you're there. Are you in tonight?'

'No, I'm not for once. Do you need to get in?' *How's your wife?* she wanted to say. *Baby doing nicely?*

He only wanted to check those shrubs they'd transplanted, he said, and had she remembered that he couldn't work tomorrow but that he might pop in, and that Douglas should be coming at 11? Was she off somewhere nice?

'Mmm. Just, you know. Out.' Bet he thought she had some pathetic crush on him. 'On a date actually,' she added.

'Oh.' He coughed. 'Have fun then.'

* * *

Julian wasn't there when she arrived by the east door of the cathedral, a little breathless as she was slightly late, so she leant against a bollard and simply enjoyed the sun on her face while she watched people walking by. The sea-green silk of her skirt fluttered around her in the breeze. She pushed aside a straying tendril of hair that had adhered to her Mulberry Dew lipstick.

Two teenage boys loping past in bodies they had not yet grown into attempted a wolf-whistle that emerged as a shrill squeak. They shoved each other on the arm to show that they were still very manly all the same and laughed. A mumbling man marched by in a battered straw panama and a blazer that had long since shrugged its shoulders and given up any thought of passing for smart; he seemed to be towed by his unlikely-looking companion, a small, snuffling terrier that resembled a shaggy bathmat gone grey in the wash. She should have brought her sketchbook. This was a perfect spot to catch people. She closed her eyes, trying to imprint the pictures in her mind.

A shadow stepped into her sun.

'Do you know you look even more delectable today than you did in that sexy dress?' said Julian. 'So, do I get a kiss?'

It went on and on. Julian seemed to be taking immense pride in the fact that he could carry on for a long time, as if a marathon were in some way inherently better than a sprint, no matter how dull it was. Boring sex was bad enough, but if the person had staying power as well... Bella felt she was starting to go numb. She'd have had more fun doing the crossword on her own. Perhaps she could reach for the paper and do it looking over his shoulder. He was so enraptured by his physical prowess that he probably wouldn't notice. Although it might be pushing it to ask him to help with the clues: 'Mmm, mm, ride me, Big Boy. What do you think "illusion" is? Seven letters, ending in "y".' Maybe if she squeezed a bit more, that would speed him up. She should have been more diligent about doing those pelvic-floor exercises.

Her gaze roved around the room. That lampshade wasn't ideal in here. The shape was a bit odd and you could see the bulb, especially from this angle. Perhaps she could make one from that parchmenty stuff and draw on it? She'd better get some shopping in tomorrow, too – she was definitely running out of loo paper. And bleach. More olive oil. She mentally sifted through the kitchen cupboards. Pasta – rigatoni or tagliatelle? Shells? *Do try a little conchiglie alla genovese.* Better check detergent, too.

He was still going.

'Mmm,' she said encouragingly, trying to urge him on. What did he want – a medal? 'That's nice.' She closed her eyes, letting her mind drift, her thoughts float free, watching herself from the outside. When she was alone, touching herself, she fantasized. Now, she willed Patrick to be here, warm and alive, reassuring and known, loving her, absolving her.

His face before her, now, smiling his familiar smile. He kisses her once, hard, then reaches up under her skirt. As he lifts it, she feels the thrill of their long-disappeared brocade bedspread, textured like a low-relief map, rough beneath her naked thighs. Surprised by his sudden urgency, she starts to pull away, to look at him, read his eyes. But, even as he touches her, his brown eyes swim to sea-grey, his jaw broadens, his hair gets lighter, shorter, growing springy as cushion-moss beneath her hand – and it is Will's face she sees. His tender face. She feels her eyes well with tears and she moves towards him then, her lips on his, their mouths hungry, greedy, grateful.

He puts his hands under her now and pulls her hard onto him. She gasps at his intensity, at her own, and pushes towards him, moving faster and harder, pulling at his back. And he clutches her, clinging onto her as if for his life. Then there is only the heat and the smell of him, and the pulse – starting like the low notes of a bass, throbbing and thrumming, then rising and spreading and – she arches back, stretching away from him, then clinging to him once more, her insides warm and soft as melting butter.

At last, her breathing eases and she lies there, her skin hot and prickling, her thighs tingling from the friction of the brocade spread.

'Well, well,' said Julian, 'you certainly warmed up all of a sudden. Bit of a slowcoach, eh?' He slapped her bottom playfully.

'Guess so.' She lay back, flushed with lust and pleasure and guilt. She rolled over then on the rumpled sheet, suddenly appalled at its unfamiliar, reproachful softness, her body still alive to the touch of the rough brocade.

'So, then this guy says, "You'll have to move it, sir." I mean, he was just totally non-helpful about it. Unbelievable.'

It certainly is, she thought. I can't believe I've actually gone to bed with someone who says non-helpful. This was such a bad idea.

'Really?' she said out loud, injecting interest into her voice as much for her own benefit as for his: he was interesting, she told herself, really he was.

'Do you want some tea or something?' She slid out of bed.

'A brandy if you have it.' Julian watched her reach up for her robe from the back of the door. 'Nice arse.'

Waiting for the kettle to boil, Bella stared down at her feet, pale and soft against the cold quarry tiles. Her toe-nails could do with a trim, and her nail varnish was chipped.

What on earth did she think she was doing? She had just leapt into bed with a virtual stranger and had to fantasize about another man – two men – she was getting seriously weird – and yet here she was thinking about her toenails. Still, it was better than thinking about how extraordinarily, incredibly, mind-bogglingly stupid she'd been. And it hadn't even worked anyway. She still felt horrible about Will, worse if anything because thinking about him had made her so turned-on, only now she felt bad about Julian and guilty about Patrick as well. Three for the price of two. Marvellous. A complete matching set.

But what if she could never enjoy sex again without pretending it was with Patrick or someone else? Her sense of shame stung her afresh. Embarrassed, she poured Julian an extra-large brandy and wiggled her hips provocatively as she took it up to him.

'You were great,' he said. 'You really got into it.' She smiled, then buried her face in his neck so that he could not look into her eyes.

. . .

The doorbell rang. She rolled over, dopey from lack of sleep. The shock of another face on the pillow next to hers.

'Expecting visitors?' asked Julian. 'Not the vicar, I hope.'

Bella laughed and shook her head. Why was she humouring him? Glanced at her watch. Nearly ten thirty a.m. Could be Douglas a bit early. A horrible thought: it might be Will. Perhaps she should ignore it.

The bell rang again. No time to get dressed. Well, what did it have to do with him anyway? It was certainly none of his business whom she chose to sleep with. Have sex with. Absolutely none. She pulled her robe close around her, crossed her arms over her chest and stomped downstairs to open the door. Framed her face in a look of defiance.

'Morning,' Will said. 'Sorry if I got you out of bed, but you should be up anyway. Glorious day. Come out to the garden. I promise not to look at your stubbly legs.' He steamed through to the kitchen.

'They're not stubbly.' She covertly rubbed one against the other. Hmm. 'I only did them yesterday. See?'

'They look lovely to me anyway.' How had he managed to make it sound as if she were trying to get him to notice her legs? He had such a way of twisting things around.

'Any chance of a cup of tea before I head off?'

'Why? Have you lost the use of your hands?'

'I didn't want to just barge in and make myself at home.'

'Why not? You do normally.'

Will turned to look at her.

'You're as prickly as a hedgehog holly this morning. What's up?'

'Nothing's *up*.' Why couldn't he go away? She crossed her arms again and looked down at her feet. 'I'm just in the middle of something.'

'In your dressing gown?' Will laughed, then flushed. 'Oh. Right.

Sorry.' He clunked the kettle back down on the worktop. 'Why didn't you say? I'm only the gardener after all. You don't have to pussyfoot around my feelings.'

'No, I – it's not. I—'

'There's no need to look embarrassed.' He was looking at her directly now. 'I'm sure you don't need to justify yourself to the hired help.'

Bugger him. How dare he try and make her feel ashamed?

'No. I certainly don't. You've got a fucking cheek, trying to make me feel guilty when you've been flirting with me all this time and you've got a wife and babies and everything.'

'What?' Will looked behind him. 'Are you talking to me?'

'Yes, don't pretend. It doesn't suit you. You didn't exactly advertise it, did you? How very peculiar that this minor detail of your life seemed to have slipped your mind during all the talks we've had. But I *saw* you. In Tesco's with *millions* of *nappies*.'

He sighed loudly and shook his head.

'Have me put down now and put me out of my misery. Did it not occur to you to speak – try communicating sometime, why don't you? Try saying: Will, why have you bought a load of nappies? Then I say: Bella, I'm glad you asked. It's because I'm a proud and devoted uncle which, in fact, I believe I'd already told you. I was helping my sister out because what with her five-year-old girl, her baby boy and her workaholic husband, she's bloody knackered. OK?'

Bella was silent, bunching and unbunching her fists by her sides. Her breastbone felt tight, as if it were clamped against her lungs, squeezing, pressing the breath out of her.

'I just sort of assumed...' Her voice a croak.

'Why didn't you ask if it was bugging you?' Will took a step towards her.

'Why on earth should it bug me?' She rallied, defiant once

more, moving away. 'It's nothing to do with me how many babies you have. You could have a whole crèche-load for all I care.'

'Thanks. I'll bear in it mind next time I come into season. Anyway, for the record – not that anyone's remotely interested in me or my life or my marital status – I am: a) childless, b) single, and c) open to offers. Thank you. I am now going into the garden to check those shrubs, then I'll be out of your hair.'

'There's no need. Take as long as you like.' She bit the inside of her lip. She wouldn't cry. Would not. Dug her fingernails hard into her palm. I *don't care,* she told herself, I *don't care, I don't care, I don't care.*

'Just make sure you drag yourself out of bed to give them another watering tomorrow if there's no rain. I'll be back on Monday anyway before you go to work – eight a.m. sharp. Please make sure you're up.'

'Sir! Yes, sir!' She saluted him, but he had already turned his back on her, so he failed to see the joke.

14

'A small token of apology.' Will pushed a small plastic bag into her hands. 'Still a bit early for roses.'

The bag was filled with stems of rosemary from his garden. Rubbing it between her fingers, she dipped her head to breathe it in: heavenly – rich and pungent, but a clean smell, almost antiseptic.

She should apologize, she knew. It had been entirely her fault. Making assumptions. And then she'd practically thrown herself at Julian to make herself feel less crappy. Another inspired idea from the woman who brought you Moving to a City where She Knows Only Two People, Moving House and Starting a New Job at the Same Time, and that old favourite, Dreaming of Being a Painter. What was the point of indulging in a brief bout of meaningless sex if it made you feel so bloody miserable afterwards?

Once Will had stomped off on Saturday morning, she couldn't get Julian out of the house fast enough, babbling about vital work – she had to go into the office, she'd said – would love to loaf in bed all day – still it couldn't be helped – ushering him down the stairs – giving him coffee in a small cup so he'd drink it quickly – kissing him in the hallway, her hand already on the doorknob – saying yes, yes, it had been wonderful – would love to see him next time he was over – yes, of course – have a great trip – kissy, kissy, bye-bye.

'I know you're a bit of a foodie. Sorry about the inelegant wrapping.'

'Isn't that a euphemism for complete pig? Thank you. I love it. Why are *you* apologizing anyway?'

He gave a small cough. 'I'm just sorry if I was a bit snotty on Saturday.' No sweat, she said, it didn't matter.

Definitely, she should apologize. She scrunched her toes in her shoes at the thought of it, the shame, admitting she'd been wrong. As a child, her head dipped like a wilting flower, she'd seemed to be having to say sorry almost every day: Sorry, Mummy, I didn't mean to – sorry, I forgot – sorry, I didn't know – didn't realize – thought it would be all right – sorry, sorry – sorry for being a nuisance – sorry for being naughty – sorry for being me. Her mother's mouth, twitching in silent triumph, suddenly gracious in victory: *That's all right, Bella dear. You'll know better next time, won't you?*

'Yes,' Will nodded, 'it does. I – was – well. I apologize.'

'Me too. Really.'

'Me three.' He smiled. 'Really.'

'You can make the tea – if it'll help you feel better.'

Will said he couldn't stay now, had only come to check a couple of things and drop off the rosemary, but was she still all right for Saturday?

'Or are weekends likely to be a problem in future? For any reason?'

'Is that Will-speak for is there likely to be a recurrence of last Saturday? I'd say it's about as probable as my being commissioned to fresco the dome of the Albert Hall.'

He shrugged. 'So quite possible then?'

'And you say *I'm* a dreamer?' She shoved him playfully.

'You *are*. Now, have you started the mural on the far wall yet?'

'It's still in the planning stage.'

'That'd be a no then, as you would say.' He turned to leave. 'Better get on with it, hadn't you?'

'You're *so* bossy!'

'I know you, you'll float around in a dream all week otherwise and I need you to be useful at the weekend.'

'But I'm not designed to be useful.'

'You'll love it. It'll be a new experience. Trust me.'

* * *

Bella resolved to ignore the fact that she was now drawing every day as well as in her weekly life class and had started to paint again in the evenings. It was presumably a temporary quirk, a mere glitch in the fabric of the Universe that would shortly be righted. It was easier when she tricked herself into it, casually picking up a pencil, balancing her pad awkwardly as if making a brief note. If she made it too important, treating herself to the luxury of thick paper, buying new brushes, clearing her studio properly, it would never happen. It was like walking a tightrope over an abyss – you mustn't stop and look down or you'd suddenly realize what you had been so daring, so foolish to attempt.

Starting the mural on the garden wall, she felt once more that old rush of excitement, giddy and disturbing. Years before, when she'd been accepted for art school, she'd considered herself a lucky fraud: being allowed – encouraged! – to draw and paint all day! A licence to play. Remembered Alessandra's baffled smile, explaining Bella's peculiar peccadillo to the neighbours, 'Of course, dear Bella could have gone to university, Oxford or Cambridge, but she's set her heart on being an artist!' It sounded no less ludicrous to her own ears, like wanting to be a ballet dancer or an astronaut, a silly childish fantasy. She'd kept herself in check. Opted for graphic design. Practical. Commercial. Focused on building her career.

On Saturday morning, Will stood back to admire the bunch of rosemary stems standing in a blue jug on the kitchen window-sill.

'Rosemary's lasted well then? See, aren't you glad I didn't get you a boring old bouquet of roses?'

'Tremendously glad. Every morning I wake up and think "Thank God Will didn't buy me any roses." Stick the kettle on, will you? I'm all paint-spattered.'

'So you are.' He reached out and touched the side of her nose. 'You've got a dab of grey just... there. Or have you not quite got the hang of doing your eyeshadow?'

'Glad to see you've started to obey my every command.' Will looked at the beginnings of the *trompe-l'oeil* arch on the garden wall. 'You probably want to carry on, or shall I show you how to plant and stuff?'

'The Henderson patented Instant Green Fingers Course? Will that really make me a proper gardener?'

'Oh no, my lovey, takes years 'n' years to become the real thing. See? Look at those hands.' He held his palms outstretched towards her. 'That's ingrained that is, never come out.'

Bella started to stretch out her finger, to trace the lines in his hands. She wondered what his skin would feel like beneath her fingertip, how he had got that scar at the base of his thumb. Their eyes met.

'Nonsense,' she said, withdrawing her hand and diverting its direction to push back a strand of hair from her eyes. 'You just need a good scrubbing, that's all. Show me the secrets of the soil then. I can't paint with someone else watching me anyway.'

'Really? Why's that?'

'You're very nosy, aren't you?'

'Yes. Why can't you?'

She stopped, not having really thought about it before.

'I think it's a bit like having someone in the same room when you're in the bath or on the loo. Kind of –'

'Intimate?'

'Mmm-mm.' She nodded. 'Does that sound wanky?' Will laughed through his nose.

'Tremendously, you old pseud. No, not at all. Makes sense. But what about once you've finished a painting? People are going to look at it then, aren't they? It's still revealing.'

'Ye-e-e-es. But it's separate from you then. Like an ex-husband or something. You had a relationship once, but he no longer has quite the same power to embarrass you in public.'

He showed her how to plant, carefully firming the soil around a lemon verbena, giving it his undivided attention. He passed her another pot.

'Here. Your go. About there, so it has room to grow.'

'You really love this, don't you?' she asked, looking across at him. The tips of his ears went slightly pink, then he nodded.

'Always have. Ever since I was a kid. Used to sow sunflower seeds, radishes, anything I could get my hands on. My mum gave me my own little patch of garden when I was eight. And Hugh, my stepdad I told you about – ex-stepdad now, I suppose. Whatever. He helped me lay a course of bricks all round the edge to make it my own little kingdom.'

'They sound nice. You must miss him. My dad's a keen gardener.' Bella got up from where she'd been kneeling on the ground and stretched herself. 'You'd like him.' She said it without thinking, seeing Will and Dads in her mind, the two of them together, bending over plants, pointing, talking, at ease. Swung her arms, pushing the thought away.

'Are you stiff? Sorry if I've been too much of a slave-driver,' he said. 'And your mum? Does she garden too?'

'Ha!' The thought was amusing, absurd. She looked down at him. 'She might snip a few flowers, but the rest of it – too messy. Might spoil her hands.' Bella held up her own hands and stroked one delicately against the other, as if admiring their charms in the sunlight. 'Oh no! National crisis! Call the Emergency Services! Bella darling, I've chipped a nail!'

Will laughed.

'I'm sure she can't be all bad as she produced you.'

'I'm a changeling. Didn't I tell you?'

They fell into a routine over the following month, working each weekend, stopping too often to talk or to survey their progress, adjusting the plan slightly here and there as they went. As she dug her trowel into the soil, she could hear the confident clipping of his secateurs, methodical and comforting, his quiet humming as he tied in a climber or cut back a wayward stem.

The mural was completed, the painted arch offering a glimpse of another garden beyond, with a moss-cushioned woodland floor in the foreground, opening to a sunlit clearing, at once tantalizing and out of reach.

'This will be the main scented area,' Will said, putting in the lavender plants alongside buddleia, daphne, sar-cococca, 'near your willow seat.'

Bella inhaled as if she could already smell the plants, as if the air was thick with fragrance. She smelt just-laundered cotton, a touch of soap but not too soapy, a hint of fresh sweat, warm skin, the faint tang of something citrusy. Nice. Not too much aftershave.

Silently, he leant past her, stretching into the cupboard for two mugs. They moved around each other in the narrow kitchen, a silent dance, sidestepping, anticipating, not touching. The gaps between them fizzed; she felt the air charged and trembling, making her skin prickle, her body light and buoyant. She wondered what he would do if she were to touch his back as he stood by the sink washing his hands, imagined his warmth beneath her palm, her fingers. She swallowed. Avoided looking at his face. Clattered about in the cutlery drawer, hunting for a particular teaspoon. A hollow ache in her gut. A slight feeling of nausea. Low blood sugar, she told herself, that's all it is. Wished he would go away, leave and not come back – ever. Wanted him to stay – always. Wanted him to hold her, stroke her hair, make her safe. She banged the cutlery drawer shut.

'Having fun there?' he said.

'I can never bloody find anything in this bloody stupid house!' Will threw back his head and laughed.

'I'm glad you find it amusing. I'm surprised you ever get any work if you treat all your clients this way.'

He giggled into the depths of his mug, his eyes shining over the curve of the rim.

The work, inevitably, took longer than he had originally estimated – 'It's your fault, of course,' he said. 'Too easy to talk to' – but, finally, it was done.

'Well then.' Will lingered on the doorstep. 'I'd better be off.'

She thanked him again for all his hard work. It was stunning, she said, she would try to look after it properly.

'You better had or I'll come round and deface your mural. Oh and – nearly forgot.' He turned back towards her.

Her heartbeat quickened.

'Would it be OK for me to come back soon to take some photographs?

For my folio?'

He waved at her, once, from the end of the street, and then he was gone.

15

Bella stood at the door for a moment, then went into the kitchen to fill the kettle. Wiped the surfaces, opened first one cupboard then another, as if looking for something. Padded through to the sitting-room to plump the cushions. It was a good thing, she told herself, pounding the cushions, tweaking at the corners to make them pointy, that he hadn't kissed her goodbye or anything silly like that because then he would still have left and she'd be feeling a whole lot worse. Yes, all things considered, she was very lucky that he hadn't kissed her. She picked up the phone and called Viv, to see if she wanted to come and admire the garden before Bella had a chance to mess it up.

* * *

'Wow. It looks stunning now it's all finished. Lemme out there.' Viv rattled at the French windows. 'Is this all the work of the wunderkind Will?'

Bella unlocked the doors. 'Yup. And me. I have the scars to

prove it.' She shoved back her sleeves to reveal the long-gone marks on her brambled forearms. 'Well, they were there.'

'So, tell me more.'

'More what?'

'Since you found out he was single – has he—'

'Declared his intentions? No. I think I've lost the knack, Viv. Anyway, it's too late to impress him. He knows me too well.'

'But?' Viv raised her eyebrows into an exaggerated arch. 'But what?'

'Oh, come on. But you do think he's a bit of a potential shag-meister, don't you? I know you do.'

'Good grief. I told you before, he's not drop-dead gorgeous or anything...'

'Orange toupee? Nicotine teeth?'

'I admit I do think he has a nice face – the kind that makes you think you must always have known him. Comfortable-looking, like an old sofa. And he's got this little scar here—'

'I know, I know – you told me, it makes him look vulnerable. Never mind all that.'

'I keep wanting to reach out and touch it.'

'You're bloody smitten, woman. Admit it.'

'Nonsense.'

'Yes you are. You're all glowy and smiley. You're in l-u-u-r-r-v-e.'

'Am not. You know I'm immune to that sort of thing. And please don't use the "L" word before the 9 o'clock watershed or I'll have to report you.'

* * *

'Hello.' It was Will. 'It's me,' he said.

'You're right,' she said. 'How could you tell?'

'Don't be annoying. You're probably wondering what reason I

could possibly have to call you when I only left your house a few hours ago and the garden's all done?'

'You're calling to tell me to check the peonies every half-hour and to tie in any traily bits on the clematis. You told me.'

'Did I? Good. And don't forget those newly planted shrubs. Don't let them dry out.'

There was a pause.

'And I've got a possible commission for a Kreuzer mural.' He told her about an urgent civic project he had, two alternative designs for part of the area behind the mayoral offices. It was a plum job, high-profile, could bring in lots of new clients. Would she be interested in coming up with a couple of ideas for a mural at the back? Only on spec, but could be worth it.

'Thing is, we'd have to meet up to go through the brief. I could pop round or we could go out, save me always using up all your provisions. How would tomorrow suit you? Evening?'

It was a first-rate opportunity, so why did she suddenly feel disappointed? A large-scale commission – what could possibly be better? You're just scared, she told herself, scared to try anything new.

* * *

Could it really be true? *Another* spot? Smack dead centre on her chin. It couldn't have been more perfectly centred if she had used a measuring tape and painted it there herself. She had managed to steer through the entire spot-minefield of puberty, and some years afterwards, with an almost unblemished record. She had dared to believe – naïvely and somewhat mistakenly it now appeared – that she 'just wasn't the sort of person who gets spots'. She had, of course, been suitably sympathetic to her more carbuncular friends, offering them such small consolation as: 'It's only because I've got such dry skin. I'll age really badly' while telling herself that she could bathe in moisturizer morning, noon and night if she needed to in that then far-off time of ageing.

God evidently did not believe 'Blessed are the smug' for she was paying for her complacency now. Perhaps He got some cheap thrill from watching her relax in a non-spotty identity, only to spatter her when she was off guard – at an age when any sensible person would be worrying about wrinkles, not spots. She teased her reflection in the bathroom mirror: why are you so nervous, you idiot? It's not a date or anything. It's only Will. He's seen you with a spot before. He's seen your stubbly legs, tangled hair, smudged panda eyes because you're too lazy to take off your make-up.

The spot gleamed back at her from the mirror. Will wouldn't be able to take his eyes off it; it was like a homing beacon. Ships at sea could probably use it to navigate by. He wouldn't be able to think of anything else, only 'Don't mention the spot, don't mention the spot' cycling through his brain, terrified to speak in case he blurted out 'So, can I get you another spot?' Perhaps she should try to cover it up? But that always looked so obvious – so very like a spot with a blob of cover stick on top of it, never quite the same tone or texture as the surrounding skin. And anyway her cheerily named 'Hide the blemish' stick must be somewhere in the crammed-full bathroom cabinet, the Cupboard that Time Forgot with relics in layers displaying her personal history like a cross-section of an archaeological find: purple eyeshadow, too-pink blusher, various hopeless hair-taming products, dental floss still hermetically sealed in its bubble pack purchased after a resolution to Be Good and floss every day, bronzing gel – abandoned after one use which made her look as if she had bathed in orange squash.

If she wore the black top that was quite low-cut, he might not notice the spot. Sort of like creating a diversion. Good grief, it was a meeting, not a seduction, will you be sensible, she told herself. Her fingers wandered over her smart charcoal suit: too formal. Back to the black top, teamed with a sober skirt to show that she was capable of being a serious, professional person. She looked at herself in her old barley-twist mirror: first, the top half – the black top clung as closely as a drunken friend. Better cover herself up with a jacket.

She tilted the mirror to inspect her lower half. Perhaps she should go wild and buy a full-length mirror one day. Then again, perhaps not; she felt she was best seen only a small portion at a time.

The doorbell rang.

'Wow – have you dressed up just for me?' he smiled.

'This is my official impressing-a-prospective-client outfit, not that you bothered when it was the other way round. And it's to distract people from the repulsive spot on my chin. Don't worry – it's not contagious.'

Shut up, shut up, she told herself, that sounds like you're planning to press yourself against him all evening. Change the subject and just try to be normal.

Drinks drifted into dinner. Dinner stretched into coffee. More coffee. It was getting late.

He said he would walk her home. They meandered through the streets, talking, walking slowly. Zigzagged along the high street, pointing out their favourite hideous objects in shop windows and searching for the ultimate Gift You'd Least Like to Have to Display in Your Own Home.

'So then.' She paused at her door. 'Can you stand yet another coffee? Or will it keep you awake?' What the hell was that supposed to mean? Now he'd think she was trying to seduce him when she was only being friendly.

'It's late.' He smiled. 'I'd better get back.' She turned to put her key in the door. 'Still. If you insist. Just for a minute.'

When Bella came down from the loo, Will was looking at the kitchen pinboard while drinking his coffee.

'Sweet-looking kid.' He nodded at the picture of Patrick's nephew, which had survived the move from London still attached to the board. 'I always meant to ask you who it was.'

'Yes, isn't he? That's Lawrence in his school nativity play. Patrick's nephew,' she continued. 'My old boyfriend.' She gestured at a photo of a drenched Patrick standing by a Scottish loch, his straight hair plastered to his skull by rain. 'There. That's Patrick. Not looking his best there though. One of those Scottish holidays where it rains non-stop, day and night, you know, on and on. We got soaked. Rain, rain. Endless.' She must stop talking about Patrick. She was starting to babble. Will you shut up, woman?

'Oh? Right.'

She saw his eyes drop to the picture at the bottom of the board, the one of her Patrick together, sporting red Christmas antlers in bed.

'That looks horribly aren't-we-wacky.' She made a face. 'I must take it down sometime.' Bella turned away and foraged in the cupboard for some chocolate.

'I've got a bit of a confession to make,' Will said.

'I knew it. You used to be a woman. You're an international drug-smuggler. Out on parole. Worse – you're really a journalist?'

'The roughs for that project. I may have exaggerated its urgency just a tad.'

'When are they needed by?'

'Not for six weeks. I got home and then realized I didn't have an excuse to see you again. And I felt lousy.'

Her stomach felt tight, knotted. She couldn't do this – she couldn't have this kind of conversation – she must stop him – she'd thought she was ready for this, but she wasn't. She turned to the sink, poured herself some water, holding onto the cold metal of the tap.

'Do you think you could turn round, Bella? I'm trying to talk to you.'

'OK, OK. I was just thirsty. You're supposed to have eight glasses of water a day. I read it somewhere. Good for the skin.'

'Thanks for letting me know that. Nice timing. Now I've started and I don't know how to – I've never, you know, really *liked* a client before. It's probably a breach of professional ethics or something, perhaps I'll be struck off and never let within a hundred feet of a hebe again, but there's always been – something – between us, hasn't there? I'm not very good at this, am I?'

Bella crossed her arms and shrugged. 'Good at what?' Behind Will's left arm, she could see part of Patrick's photograph. Half a Patrick: one brown boot, one corduroyed leg, one waterproof jacket sleeve, a corner of closed mouth, one dark eye.

'Oh, shit. Good start, Will.' He clunked down his mug on the worktop. 'I feel like such a prat. So you don't think there is?'

'Why should there be?'

'All the hours we've spent talking mean absolutely bugger all to you then?'

'I've enjoyed our conversations, of course.'

'You make it sound as if we belonged to a debating society.' She shrugged.

'And every time we've looked at each other, that meant nothing either?' He moved towards her.

She would not look at him. Could not. Opened her mouth to speak.

He was standing close, so close. She could feel the warmth of him, smell his skin, his Will-smell that she had sniffed a hundred times in the garden, when he'd leant close to her, showing her how to prune correctly, when he'd squeezed past her in the kitchen to get to the sink. She pressed herself back against the draining board, clutching the curved edge of the worktop. Noticed her knees were shaking. Surely she would pass out. If only he wouldn't stand so close.

'Oh, Bella...' His voice quiet. Then, he held her suddenly by her arms, but she turned her head as if she had been slapped. In her short-sleeved top she felt suddenly naked, conscious of her bare flesh beneath his fingers.

'Look at me!'

His hands were strong, holding her, anchoring her to the ground. His hands on her arms. His skin touching hers.

'Look me in the eye and say, "Will, you're imagining the whole thing. I'm not interested. I never have been." Come on. Say it. I'll believe you.'

At last, she raised her face to look into his eyes. She couldn't speak. Her lips parted but there were no words. Her throat felt tight and full as if she were about to cry. Once more her mouth opened, forming a single silent word:

Will.

And then she was in his arms. He was holding her, drawing her tight to him, his face buried in her hair, her neck, saying her name again and again, spilling out as if it had been a great secret stored up in him. She tilted her face up towards him and his face was so close, his mouth found hers, but a curl of her hair was caught between them. Bella tugged it out of the way and they both laughed with relief. He was kissing her now, his mouth warm and real, and she was drunk with it and the two of them were gasping and laughing and kissing. He dipped his lips to her neck, kissing it sweetly, tasting her skin, wanting every inch of her. She pressed herself against him, feeling that he was indeed like some great tree, standing firm, safe and strong and true.

There was no way he would phone the next day. At least they were old enough to have left all that tedious treat-'em-mean-keep-'em-keen nonsense far behind them, so she wouldn't have to wait a whole week or anything, but he definitely wouldn't phone the next day. *You phone him if you want to. You're thirty-three for God's sake.* Well, she might just do that. But not yet. If he didn't phone her at work, then she would give him until, say, nine this evening, OK, eight thirty. After that, she could legitimately call him to ask vital questions about the mayoral mural because they hadn't really gone through the details properly and she wasn't sure if she'd noted down the dimensions correctly and she ought to be making a start on it; yes, she decided, she probably should give Will a ring anyway about that, whether she wanted to speak to him or not.

She had awarded herself bonus points for not going to bed with him straight away, propelling him out of the front door, telling him she wanted to take things slowly, making out she was mature and sensible and not just someone annoyingly on the first day of her period. Her mother would have approved, she thought. *Say what you like, Bella darling, but men don't respect a woman who falls into bed on the first date. Don't show your whole hand at once.*

* * *

Even from the other side of the office, she saw that she had a message, signalled by the semaphore flag of a yellow stickie – SOMEBODY WANTS YOU. She tried not to run to her desk. It was probably only a client. Clients always loved to phone first thing in the morning to catch people out when they were late in, while a colleague covered – 'She's not at her desk right now. I believe she's in a meeting...' Or Viv, wanting to know whether Bella had at last broken the longest snog-free spell in recorded history. Bella had managed to suppress the urge to recount the full hideousness of the Julian saga, but Viv had given her that pursed mouth, something's-going-on-and-you're-not-telling-me look.

WILL PHONED. PLEASE CALL A.S.A.P.

'Hi,' she said, phoning him while she was still standing, her bag hunched on her shoulder. 'It's me. Anything wrong?'

'Hello, you. No. Just being a sad sod who can't get enough of you. When am I seeing you? How about now? I need to kiss you again. They can survive without you there for a day, can't they?'

'One moment, Mr Henderson. I'll have to put you on hold while I check Ms Kreuzer's diary—' She clucked her tongue officiously. 'Looking very busy, Mr H., especially with dull clients having just come into season. Oh, but, there may be a small *window* this evening.'

'I'm not sure I could fit into a small window. I'm not the svelte little snip I once was, you know. Now I'm a man-sized hunk of 100 per cent pure, bulging flab.'

He was working outside the city in the afternoon, he said, over-seeing the landscaping of the area around a swimming pool at a swanky health club, but he could be back a bit after seven. They arranged to meet in the little garden behind the cathedral.

* * *

There was still over an hour to spare after Bella had left work, so she went inside the cathedral and leant against one of the massive pillars to draw the tourists. She wondered whether it might be considered blasphemous, drawing in a cathedral. She'd never noticed anyone sketching there before, though it was certainly less intrusive than taking photographs, which no-one seemed to bother about. How odd it must be to try to pray when all around you the stately gloom was pocked by white flashes, the solemnity punctured by discordant voices – 'Say, isn't it *big*? It's, like, really *old* too.' Perhaps drawing was her personal form of prayer; that complete absorption in itself, that reverence for form and line, light and shadow, that willing subjugation of self – surely it was a kind of worship? And if so, why couldn't they turn up the lights a bit? – she could hardly see to pray.

Outside, by the cloisters, she quickly sketched a couple pointing up at the carved masonry, a toddler journeying across the central square of grass. As she looked up from her pad, a woman settled to lean on one of the stone ledges, crossing her arms over her body like an Egyptian mummy, holding her shoulders. She stood watching the child for a little while. *Please don't move,* Bella willed her, *please don't move.* Speed gave her strokes greater boldness, confidence, mapping the angle of the woman's arms, the shape they formed around her neck, capturing the tilt of the chin, almost defiant. Her pencil set down the symmetry of the arch, framing the woman, echoing the line of her arms.

If only she had her paints with her; the evening sun falling at an angle seemed to pick out every element: the single strand of hair in front of the woman's eyes, the shadow her arm cast, the drape of the fabric around her shoulders, the shape of her elbow leaning on the flat stone. As if Bella had willed it, the woman suddenly looked up and straight towards her, without moving her head. It was hard to read the expression in her eyes, half-shaded as they were by the swag of her loosely pinned hair. There was something wistful about the angle of her head, as if she were trying to catch the faint strain of far-off music. Bella's pencil moved over the paper once more; she must paint this later, must, must, *must*. She closed her eyes, drinking in the image, the light, the shadows, feeling the picture sinking into her skin in thousands of points of colour like a tattoo.

'You've missed a bit.' Will's chin appeared over her shoulder. 'I may be a complete oik where art is concerned, but that's bloody good. Why aren't you in the little garden where you should be?'

A glance at her watch.

'I'm only five minutes late. Sorry. I got immersed.'

'Just as well I spotted you on my way there. Can pick out your squiggly hair from a mile away.'

'What do people *do* on dates? We should probably go see a movie or something.' Will rubbed his chin.

'You're hardly a toyboy. What do you normally do? Even you must have found the occasional female to take pity on you.' She felt his hand gently laid on the small of her back.

'So you're just doing this out of pity? Excellent. If I'm truly pathetic, will you seduce me?'

'Nope. It's just part of a local initiative to help keep our city clear of roving bands of garden designers rampaging along the high street, dead-heading the petunias.' Bella veered off into a newsagent. 'Shall we get a paper? See what's on?'

'But then we can't talk.' Will followed her in. 'I wish we could do everything, all at the same time.'

'We could whisper all the way through the film; don't you love people who do that? Give a running commentary even though the other person's right there watching it too: "This is the best bit. This is when he jumps out and you're really not expecting it."'

They strolled to the public gardens just inside the city wall, spread out the paper on the grass. Will ran his finger down the columns.

'Daft thriller? Daft courtroom drama? Or daft kids' film with talking animals? Not much choice. What haven't you seen?'

Bella leant closer to look. 'You smell nice,' he said.

'Thank you.' She focused on the paper. 'Anything at the Marlowe? "Leo Sayer – one night only." Does he still exist? For a theatre, they don't seem to have any actual plays on very often, do they?' She turned to see him looking directly at her.

Her eyes returned to scanning the columns. 'Will. What are you doing?'

'What? This?'

'You're making me nervous.'

'Are we too crumbly to snog in the park do you think?' He moved closer.

'We? I'm not, but I'll let you join in if you like.'

Lips on lips, his tongue finding hers. Her insides felt as if they were unravelling. Will steadied her with his hand and drew her closer. They stopped for a few seconds, only to indulge themselves with the delight of looking at each other and moving together again, to relish that first touch, teasing themselves with anticipation.

How many kisses? she wondered. How many would there be between now and – afterwards? You're only making it worse for yourself. Don't say I didn't warn you. Closed her eyes, blocking it out.

'We don't really want to go to the cinema, do we?' Will lightly nuzzled her cheek. 'You're probably desperate to invite me back to your place, but worried I'll lose all respect for you, so I just want to assure you... that I've never respected you anyway.'

'Thanks for reassuring me on that point.' She got to her feet and held out her hand to him. 'Come on, you. We're going to your place. I want to see *your* garden.'

* * *

She stood in his hallway where he insisted she wait while he did a lightning clear-up.

'Two minutes! Give me two minutes!' A clattering, as of cutlery being hurled into a sink. The sound of water running.

'Coming, ready or not. I'm not hanging around out here while you try and do a year's worth of washing-up.'

'Only my breakfast things. Just because I'm a bloke doesn't mean I'm a complete slob, you know.'

'Of course it doesn't.' She bent to pick up something from the floor. 'Oh, what an unusual miniature rug!'

He took the sock from her hand and tucked it into his trouser pocket.

'Oh, Will...' Bella laughed with the pleasure of it.

'I thought you might like it.' She thought she had never seen him look so pleased.

It was large by town-garden standards, and Will said he shouldn't be showing it to her and she must sign a confidentiality agreement because it went against all the current thinking about town gardens, which was that they should be fairly formal so that they related to their architectural surroundings, and he wouldn't have recommended it for any of his clients because it could easily slide into chaos without careful management. It was like stepping into the most beautiful countryside. There was a pool, fringed with rushes, irises and a clump of giant gunnera, like an alien forest, each leaf an inverted umbrella; this melded seamlessly into a bog garden, filled with lush foliage plants and candelabra primulas, as neat and straight-backed as convent girls.

A small dining-table and two simple benches were set beneath a pergola swamped in blue and white clematis and the acid-green leaves of a twining golden hop.

'Now it's warm I'll bring out my lanterns so we can sit here after dusk.'

She hurried from one part to another, descending on each delight like a butterfly alighting for a draught of nectar: a cherry tree with bark gleaming like polished mahogany, tubs splurging with white bell-flowers and silvery filigree foliage, tiny ferns growing in the crevices of a wall, like the ones he had planted in her own garden.

'Can I?' Her eyes were wide with anticipation.

'Course. You've been eyeing it ever since you came out here.' Bella ran to the far end of the garden.

All her life she had wanted one. Dreamed of having one. None of her friends had ever had one when she was a child. Now that she stood right beneath it, she realized how big it was, a proper, scaled-up, adult version. Quickly, she clambered up the ladder.

The tree house had been built into the branches of a large oak. It had a proper pitched roof and a glazed window; inside was a chair, a tiny table and a small wooden chest. How wonderful it would be to live here, she thought, away from all the irritations and nonsense, away from everybody; here a person would be safe, free to dream through the days alone with only the birds and the wind.

Leaning out of the window, she waved at Will standing below on the ground.

'Rapunzel, Rapunzel, let down your hair!'

'Too short.' She held out a strand.

'Better come back down to earth then, hadn't you?'

'Not much of a dashing prince, are you?'

'No. Come down. I need to be kissed.'

'Do you use it much?' she asked.

'No. I thought I might be able to work there, but it's not light enough and it's almost too quiet. Stay up there for an hour and you feel quite unreal. I prefer the clutter of my workroom.'

After supper, Will pulled her onto his lap.

'Is it too soon to whisk you into bed yet?' he asked, kissing her.

'Oh, stop beating about the bush, Will. I have a teeny hunch you're trying to make a pass at me.'

'Well, is it? Not that I've been thinking about it nonstop for two months or anything.'

'Why? We're not in a rush, are we? Have you a plane to catch?'

'I don't know why I feel like such a teenager when I'm around you. At school, the tough boys used to say, "Get yer leg over, did yer?" with much nudging and shoving and winking but most of us hadn't a clue.'

'We had stages called, predictably for then, Close Encounters. Maybe that's a bit of a girlie phenomenon.'

'Where are we up to?'

'Really only a Close Encounter of the Second Kind: kissing with tongues.'

'Mmm, how appetizing. What are the others? Give me the low-down.'

'Okey-doke: The First Kind – that's just baby stuff: English kiss (lips, no tongues). The Second Kind: French kissing (with tongues). The Third Kind: Touching of upper half (through your top). The Fourth Kind: Touching of lower half (through clothes) or upper half (under clothes). The Fifth Kind: The unbelievably grown-up fondling of personal parts (inside pants). The Sixth Kind: That's when you shag 'em.'

'We ought to be at least at the Fourth Kind by now.'

'No we shouldn't. And I hadn't finished: Close Encounters of the Seventh Kind—'

'Is that some weirdo schoolgirl thing: doing it on teacher's desk or something?'

'No. It's oral sex. It seemed unthinkably daring and outrageous at the time. Anyway, we're only on our second date, so...'

'But I'm thirty-seven. Doesn't that rush me up through the grades a bit faster? It ought to count for something. Besides, I've done your garden and we've had proper, grown-up conversations, so we probably should be at the Fifth Kind by now. We're lagging dangerously behind.' His arms slid around her waist.

'Third Kind. That's my final offer. No trying to sneak past my vest.'

They kissed and Bella stroked his back, as if she could absorb him through her fingertips. His hands stayed at the sides of her ribcage for a moment, not quite touching the soft rise where her breasts swelled away from her body. Her mouth watered. She drew his bottom lip gently between her teeth, sucked its fullness briefly, opened her mouth to his. His thumb eased across her left breast, circling the nipple. Their hands roamed over each other, exploring, stroking, teasingly avoiding erogenous zones, creating new ones. 'So much for not rushing,' she thought.

'You have to wait anyway.'

'Why? Did you promise your mother you wouldn't frolic with manual workers?'

'Yes. Plus I've just remembered I'm not wearing my best knickers.'

'That's OK. You can take them off. I've found it makes sex a whole lot easier.' He gathered her to him in a tight squeeze, then pulled away.

'You'd better go while I'll still let you. I'm getting too turned-on.' He adjusted his jeans.

'I daresay you can handle the problem.'

He laughed, pulling her close for another kiss.

'Don't get me started again.' He removed his lips with a loud smack, as if they had been stuck together. 'And call me, Gorgeous.'

'You're gorgeous.'

'That's comma, Gorgeous – Gorgeous.'

'I know, Gorgeous.'

'Thank you and good night.' She stood on the doorstep.

'Hang on,' he said. 'I'll just get my jacket. I'm walking you home. That way we can spin out this goodnight kiss for at least another hour.'

* * *

'Hurry up and go away so I can ring Viv and bore her about you.'

'God, you're like one of those tourists who can't wait for the holiday to be over so they can get home and develop their photographs.'

Bella kissed him on the nose. 'Bugger off.'

'Sleep tight, sweet pea.'

'And you.'

'Last chance. You sure you don't want to show me your grotty knickers?'

'They are NOT grotty, thank you. Just a bit...'

'I know. Baggy grey drawers with the elastic gone? But they're my favourite.'

'Good,' she said, propelling him out of the door. 'I'll wear them next time.'

'But black lace would do,' he called back through her letter box. 'Or silky ones.'

She ducked down to blow him a kiss through the slot.

'Go away. You can't talk about women's underwear through letter boxes. The Neighbourhood Watch will be onto you.'

17

'I could lie like this stroking you for hours. Days.' Will's finger paused in the dip above her collarbone. 'On the other hand...'

'Mmm-mm?' She spoke as in a dream.

'...I also want to shag you senseless, so get your knickers off.'

'I could tell you were a hopeless old romantic.'

Bella reached for the top button of his shirt. Their arms bumped together as they raced to unbutton each other, stopping to kiss, to whisper.

'Stop kissing me. Can't concentrate,' she murmured. 'Too many buttons.'

'All part of my cunning plan to have you naked first.'

'Ha! I'm winning, I'm winning.'

She removed his shirt. Her top came open and he peeled it off, traced the curve of her breasts through her silky camisole and lace bra. He raised her arms above her head and the camisole poured off her like cream.

'Slow down a sec, will you?'

'Sorry. Am I rushing?'

'No, but – new underwear – appreciate it, damn you.'

'You went and got new underwear? Just for me?'

She tried to backtrack – not really, she needed some anyway, she hadn't got round to doing her laundry.

'Uh-huh. I believe you, really I do. So, in fact, you were planning to get me into bed all along? Jury, please note.'

He bent to kiss her breasts above their frame of lace, reaching round her back to unhook her. His voice was low, deep in his throat, murmuring. They pressed close together. His chest felt warm and hard, solid against the soft swell of her breasts.

'God, you make me so nervous,' he said. 'Look at my hands.'

'Me too.'

'Me three.'

His fingers moved over her leg, stroking upwards, then exploring, teasing her through the lace. He traced the boundary along her thigh. Pushed aside the fabric, questing for her. She inhaled sharply and pushed against him. Fumbling for his belt buckle, she had to pull away from his kiss to see, to concentrate; her fingers lagged behind her mind.

'Here, here. Let me.' He moved back, hopping across the floor to tug off his socks, shake off his trousers.

'What,' asked Bella, pointing, 'are those?'

Will looked down at his black and white striped boxer shorts. 'These are my best pants. I thought they were rather chic.'

'You look like an Everton mint – come here.'

He shuffled over, his eyebrows raised suggestively. She shook her head.

'So predictable. That wasn't meant to give you ideas.' She tugged down his shorts. 'I just want to take them off. Oh, hello, you've got a head start.'

'Have you noticed how they never use condoms in movies?'

'Or books. Can't think why.' Bella peered over Will's shoulder as he sat on the edge of the bed. 'Maybe they think it interrupts the action too much. You can't cut straight from all that panting and drooling and closeups of beads of perspiration to "Er, hang on a minute." It doesn't have quite the same dramatic... thrust.' She nuzzled his neck. 'Having fun there?'

'Oh, bollocks. It's inside out. I see my suave Casanova image is fast going out the window.'

Bella tried to tear open another foil packet.

'I'm so glad these are made of industrial-strength aluminium. So this is what they mean by safe sex. Here, you have a go.'

Will charged around the room wrestling with it as if it were a savage beast.

'Success! These things must be designed by anti-sex campaigners. I'm too knackered now.'

'Nonsense. I was promised sex. It says right here in the brochure. I know my rights.'

He crawled back onto the bed.

'You'll have to do all the work then. Take me, take me.'

'I'm sorry,' he said. 'That was a shambles. A bloody disaster.'

'No.' Bella snuggled against his chest. 'A disaster would be if a tornado had plucked up the house and redeposited us on the fast lane of the M25. It's no big deal.'

'It is for me. That hasn't happened to me for ages.'

'So it's my fault? Thanks.'

'No, silly. I think it was just because I was so nervous. I wanted – want you so much. I don't want you to go off me just because you think I'm crap in bed.'

'Good grief. What kind of women have you been seeing? Do you really think I'd go off you because of that?' She saw his expression. 'Not that you are crap in bed anyway. I love the way you touch me. This just gives us an extra excuse to get in lots of practice.'

'You are nice, aren't you?'

'Ssh, it's a well-kept secret.'

'No, seriously.' He pulled her closer and stroked her nose softly. 'You know what I thought when I first saw you?'

''s lovely,' she sighed as he stroked rhythmically. 'No, what?'

'I thought that you were gorgeous...'

'Nah, you never.' She shoved him.

'Certainly did. And that you looked a bit scary. Formidable even.'

'Me? Not now you know me though, hmm?'

'I'm much more scared now. I think someone could know you for a long, long time and not really know you at all. Sometimes, it's like looking through frosted glass – I can see an outline of you but it's all fuzzy and elusive and I think if I were to reach for you, you'd dissolve and slip through my grasp like a, a Disprin or something. I want to know you properly, get inside your head.'

'Oh, you don't want to rummage around in there. Horrible mess. Full of old recipes, humdrum neuroses and slightly used jokes.'

They lay with just a sheet over them, blowing cool puffs of breath on each other.

'Come here, you,' Will said.

'Are you sure? I am *so* sticky.' She fanned the sheet up and down to let in more air.

'Good. Come and stick to me.' He pulled her close. 'Please, please tell me that was better than last time.'

She sucked in her breath and shook her head, like a builder appraising poor workmanship.

'Actually, I'm not quite sure. We probably ought to – you know, just to check that we're on the right track.' He started nibbling her shoulder. He whispered how he loved her smell, her taste. He wanted to inhale her, absorb her. Kisses traced a circuitous course down her body. He nuzzled at her belly, gently pinched her flesh between his lips, ran his tongue over her curves.

'You know I'm going to have to make you come again? You look so amazing.'

'Not possible. No energy left.' She lifted her head from the pillow. 'Still, you're welcome to try if you insist.'

'I insist.'

His mouth found her and her breathing quickened and grew thick.

A line of light squeezed through the gap in the curtains, slanting across the bed. Bella lay on her front, half-asleep. Will leant towards her and blew the ghost of a breeze on her lashes. Her eyebrows dipped and furrowed in the centre, puzzled, then she peered at him through half-open lids. She smiled, a cat gorged on cream.

'Hello.' Her voice soft with sex and sleep.

'Hello, you.' Will brushed her lips in a morning kiss. 'Do you have a permit to look so sexy in the morning? Shall I make some coffee or do you want to take advantage of me again first?' He flopped back on the pillow. 'I'm completely defenceless.'

Her lips curved again. 'Mmm. Coffee.'

'I can see I'm not going to get much intellectual discourse out of you at this hour. Or unbridled passion. Coffee it is.'

He got up and tucked the duvet carefully around her shoulders.

She nipped to the loo and brushed her teeth. Glanced in the mirror. Oh terrific: mascara smudges under her eyes. She hopped back into bed as Will reappeared with a tray: coffee, toast, apricot jam. He was wearing her crimson kimono, which reached only to his shins. Its soft fabric looked unlikely on his body, the silken V framing the curling dark hairs of his chest.

'Make yourself at home, why don't you?' Bella nodded at the kimono.

'These sleeves are impossible. I'm afraid I may have dipped them in the coffee. How on earth do you manage with them?'

'I have slaves who come in to do my every bidding.'

'Ah-ha. So that's the secret. Need any more?'

'Yes, but you will be expected to perform certain *personal* favours.'

'Well, if I must, I must,' he said, reaching for her.

'Such as pouring me some coffee. Thank you.'

Will went through to the bathroom to shave and shower – 'Feel free to come in and lather my personals at any point.' Bella lay back against the pillows and closed her eyes. She let herself relive last night, savouring the best moments again and again: Will moving towards her, the feel of his hands, his touch surprisingly tender; his eyes, shining with silent words; the small scar on his eyebrow, that tiny difference in texture beneath her fingertip. A world away from that fiasco with Julian. What the hell was all that about? she wondered. Why couldn't she have been more patient? Waited for... for. The long-banished phrase *The One* stubbornly resisted eviction from her head. *Don't be so stupid,* she told herself. *Don't be such a pathetic, fairy-tale-fantasizing girlie. There's no such thing.* Still, at least this time there had been no group orgy with Patrick roped into the proceedings.

She regretted the thought as soon as it had popped into her head, knowing at once that she couldn't banish it now that it was there. And now he was there, conjured up like a genie in a bottle, waiting for her.

In her mind, she called him, her voice echoing around shadowy recesses. 'Patrick!' she called softly, then louder, 'Patrick?'

When she enters she sees he is reading, lounging with his legs over the side of the armchair. He doesn't look up when she opens the door, but she knows he must have heard her.

The fire is lit in the grate, but the flames yield no comforting heat. 'Busy?' he says.

'Mmm.' She stands facing the fire with her back to him. 'But I do think of you. Often.'

'Yeah.' And now she senses him look up. 'Right.'

'I'm sorry.' She turns to face him.

He shrugs and returns to his book.

'Doesn't matter. You can't be bothering about me all the time.'

'Don't be like that. I'm with you now. I'll stay for a little while.'

'If you like,' he says, not looking up from the page. 'It's up to you.'

'So what happened to surprising me in the shower?' Will came into the bedroom with a towel over his head, drying his hair.

'I didn't come in. That was the surprise.'

'Hey – you OK? You look a bit pale.'

'Fine. Don't fuss.'

Will made a face and asked her what her plans were for the rest of the weekend. Painting, she told him, working up one of the drawings from her life class or the one she'd done in the cathedral cloisters.

'Good. Why don't we meet up later then? This evening?' He buttoned up his shirt.

'Mm. Quite a lot to do. Maybe another day.'

She sensed his eyes scanning her face, trying to read her.

'Shall I call your secretary? Sorry. Am I being too intense? I sort of assumed...'

Bella laughed and patted him lightly on the head.

'Relax, will you? What's the rush? At this rate, we'll be married by next week and divorced the week after. And, by the way, I don't care what your lawyer says, you're not having half the blue dinner plates.'

* * *

The phone rang. It was Viv.

'I was going to call you anyway,' said Bella. 'It's official. I've finally lost my virginity. Again.' She refused to count Julian, mentally sweeping the incident under the mat, best forgotten. The management cannot be held responsible for the occurrence of embarrassing one-night flings.

'Oi, Nick!' Viv shouted away from the phone. 'Guess what? Bella's got herself a shag at last!'

'Oh, feel free. Tell everyone. Semaphore ships at sea, why don't you?'

'Nick's not everyone. He's really an honorary girlie. Garden man, right? Or have you had someone else up your sleeve?'

'Certainly not – that would make a disgusting mess. Garden man it is.'

'You really like him. I can tell.'

'No I don't. Well. I do a bit. But don't tell anyone.'

'OK, OK. But, Bel?'

'What? Yes, it was good. No, I'm not giving you a blow-by-blow – let me rephrase that – detailed account so you can tell Nick.'

'Bel – don't forget to let *him* know you like him, will you?'

'I'm sure he does.'

'No, really. Men can be amazingly stupid about things like that. You have to spell it out.'

'Perhaps you could coach me via an earpiece?'

'I may have to. Are you taking him to meet your mum and dad?'

'Sure. Of course. Excuse me? Do you think I'm completely

stupid? He can meet them once we've made it to our golden wedding anniversary and not before.'

'Oh, come on. They're lovely really. He'll probably charm your mum to bits.'

'We'll never know. I can just see her smirking at his springy hair – "Oh, *William,* there's a clean comb in the bathroom if you want to tidy your hair at all. I suppose all that manual labour does take its toll on one's appearance."'

'She's not that bad. She's always been very nice to me.'

'Teacher's pet. It's only because you didn't have the misfortune to be born her daughter.'

'Give the woman a break. She's only human.'

'No she's not. She was put here by aliens to make humans feel so flawed and inferior that we'd all top ourselves.'

'Why are you sounding so miserable anyway? You're supposed to be full of post-shag afterglow.'

'I am, I am. I just feel a bit, you know...'

'What?'

'Weird. Like I've been un— I can't explain it. Got to go. I can hear Will coming downstairs.'

18

Three o'clock in the morning. The yellow light from the bedside lamp shone on a tangle of limbs, heavy with sleep. Bella shifted and took in an eyelid-slit view: the light, the pillow by her cheek, Will's face from below. The stubble on his chin, dark pinpricks. His hair, flattened against the pillow. Even his nostrils were lovable, she thought. She moved slightly to nuzzle his neck.

'Hello, you,' he said, opening his eyes a peep to match hers.

'Hello, you.'

'You know—' He yawned, catlike. 'You know when I first realized I was in love with you? You had this incredibly sexy dress on and you came running down the stairs and – you looked – so – beautiful I couldn't speak.'

'Makes a change.'

'Shut up. Then you started wibbling on about your tummy and you suddenly seemed so young and vulnerable, as if you were going out with the grown-ups for the first time.' He closed his eyes again and his mouth smudged a kiss across her left eyebrow before he settled back to sleep.

She nuzzled closer to his chest, as if she might absorb him

through every pore in her body. Her eyelids shut tight, clenching onto the moment, feeling tears start to well. *Let me have this,* she prayed silently, like a child not daring to jinx her wish by speaking aloud. *If I'm good for ever, can I? Please let me have this. Please.*

Bella woke first and slid out of bed, carefully lifting the covers so as not to wake him. She made a pot of tea and brought it up to the bedroom. He was lying on his back in a straight line instead of his usual diagonal sprawl, taking up most of the bed. His body was absolutely still, his face expressionless. She put down the tray and drew closer, leant over him.

'Will?'

No response. Her brows bunched into a frown. Dry mouth. Her hands clammy and cold, heartbeat loud in her ears.

* * *

Patrick's father gets slowly to his feet as Bella is shown into a side room. He holds her by her upper arms.

'I'm too late, aren't I?' Joseph nods.

'He never woke up. They said he didn't suffer.'

She hears the words, thinking, 'That's what they say in hospital dramas.' *He didn't suffer.* Does that mean you're supposed to feel OK about it? Joseph crushes her in a tight hug so she can barely breathe. Rose, Patrick's mother, looks blank and numb. Bella dips to hold her and they clasp each other for a minute, survivors in a storm. Sophie is on her way down from Newcastle, Joe tells her. They still haven't managed to get hold of Alan. Bella can tell that his parents need her presence, they need youth around them, some reminder of life.

'Do you want to see him?'

A silent, screaming 'NO' echoes inside her head, ricocheting around her brain. She is afraid and then ashamed. 'What would Patrick want?' she asks herself. 'What would Patrick do if it were me?'

She nods once and a nurse leads her to just outside the room, saying she can take her time, have as long as she likes.

She peers through a small glass panel in one of the double doors. Patrick is lying on a narrow, trolley-type bed in a small room. She breathes a slow breath, squashing down a wave of nausea and palpable dread, and pushes open the door. A side table covered with a crisp white cloth holds a cut-glass vase of fresh flowers: pale lemon-yellow carnations, feathery fronds of maidenhair fern, orange trumpets of alstroemeria, flecked with brown.

She looks down at Patrick. His mouth is open and she can see the dull silver glint of his old fillings and the small chip in his front tooth that he had never got around to having fixed. He should have gone ages ago. That was typical of Patrick. Absurdly, she starts to cry at the thought, small, tight, breathy sobs. She wipes them away impatiently with her hand. Not much point getting his tooth done now.

She wishes they had closed his mouth. Weren't they supposed to do that? His eyes were shut. She half-wanted to close it herself, but – but she couldn't. What if it sprang open again?

He looks slightly paler than usual, as you might expect under the circumstances. And there is a padded bandage covering half his head, though Bella suspects that, as this looks pristine, it is to protect the bereaved from the sight of their loved one with a squished skull. Bereaved. That's what she is, she realizes – a bereaved person. People will look at her with pity in their eyes, speak to her in hushed tones. They'll be embarrassed and won't know what to say. Aside from the bandage and two scratches on his forehead, Patrick looks surprisingly normal, as if he's dropped off, as he tends to do, for a quick doze. Perhaps if she prods him, he'll sit up with a jolt and say 'I wasn't snoring. I was just breathing deeply' the way he does. Did, she corrects herself.

She looks at the flowers again, traces the crinkled edge of one carnation with her finger. Someone has bothered to arrange these flowers, trim the ends, pull off the lower leaves; laid this cloth on the table, smoothing the iron-creases with a cool palm. They must have known that the bereaved see everything, that no detail is too small to be significant.

One arm lies outside the crisply turned hospital sheet. She wants to touch his hand, reach over and give it a reassuring squeeze, though whether for Patrick or herself she can't be sure. She wants so much to feel his warmth, to feel him return the pressure of her hand. Perhaps she should touch it? Shock herself with its coldness, its waxy softness, so she would understand that it was true, know that he was really dead.

But she can't. Instead, she pats the other arm, the one safely under the sheet.

Her voice, when finally she speaks, is a hoarse whisper, sounding to her ears as if it comes from someone else.

'I'm sorry,' she says.

Joseph comes in then, and stands behind Bella, solid and comforting. He squeezes her shoulders.

'Do you want to stay longer?'

'I don't know.' A small shake of her head.

'Come on.' He puts his arm around her, supporting her and steadying himself.

'Come and have a cup of tea. The nurse has made us some. It'll do you good.'

'But I can't just leave him here all alone.'

'It's all right.' Joseph strokes her hair back from her eyes and dabs tenderly, clumsily at her cheeks with his cotton handkerchief. 'He's gone now. It's not him any more.'

He leads her from the room, but she turns at the door for one last look. 'Bye,' she whispers.

* * *

'Will?'

Silence.

She tweaked his nose.

Will.'

He opened one eye. 'Boo,' he said.

'You pig.' She pinched him. 'You bloody scared me.'

'Hey, sorry. Ow. That hurt.'

'Good. Don't do it again. I'm confiscating your tea now.'

'Tea in bed?' He lifted his head from the pillow and whimpered. 'Oh tea, tea, oh please.'

She poured it out, then took her own cup and went to run herself a bath.

Will picked up her post from the doormat. As he handed it to Bella, his gaze dropped to a postcard on the top. His eyes met hers, then he glanced down again. She looked at the card: 'Hi Sexy!' it said in large capitals. Bella felt herself flush slightly and Will quickly turned away. The card was postmarked from Washington. Julian.

> *Sorry we couldn't get it together again before I had to leave – the price of being a jet-setter! Great to spend time with you. See you on my next visit!?! Best to Nick and Viv. Luv, J XXX.*

She put the card on the mantelpiece, next to one she'd recently received from Patrick's parents:

Very glad to hear you've escaped from the big smoke. We did worry about you in London on your own... Do keep in touch... visit any time...

As well as the occasional card or letter, there were still periodic phone calls. Rose would ring and ask with maternal concern how she was doing, as if she were a child struggling with a too-advanced sum. Bella would call and speak to Joseph. They were bearing up, he'd say. Things were, you know... his pauses closed by a small cough, just like Patrick. Sophie was doing well, he reported. Alan and his wife had had another baby. Rose was raising funds for a village in Bangladesh. He himself had taken up bowls to pass the time. Life ticked on.

She felt she should ask them for permission to be happy. Knew, of course, what they would say: 'You've got your own life to lead now, Bella. Don't waste it. He wouldn't have wanted that, not Patrick.' And no, she realized, he wouldn't, not exactly. How would she feel if it had been the other way round? 'You wouldn't feel anything, stupid, you'd be dead,' she told herself. But still – what if she died and Patrick had been left alone? Or – her scalp prickled – what if it were Will? Would she want him to grieve for ever? In a horrible way, she would – at least in some small corner of himself. What a vile, mean-spirited person she was. How could she ever want Will to be unhappy? No. That wasn't it. She'd want him to remember, that was all, only so she wouldn't be lost without trace. She wouldn't want to have him hunched over his grief, treasuring it and hoarding it like a miser, allowing no-one near – a second death.

. . .

'Can I ask you something?' Will said after breakfast. Then, without pausing, 'Are you seeing anyone else?'

'No. Whatever gave you that idea? I can barely cope with you.'

'Nothing. Just a feeling.'

That postcard from Julian, she thought. HI SEXY! He must have read it.

'Um, do you still see your ex at all? Patrick. You look like one of those civilized types that manages to stay on good terms with their exes.'

Bella rootled in the fridge for some mineral water.

'Hmm?' Her voice floated from inside the fridge. 'No, I don't. Do you want some water?'

'No thanks. Sorry. I didn't mean to be nosy.'

Bella shrugged. 'Doesn't matter. Anyway—' she opened the newspaper and leafed through to find the listings. 'Do you still fancy seeing a film tonight? I could give Viv a call, see if she and Nick want to come too. We don't have to be stuck just with dreary old us all the time.'

'Is that how you see us?'

'Hmm?'

'Dreary old us?'

'No, course not.' She banged the fridge door closed. 'Still, we don't want to get too couply, do we?'

'Why ever not? I like being couply.'

'Oh, *Will*. I'm just teasing. Where's your sense of humour?'

'Had to give it back. Only got it on loan.'

* * *

Viv rang the next day to recap on their cinema outing, as Bella knew she would.

'Lousy film,' said Viv. 'Why does everyone keep going on about how sexy she is?'

'Because she's blonde and can't act.'

'But *Will* – he's so lovely! And he's got you sussed, hasn't he?'

'Meaning?'

'Meaning he knows how to handle you.'

'You make me sound like a deranged leopard.'

'Well, you're no giggling pushover, matey, are you? You need someone like that to stand up to you. But the way he *looks* at you. When's the wedding?'

'Oh, *behave*. I'm not thinking about the future or any of that bollocks.'

'Why do you do this?'

'Do what?'

'Pretend not to like him. A child of three could've seen that you were mad about each other.'

'Get me a child of three then. You read too much into everything.'

'Babe? You bloody well hang onto him.'

'Yeah, yeah. You just want the chance to wear a puff-sleeved number in apricot sateen.'

'With flounces?'

'You can have flounces, sweetheart neckline, basket of rose petals, all the trimmings in the unlikely event of my ever getting hitched. Ladbrokes are offering four thousand to one against, you might like to know, before you hotfoot it to Fabrics 'R' Us.'

'Bel? You do know about being happy, don't you?'

'Is this a trick question?'

'No. It's just – well, it is *allowed*, you know.'

19

'Which is my best side, do you think?' Will turned his head this way and that.

'It's a well-kept secret apparently.' Bella balanced her sketch-pad on her knee.

'Oh, tee-hee.'

'Turn to your left. More. Bit more. That's lovely.' She was now looking at the back of his head.

'Hilarious. Look to your laurels, Oscar Wilde.' He got up and went to the window, gazing down at his garden. 'That honeysuckle needs a good prune.' He half-turned to look back at her.

'Stop! There, like that. No, no, don't move.'

Standing by the window, his face half in light, half in shadow, his body twisted towards her, he looked alert, expectant, as if he had heard an unfamiliar sound, or suddenly noticed the extraordinariness of something ordinary.

'Can I see some of your paintings yet? I know you've been secretly beavering away.'

'Not secretly. And no you can't.'

'Yes secretly. And why not? You must have enough for an exhibition by now.'

'Don't be absurd. Anyway, will you ssshh! Concentrating.' Looking down at the drawing, she sensed his making stupid faces at her. Patrick used to do that too when she sketched him. Perhaps it was something to do with testosterone, the inability to keep still. Her gaze flicked up to Will's hairline, the clear shape of his brow where the hair jumped up from his scalp, looking eager to grow, to get on with it; she smiled to herself, trying to let its enthusiasm run into the line of her pencil, her tongue touching her lip in concentration like a child. Patrick's hair was soft and fine, flopping down over the left-hand side of his forehead. She remembered the feel of drawing it, the motion of her hand backwards and forwards as if she were weaving. And the way he reached his hand up, pushing it back off his face, the way he fidgeted annoyingly while she drew, even in his sleep, never entirely at rest, never, until— She swallowed.

'Sssh!' she said again.

'What?' Will frowned. 'I never made a sound.'

When they stopped for a break, Will told her how weird it was to be looking at her looking at him as she drew.

'You seem to look at me so intensely, but right through me at the same time. I see your eyes flicking over me, scanning me, but you don't seem to be registering me as me.'

'Don't take it personally. Drawing's like that. You just become a body, a face, not Will, the man I know and— so forth.'

'Excuse me? The man I know and so forth? Is that English as she is spoke?'

'Are you ready for the second sitting?'

'What were you going to say? You can't say it, can you? Not even casually.'

'What – the "L" word? Of course I can. Don't be silly.'

'The "L" word. That's exactly what I mean. Love really is a four-letter word to you, isn't it?'

'I'll do the jokes thank you.'

'This one's not funny. Go on, have a go. You might get to like it. I L-L-L – golly, you're right, it is tricky, isn't it?' He folded his arms.

'You can be bloody irritating sometimes. You are such a big kid. Unbelievable.' She rummaged in her pencil case for her putty rubber. 'The man I know and love. See? OK?'

He staggered backwards.

'Overwhelmed with the force of your passion. Look, ease up on the slushy stuff, will you? I'm not sure I can handle it.'

Bella sharpened her pencil into the bin.

'Yes, dear. Pose please. Left arm round a bit. Yup. And could you twist a little more this way. Whoa, not too much. Yup. That's it.'

Her gaze flicked back and forth from Will to the paper, the paper to Will, as she set down the bones, the flesh, the form of him, but she did not see the expression in his eyes.

Will asked her if she would be free at the weekend. 'I hate it when people do that.'

'You hate it when people invite you to things? Forgive me. I'm sorry. It's unpardonable. I'll never do it again.'

'Oh, shut up. You say you're free, then they say "Ah, good, I've got tickets to see Bernard Manning." People should say what it is first so you have a chance to refuse graciously.'

'So are you free or what?'

'Yes. No. Yes. I should be doing some painting – I want to work up that drawing of you. What is it?'

'I thought you might like to meet my mother.'

'Do I have a choice?'

'Oh, charming. She's lovely. She's just like me.'

'Smug with stupid hair?'

'No. Easygoing. Loves plants.'

'It's really a bit tricky this weekend. Got loads to do.'

'Such as?'

'*Will.* I'm not on trial. I don't have to account for my movements every second of the day. You know – *things.* Washing and stuff.'

'Oh, *washing.* Well, obviously that comes first. Heaven forbid you should actually put yourself out to meet my family.'

'Deep breaths. I'm sure she's not exactly sitting there, crocheting in her rocking chair, wondering how much longer she can carry on without meeting me. Some other time would be lovely. Of course I'd like to meet her. I can't imagine the paragon of patience and fortitude who could have put up with you for so long. Now, will you please get back to your pose.'

Will moved to the window.

'Can I just ask – is there some particular reason why you don't want to meet my mum?'

'Course not. I'm busy. Please can you just drop it for now? I really want to finish this.'

* * *

Over supper that night, Will got out his diary and raised the subject again. 'If it really is that you're just busy this weekend, let's make it another time.'

'We don't have to do all that meeting the parents stuff, do we? I'm in no rush for you to meet mine.'

'Have I ever asked to meet yours? We'll come to that when you're ready, but Mum's dying to take a look at you.'

'Why is she?' Bella held her fork poised, pointing towards his neck like a lynch mob armed with a pitchfork. 'What have you told her about me, boy?'

'Nothing. Nothing. Back off, you big bully. I may have gone on about you a bit, well, a lot. I couldn't help it. It'll be painless, I promise.'

'All right, all right. Don't go on about it. Next weekend, OK? Let's get it over with so you'll stop nagging me.'

She hadn't seen Patrick's parents for quite a while; looking back, she was worried to realize she couldn't remember exactly when her last visit had been. In the beginning, she had gone almost every weekend.

* * *

She senses that they seem to need her presence, as if she emanates some essence of Patrick from her skin, as if they can remember him more clearly when she is in the room. It is a comfort to her, too. The flat is cold and echoing without him, like a stage set when everyone has gone home, and she feels frightened sleeping alone. The hall light is left on at night but still she has a horror of going to sleep. When she wakes in the early hours, for one, two seconds, she forgets. In that haze of half-sleep, he is still alive. Then the knowledge strikes her like a physical blow. Her breath seems to rush from her body, leaving her lungs hollow, her stomach aching. She closes her eyes to seal in her pooling tears. In her mind she finds her refuge, her solace. There, his voice is clear and strong, his face bright and alive, and she could breathe again.

At his parents' house, the family photo albums have taken up permanent residence on the coffee table, displacing the copies of *Homes & Gardens*, the neatly folded *Daily Telegraph* and *Daily Mail* relegated, unread, to the hall stand where their callous normality can be overlooked.

'Look,' they say. 'Here he is ready for his first day at school. That grey cap kept sinking over his eyes. Remember when he went off to college and he was tall and lanky but he suddenly looked like a little boy again.' *Do you remember?* they say. *Do you remember?*

Seeking refuge in the kitchen, Bella cooks and clears up, grateful to lose herself in the rhythm of topping and tailing beans, the predictability of cooking: you put a shepherd's pie in the oven, it comes out brown; you whisk a sauce, it becomes smooth.

Rose fusses around her.

'You're doing everything again, Bella. You're a treasure.' Rose removes the colander Bella is about to use and puts it in the dish-drainer. 'I don't know where I am today. Have you seen my reading-glasses? I found my fountain pen in the fridge yesterday. I wonder where...'

Rose drifts in and out of rooms, leaving behind her a trail of untouched cups of coffee, miscellaneous bits of sewing bristling with wayward pins, her spectacles, her wristwatch, her unfinished sentences.

Joseph, Patrick's father, pats Bella's shoulder as he passes, his affection, his gratitude all the stronger for its silence.

'We always hoped...' he begins late one night, then stops, knowing it is better left unsaid, that there is nothing to say.

Sophie times her visits to coincide with Bella's, dragging her to the pub at every possible opportunity.

'They're driving me mad, Bel. Mum can't remember anything for more than ten seconds and Dad phones me twice a day just to check that I'm still breathing.'

'I know,' says Bella. 'Be patient. It's hard for them. It's just too hard.'

* * *

Pleading tiredness after a long and draining week at work, Bella managed to talk Will out of driving to his mother's on Friday night.

She would get up at the crack of dawn on Saturday, she promised. She would bring him tea in bed. It would take her only one minute to pack.

It was after 11 a.m. by the time they left.

Several tapes clattered onto the floor from Will's overstuffed glove compartment as Bella poked about in it.

'What's up, pumpkin?'

'Nothing. Just *trying* to find the Ray Charles.'

Had she looked in the side pocket? She had. That was just the empty box.

'Why don't you keep the tapes in their boxes? Then you wouldn't have this problem.'

I'm sounding just like my mother.

'I don't have "this problem" because I don't care. I just plunge in and play whatever comes to hand. Potluck.'

'Men are just so annoying.'

'That's always a good answer – dismiss half the human race in one fell swoop. Keeping the tapes in their boxes doesn't bring about a cure for cancer or herald the dawn of world peace, does it?'

'What's that got to do with the price of fish, as they say?'

'Because you are fretting over a speck of dust in this Great Creation. But it's not about tape boxes, is it? Oh-oh, I feel a bout of smugness coming on. Why are you so nervous?' he asked, looking at her sidelong. 'She's not an ogre or anything.'

'I'm not nervous. Isn't it an ogress?'

'Bzzz. Pedantry alert. Stop trying to change the subject. She's fine and she'll love you.'

Bella delved into the depths of her handbag, foraging for a mirror. Will snorted with delight.

'Not nervous. No, course you're not.'

He rootled around under his seat, retrieved a tape with the tips of his fingers and clunked it in.

'...dah-dah dee, dah dee dee – dee...' Will hummed along with the tape. *Ray Charles.*

She stuck her tongue out at him covertly.

'I saw that.' He squeezed her leg and left his hand resting on her thigh.

'So, should I call her Mrs Henderson or Frances or Fran or what?' She licked her finger and smoothed down her eyebrows, frowned at her reflection.

'You look fine. Relax. Not Mrs Henderson, mainly because she isn't anyway; minus five points for not listening when I was giving you the fascinating details of my family tree. She's Mrs Bradley because of Hugh, my stepdad, ex-stepdad, whatever. She prefers Fran, but, frankly, I don't think she'd care if you called her Chatanooga Choo-Choo. She's a tad eccentric.'

'How eccentric?'

'Hardly at all. Barely noticeable. Can't think why I mentioned it. But thank heavens she lives in England where behaving peculiarly is cultivated as a national pastime.'

* * *

Fran's cottage was set back a little way from a narrow track with three other houses. It looked old to Bella, perhaps seventeenth-century, with a low doorway and steep 'catslide' roof that swept right down to her eye level. Succulent houseleeks clung to the roof-tiles in compact clusters. An uneven brick path led to the front door, flanked by beds packed with scented clove pinks, outsize oriental poppies with petals like salmon-pink tissue, a haze of pale blue love-in-a-mist. Will dipped to smell the pinks as he passed.

'Here, have a sniff,' he said over his shoulder to her.

A few strands of badly painted ivy trailed across the blue door, continuing from the real ivy that grew around it. There was no answer when they knocked, so they went round to the back.

'Hello-o-o-o-o,' Will called down the long garden.

A figure sprang up from a fuzz of fennel halfway down. 'Hello-o-o, yourself.'

Will led the way along a narrow path that wove between lavender bushes, feathery artemisia, waving blue delphiniums.

'Hello, Ma.' He gave Fran a big bear-hug.

'Willum,' she said fondly, squeezing him back. She was wearing a voluminous blue boiler suit, its pockets bulging with lumpy artefacts, and what looked suspiciously like a pair of men's leather slippers. Her grey hair was piled on top of her head in a rough heap. There seemed to be a pen stuck into it, though Bella couldn't tell whether it was to anchor the hair vaguely in position or if it had just been poked in there as a temporary resting place. Will reached forward and removed a bit of twig from her hair.

'So you're Will's light-o'-love then?' Will rolled his eyes.

'Ma, do make some effort not to embarrass me completely.' Fran took both Bella's hands in her own and looked at her.

'Oh, peachy cheeks! Will said you were a beaut but I presumed he was biased. What wonderful eyes. Tell me – do you like rosemary?' She waved her secateurs around alarmingly.

Bella was grateful for the sudden change of tack.

'Here, have some cuttings. This one has the bluest flowers ever. Do you know which it is, Willum? I never remember the names.' She leaned towards Bella. 'I'm sure he must despair of me.'

'Nonsense. I do not. The plants don't know their names either, do they? I only need to know to impress my clients. It might be *Rosmarinus officinalis* "Prinley Blue" – that's very blue.'

'Certainly worked with me, at any rate,' Bella said. 'He bewitched me with his talk of *Meconopsis* and *Salix* and *Lavandula* whatever it is.'

Angustifolia, mostly.' He looked suddenly very serious and very young. 'This one,' he patted a nearby bush with wing-tipped purple flowers as if it were a small child, 'is French lavender, *Lavandula stoechas.* Like we put in your garden. And I thought you'd fallen for my brains, wit, charisma and dashing good looks.'

'And simple humility, obviously.'

'Obviously.'

Fran laughed and linked her arm through Bella's.

'How nice to see he's met his match. Lunch isn't quite ready, but come in and have some tea. You must both be gasping.' She stuck her secateurs into her pocket. A length of green garden twine dangled down behind her like a tail from the other pocket, trailing on the ground. Will picked up the end and processed after her, carrying it like a bridal train.

'There's a casserole on the go, but the meat's a bit tough, so we'd best leave it as long as we can stand it, I think.' Fran lit the gas under an outsized enamel kettle. 'There're some scones somewhere if you want to keep yourselves going. Have a rummage in the bread crock there – they're fresh today. Or yesterday. Anyway, they're absolutely fine.'

Bella reached deep down into the stoneware crock. 'I feel like I'm doing a lucky dip.'

'More likely unlucky dip in this kitchen.' Will shifted a sprawling pile of papers from the table to the dresser and set out an assortment of cups and mismatched saucers. 'They're not home-made, are they, Ma?'

'No, you needn't worry, rude boy. I knew I should have paid more attention to your manners when you were growing up.' Fran's voice echoed from the depths of the larder. 'My scones are legendary, Bella – flat as stepping stones and twice as hard. Hughie cracked a tooth on one once. The dogs used to love them, though. But these are proper shop-bought ones as you're a real guest.'

'Consider yourself honoured,' Will said. 'Any jam, Mother dear?'

'Strawberry and elderflower. And that is homemade.' Fran caught Will's look. 'Recent vintage, so don't look like that, but it might be a bit gloopy; it didn't seem to want to set. It's fine. Just eat it with a spoon and alternate it with bites of scone.'

* * *

That night, Bella lay cuddled up close to Will in the narrow double bed in the 'rose room'. Fran had said they could have the proper guest bedroom, but they'd have to shove the beds together or they could squeeze in here.

'It's very cosy, but – be warned – the walls are a bit thin and I'm right next door.'

'God, Ma, you are so embarrassing.' Fran breezed on, unabashed.

'I only do it to annoy. I know, how hideous – a parent alluding to sex. Yuk. Children always think of their parents as permanent virgins or asexual, like amoebas. Or is it amoebae?'

Will was cringing. He pulled Bella by the elbow into the room.

'Fine, fine. We'll have this one. Thank you. Come on, otherwise she'll be off on her I've-had-quite-a-few-interesting-escapades-in-my-time speech and we'll have to hear about the bank manager who fell madly in love with her and kept calling her with trumped-up queries about her finances, then tried to ravish her over a pile of her statements.'

'I'm paying no attention.' Fran skipped downstairs. 'Kettle's on.' Bella told him he was being rude.

'No I'm not. We love each other to death and we both know it. So we can be as rude as we like.' Surely her family weren't *polite* to each other all the time?

'Dad and I tease each other. We always have.'

He asked about her mother. 'Do you know, you almost never mention her.'

'I'd never talk to her the way you just did. You can't tease her, it would be bound to upset the planet's orbit or something. We try to be quite civil most of the time. Like in an armed truce.'

He raised his eyebrows.

'Mmm. Have to be. If we let down our guard, boy the knives'd be out.'

'Aah, how sweet. The joys of the mother-daughter bond. I see it now: Madonna and child with beatific smiles, a small dagger glinting discreetly beneath flowing robes.'

'Hilarious.' Bella left the room. 'Coming down for some tea?'

20

'Will you really? I'll be your best friend.' Bella squidged Will's cheeks and gave him a slurpy kiss.

'You already are.'

After only minor arm-twisting and the promise of numerous sexual favours, Will had volunteered to speak to his brother-in-law-in-law about the DAMP. The phone call was made, unknown leverage put into action. Mr Bowman had moved her from his black book to his red book, the actual one where real jobs were written in with dates and everything. It would take four to five days; once the treatment had been done, the walls would need replastering then drying out before they could be repainted.

Life became even more impossible. Boxes were squished into the bedroom, pictures stacked like dominoes on the landing, pot plants gathered in a leafy convention in the bathroom.

'You oughtn't really to stay in the house while all that's going on; the dust can't be good for you,' Will said.

'I know. Viv said they'd put me up.'

'Right. Or – you could, ah, stay with me.'

Although they usually ended up at Bella's house, she had stayed the night at Will's place several times before. He had bought her an extra toothbrush to keep at his place because he thought it ridiculous that she kept taking hers backwards and forwards. He had cleared a drawer for her, in which she kept one large T-shirt and one pair of pants. But staying the night casually was different, supper followed by sex followed by falling asleep. This was planned, official. Living together for five days solid – well, it was... domestic, wasn't it? It would involve couply conversations, cohabiting-type rituals: who would pick up something for supper; you-cook-I'll-wash-

up routines; she'd become involved in the minutiae of his household: where he kept the spare loo rolls, how to master the exact jiggle-jiggle-chunk required to open the back door, which day the rubbish was to be put out.

'That's very kind of you. You don't have to do that. You've earned your scout badge, talking to Mr B.'

'I'm not being kind. You sound like a polite child who's been coached to say thank you. I know I don't "have to do that" – I want to do that. This. Whatever. What I mean is – I'd love you to come and stay. With me.'

Warning bells. What if she got to like it? Got used to seeing his face and his adorable, funny eyebrows on the pillow by hers when she closed her eyes each night? Each morning, there his face would be, her first glimpse of the world, already familiar. She'd know if he was in by the feel of the house when she entered the door, the smell of him in the air. How quickly might she adjust to his tread on the stair, his voice calling hello, the change in his eyes as they met hers? And then? Then the DAMP would be done, the walls painted and there would be no reason for her not to go home. That first evening she would go back to her own house. The chill tang of fresh paint, the clunk of her keys on the table, the fridge with its lone carton of blobby milk. It would be like the first time she had gone back to the flat after Patrick. *After* Patrick. That was how she saw her life sometimes: Before Patrick/With Patrick/After Patrick, divided into neat sections like a pie chart, with no space left over for anything else.

* * *

She turns her key in the lock, half-expecting him to call out 'Hiya. Good day?' The silence is like water, filling the rooms right into the corners. She moves through it with slow limbs, feeling it part and reseal itself behind her. In the kitchen, there is an unfamiliar stillness, a cold tidiness; nothing has moved. There is no marmalade jar sitting on the worktop with its lid off. No half-read paperback spreadeagled on the table. Automatically, she looks down. Patrick has an infuriating habit of leaving his heavy brown lace-ups in the middle of the floor where she frequently trips over them. *Had* an infuriating habit, she corrects herself. She feels a sudden pang of anticipated loss, a guessing of future pain. She is tempted to go and fetch his shoes and place them on the floor, then dismisses the thought as silly, mad even.

The bathroom is worse. Four disposable razors, all apparently on the go at once. That absurd deodorant in the just-'cause-I-smell-nice-don't-mean-I'm-not-macho black phallic spray can. Her fingers run over the head of Patrick's green toothbrush, splaying the bristles to and fro. It had what Patrick claimed were 'go-faster' stripes – 'See, I can do my teeth in 30 seconds with this.' She lifts her purple brush from the tooth mug and holds one in each hand, face to face, bouncing them up and down the way Patrick used to, giving them voices. 'Are you talking to me yet?' he'd say as green toothbrush, putting on an extra-deep voice, pogo-ing it along the edge of the basin. He'd twist the purple one from side to side, shaking its head, until Bella laughed.

She head-butts green toothbrush with purple toothbrush.

'Why'd you have to go and die on me then? That was pretty dumb.'

'Yeah.' She switches to goofy, green toothbrush voice. 'Guess I just

didn't see it coming, a-her-her.' She leaves them intermeshed – 'Kiss and

make up?' Patrick used to say, pushing their bristles together. Wipes her *stupid* tears away with her hand. Her lungs feel tight and full, as if they are packed with explosive. 'Breathe deeply,' she says out loud. She can feel ugly sobs stirring down there, churning around in her, threatening to lurch out of her uncontrollably, tearing the fragile silence. She rubs her ribcage; it is so tight, it is painful, aching for release. Her teeth clamp tight shut and she bites the inside of her lip hard, desperate for some tangible, lesser pain to cling to.

In the bedroom, the curtains are half drawn and the dim light is welcome. She undresses slowly, by rote. As she pulls back the quilt to get into bed, she stops, then crosses to the chest of drawers. Rummages in a drawer, tuts quietly to herself. She dips into the linen basket and digs down, dropping socks, towels on the floor. Patrick's blue shirt – crumpled, soft with wear. She sinks her face into it, and breathes in.

She slides beneath the quilt and folds the shirt into a bundle by her face. Fingers one of its pearlized buttons, tracing round and round the rim, until she slips into sleep. It is twelve hours before she wakes again.

* * *

Will took her in his arms, scooped her close.

'What's up, sweet pea? Have you disappeared again, dreamy?'

She rallied a smile and kissed him. Shook her head. *I must try. I must.*

'I don't want to put you out.'

'You're right. Let's forget it. It would be a huge hassle, having to lie next to a gorgeous naked woman every night, having to wake up each morning to see the face of the woman I love on the other pillow. What a drag.'

'Oh, is someone else coming too?'

'Shut up. You're staying with me. Don't argue. I promise not to make you enjoy yourself. You can hate every minute if you like, then you can say "I told you so". I know how you love to be right.'

'I do not. Are you sure you can tolerate my repulsive habits?'

'I'm sure you're merely an amateur in the disgusting-habits stakes. I once competed for the South-East. What feeble attempts can you offer – Nose-pickings on the pillow? Toenail clippings in the teapot? Peculiar sexual practices involving courgettes? What?'

'Eugh. You're disgusting.'

'Confess your dark secrets.'

'I rest half-used blobs of cotton wool by the basin...'

'Repulsive! Foul!'

'Leave the washing-up till the next day...'

'I shall be sick!'

'Bleach my moustache while I'm listening to *Woman's Hour.*'

Woman's Hour! Grotesque!' His voice shifted. 'What moustache?'

'Men always do this. Like that shampoo ad with the pouty woman –

"But you don't have dandruff." See. Here.' She jabbed at her upper lip.

He stroked the dip below her nose with his little finger. 'A few downy hairs. Nice.'

'Not a few. Lots. And *dark*. Haven't you heard the saying: Jolen is a girl's best friend?'

'What?'

'Creme bleach. Don't worry, I won't wander around the house with it on. Anyway, I have to—' She held her upper lip rigid. "tay 'ike 'is. Or it all 'alls off.'

'This I have to see.'

'Nope. Absolutely not. My mother always said "Never let a man see you shave your legs or bleach your moustache until he's signed on the dotted line."'

'You really think I'd be put off by stuff like that? You won't get rid of me that easily.'

She shrugged. 'If it's not that, it'll be something else.'

'You're serious, aren't you?' He held her by her upper arms, making her face him straight on. 'You just don't get it, do you? I am NOT going anywhere. I'm afraid you're stuck with me.'

'Why Mr Henderson, this is so sudden.' She fanned her face with her hand.

He let go of her and held her hands.

'No, it isn't actually. I thought that before I'd even kissed you.' He caught her expression.

'You look like you're about to see the dentist. Don't panic. I'm not rushing you, just telling you. I want to spend the rest of my life with you.'

The rest of my life. But how long would that be? Could be forty, fifty years, sure. Or ten years, five. Or one. Three weeks. If only there could be some sort of guarantee.

'Once you've had me stay for five days, that'll cure you.'

* * *

'Any room at the inn?' Bella stood on Will's doorstep with her holdall. 'Stable block's all full, young missy. Have to bunk in with the landlord.'

'Glad to see you've perfected your leer. So important to have a skill.'

'Oh, you can come again.' Will relieved her of the bottle of wine she had brought, the beribboned box of truffles. The big kitchen table had been freshly covered with a bright madras check cloth. On it stood a stoneware jug of scented white roses and sprays of foliage from Will's garden. Bella bent to sniff one of the blooms and sighed with appreciation. Will opened a kitchen cupboard and gestured. Blackcurrant tea, her favourite.

'And, and —' He towed her around the house: recycling crates finally shifted from the hallway where they always snagged her stockings to miraculously tidied cupboard under the stairs; more flowers by the bed in a blue glass tumbler; hangers vacated; folded towel laid out, topped with a boxed hotel guest soap; a foil-wrapped chocolate on the pillow.

'Wouldn't spoil me too much. Might get used to it.'

'That was the general idea.'

He watched as she unpacked her things, offering her hangers, clearing out another of his drawers to give her space, squashing his own clothes to make room for hers.

'I'm not moving in, you know. It's only five days, don't go mad.'

'Yes, dear. Have you got your little nightie to tuck under the pillow?'

'Don't own one. I nearly brought my irresistible baggy T-shirt which says "I think therefore I drink" on it with a picture of a bottle of lager.'

'I knew you were too sophisticated for me.'

'Yup, let no-one say I was just an also-ran in the Nifty Nightwear Stakes. It was a promotional freebie from when I worked at that ad agency – looks particularly stylish with my purple Peruvian slipper socks.'

'And you left those behind too? Don't you know I just go wild for Peruvian slipper socks? Stockings do nothing for me.'

'Oh, that is a shame,' Bella said, lowering a pair of filmy nothings back into her holdall.

Will leapt to his feet and plunged his head into her bag, like a hound in a foxhole.

'This is weird,' Bella said as they were stretched out on the sofa after supper.

'What is?'

'This. Being with you and it feeling so normal. Almost as if we're a real couple. Can't we have a row?'

'Whatever for?'

'So I can relax. I feel so *nice* when I'm with you, just as if I were a normal person. Really quite lovable. It's most disconcerting.'

'You *are* lovable, you noodle.' He blew a raspberry into the side of her neck. 'Anyway, we are a real couple.'

'Yes, dear.'

'There you go. You've been in a couple before. You remember how it's done, don't you?'

She nodded. *But,* she thought, *but.* This is *different.*

'So, why aren't you married then, Mr Perfect?'

'Nearly was. You're lucky to get me.'

'Yeah? Bet you were just shoved back on the shelf as damaged goods.' Bella stroked the scar on his eyebrow. 'How nearly is nearly? Were you jilted at the altar?'

'No. It was Carolyn – remember, I told you a bit about her before?'

'Hmm, yes. The *thin* blonde one.'

'I love your curves. Don't be daft.' He rested his hand on her tummy. 'Anyway. We were together for years: Will and Carolyn, Carolyn and

Will like fish and chips or—'

'Burke and Hare.'

'Hush up, you. But you know when things are the same year in, year out so you never question it? Like my mum's jam that's never set properly. It's not that it's good but I'm used to it that way – it is Mum's Jam. Well, Caro and I—'

'Caro. Oh, yuk.'

'Ssh, d'you want to hear this or not?' Will told her that they were getting on OK, not arguing or anything, but not really talking either, their conversations were just the exchange of information about work or gossip about their social circle. They went out frequently, together and separately, apparently having a vibrant social life, rarely staying in on their own, surrounding themselves with people, with events, with busyness. Still, they were trundling towards marriage, as if they were on rails and only something dramatic or violent could have shifted them off course. Arrangements were being discussed. Then Carolyn was offered a three-month contract in New York.

'Did she take it?'

'Yes, she did. And I encouraged her. I was the ultimate unselfish fiancé – "You must take it, Caro. It's such an opportunity. It's only three months." I didn't realize for ages that I was kidding myself. I think I was relieved when she decided to go.'

'Here.' Bella nudged him to move so she could nestle against him. 'My go. So then what happened?'

'So, she went to New York and she met someone else within a month.'

'You're kidding? How awful.'

'No, not really. I just think neither of us could see a sensible way out.

We needed—' he laughed. 'Outside help.'

He tucked Bella's head closer and stroked her hair.

'After she'd been gone about a fortnight, I was pottering about at home in a lethargic kind of way one weekend. I was moving in that slow-dreamy-Sunday-morning manner, as if I had no energy. I remember thinking, it's still so clear in my mind, thinking: "I'm feeling sluggish because I must be missing Caro." And then it hit me. It was as if someone had gone plink, plink and plucked the scales from my eyes and the world sprang into sharp focus. I thought "No. You're *acting* the part of a man missing his girlfriend because you don't want to face the truth."'

Bella rubbed at her arms, suddenly chilled. 'Which was?'

'Which was that I *wasn't* missing her, which was much, much harder to deal with. Because then – then I started looking back at our relationship and I couldn't remember the last time either of us had shown any real interest in each other. Or how long it was since I'd stopped loving her.' His fingers rested still on her hair. 'I felt horrible. Scared. Ashamed. And when her letter came saying she'd met this other bloke, God, the relief! I had been let off the hook and I hadn't even had to *do* anything. Then I felt bad, as if I'd cheated because I hadn't actually resolved it in a proper, grown-up, we-have-something-to-talk-about way. I felt like a fraud.'

Bella nodded slowly. Her mouth felt dry, as if lined with cloth, her tongue suddenly alien, sliding over her teeth, feeling each one in turn as if checking she was real. She kneaded at her stiff neck, then twisted to look up at him.

'Wasn't your fault though.' Bella cleared her throat. 'It's just life.'

'Confucius, he say "It's just life." Thank you for your words of wisdom.' She punched him softly.

'Oof.' He held her hand. 'And, *now,* I cannot believe that I could ever have thought of marrying her for even a minute. I can't explain – this is *so* different. It's like all your life you've been given strawberry-flavoured, I don't know, bubblegum or something and told "This is strawberry, this is strawberry." Then, one day, when you weren't expecting it, a beautiful, brilliant red fruit is popped right into your mouth and it's like nothing you ever saw or smelt or tasted. Or – or *knew.* And then you suddenly get it: "Oh my God, *this* is a strawberry."'

The print of his lips on her brow, his hand on her hair. She cupped the back of his head in her hand, pulling him close. His fingers on her neck. His mouth strong on hers. The evening-roughness of his cheeks, his chin, real and alive against her skin.

'Ouch, prickly.' She rubbed her fingertips across his cheek, pretending to file her nails on him.

'Shall I go and shave?' He started to get up.

'Nope.' She kissed him, shielding her chin with her hand. 'Why don't they make chin guards?'

Bella bounced the flat of her hand lightly on Will's head.

'I love this. First thing I noticed about you. I even thought of you as Springy Hair in my mind after that poetry reading.'

He tilted to look at her.

'You never said you'd thought about me after that first time.'

'What is that ridiculous face meant to mean?'

'Just pleased you'd noticed me.' He slunk down to rest his head on her chest and closed his eyes. 'You make a perfect pillow. Tell me something nice. What else did you think?'

'Well, I thought you were funny and what bright eyes you had. And, what? Your eyebrows. Definitely your eyebrows. Very sexy. And you had this sort of amused look.'

'Someone once said I looked smug.'

'No.' She thought back. 'Not smug. A funny half-smile, assessing, as if you found the world an amusing and fascinating place.'

'I do.'

'I know. That's what I love about you.'

'You just used the "L" word.'

'It slipped out. I'm not responsible.'

As they kissed, her hand rested on his chest, feeling the rhythm of his heartbeat.

'Bmm-boom.' She patted out the beat on his body. 'Bmm-boom.'

Now he placed his hand close below her left breast. His drumbeat followed.

'Bmm-boom,' they said together, beating as one. 'Bmm-boom.'

21

'How long were you with Patrick?' Will asked the next evening as they were finishing supper at his house. He looked down at his dish, chasing the last bobble of tortellini round and round with his fork.

'Five years, three months and eleven days since you ask.' Bella started clearing the table.

'Not that you were counting or anything. Can I ask why you split up? Do you mind? Did you just get bored of him or what?'

'Why do you assume that? It could have been the other way around.' Will pulled her away from the sink and back to the table.

'Uh-uh. Not possible.' He picked up her hand and lightly nibbled it. 'Infuriated, yes. Mystified, certainly. Bored, never.'

'Thank you. I think.'

'You never mention him.'

'I thought it wasn't considered polite to talk about one's exes.' She withdrew her hand and started whacking the place mats together like cymbals. Dislodged crumbs fell from their spiral grooves. 'Where do you keep these?'

'Wherever. And the answer to my question is...? I'm going to have to hurry you on this one.' Will picked up the plain glass stoppered bottle of olive oil. 'You could win this de luxe crystal decanter.'

'You were wrong. He did get sick of me.' Bella tucked the mats into a drawer, and stood at the sink, looking out at the garden. 'He did the ultimate escape trick. He died. Men, eh? So unpredictable. Just when you think you know where you are with one, he goes and gets himself killed. Still, it's cut down on the ironing.' Will came and stood behind her. His arms encircled her, held her tight. She remained rigid.

'God, I'm sorry. I'm so sorry. I wouldn't have teased you. I'm an idiot.' He whispered into her hair. 'Why on earth didn't you tell me before? Do you mind talking about it? Of course. What a stupid question.'

'No. It's OK.'

She told him the bare facts. One paragraph. News in brief. In her head, she saw it typeset on a newspaper page:

Death fuels concerns over site safety

The death of a surveyor has reawakened concerns over safety standards in the construction industry. Patrick Hughes, 34, died late on Tuesday evening after sustaining severe head injuries and internal haemorrhaging when part of a brick chimney stack collapsed on him on a building site in Vauxhall, south London. He was rushed by ambulance to St Thomas's Hospital, but doctors were unable to revive him and he died without regaining consciousness. Mr Hughes was assessing the stability of an adjacent wall when the accident occurred. The Health and Safety Executive has launched an inquiry.

Was that Patrick, those neat, flat little words in black on flimsy newsprint? When it had appeared in the newspaper, she had wanted to buy up every copy. Tomorrow, people would be using it to protect their floors, stuff into wet shoes, line cat litter trays; tomorrow, it would be thrown away, old news, forgotten.

'Bella?' Will started to turn her towards him. 'I'm OK. Honest.' An automatic smile.

'Are you?' His voice was low and gentle.

She could feel his warmth, solid and reliable at her side as he moved to see her face. She wanted to lean against him. How good it would be just to let go, give herself up to him, let herself be held and comforted.

Her head moved a fraction, barely discernible, and Will clasped her more tightly to him. For a moment, for one moment, he felt her give and he held her as tenderly as if she were a frightened child; his hand stroked her hair. Then she stiffened and drew herself straight, shook her head with small jerks. Patted his arm with distant affection.

'Come on, Will. You're not my therapist or social worker. You don't have to put on your special concerned voice for my benefit.' She turned away from his face, stung as if she had slapped him. Easing herself from his grasp, she picked up a cloth and started wiping the table, sweeping the crumbs into her cupped palm.

'I'm sorry. It's not – it's not how it seems,' she told the crumbs. 'I can't. But I'm fine. Really.'

She felt the brief pressure of his hand on her arm, then he turned to the sink and covered the silence with the reassuring clatter of washing-up.

Could she use the phone, she asked Will, to pick up her messages from the answerphone.

'Of course. You don't need to ask.'

There was a call from Viv – 'Sorry, just remembered you're staying with Mr Wonderful for the five-day shagfest. We're suffering from a lack of gossip and a lack of your chicken in lemon sauce. Don't forget me just because you've found your soulmate' – and another call from her dad; she still hadn't responded to his last one. Sorry, she said to Will, would it be all right to phone her father as well.

'You're so polite.' He shook his head, amused. 'I keep saying, treat the place as home.'

'Hi, Dads. It's me.' She covered the mouthpiece with her hand, whispering to Will. 'I can't be long.'

Will made a 'T' sign.

'Take as long as you like. No rush.' She nodded and pouted him a kiss.

'No, it's just I'm on someone else's phone.'

She heard Will's voice, deliberately audible from the kitchen: 'Yes, folks, that's me. Someone else. Not "my boyfriend", not "my partner", not "Will" even, just "someone else". She loves me, nah, nah, nah...'

Fine, she said, she was fine – house fine – damp actually being treated that very moment – OK, not at that actual moment, but that day and tomorrow and soon it would be done and she could unpack and live like a real grown-up – yes, work fine, bit dull but paying the mortgage and keeping her in croissants – painting, surprisingly fine, she was less rusty than she'd thought – no, silly, not nearly good enough for that – yes, of course he could see them some time—

'How come I'm not allowed to see them then?' Will called through. 'Don't be so nosy,' she called back. 'Get on with the tea, boy.'

'Oh. That's Will,' into the phone. 'Well, he's – y'know... hmm...

yes, I guess he is really.' She might as well admit it. She couldn't sidestep the issue for ever. 'Quite a while. He originally came to do the garden, which, incidentally,' she said as he came back into the room with two mugs of tea, 'is in dire need of attention. He's falling way behind in his duties.'

Will came up behind her, put his arms around her and whispered in her ear, 'That's because I keep getting distracted.'

She shook him off and waggled her fingers at him to wave him away. 'Yes, yes, he is.'

Will was standing very close.

'Is what, is what?' he said. 'Gorgeous? Lickable? Most Rampant Man on the Planet?'

'Is right *here,*' she hissed at him. Will wrinkled his nose.

'No, no, don't be leaping ahead, Dads. That's not on the agenda.'

'What isn't? What isn't?' said Will, nibbling at her neck. Bella covered the mouthpiece.

'Go away, Annoying Person. I'm trying to have a sensible conversation with my esteemed father here.'

Will stuck his tongue in her ear and waggled it about slurpily. She grabbed his sleeve and raised his arm to her ear to wipe it – 'You're disgusting,' she mouthed. He smiled and shrugged – 'I know.'

She dropped her voice and turned her back to him.

'Funny, playful – yes, hmm-mm, very bright, thoughtful, direct. Sensitive, too. OK, if you like that sort of thing, I guess.'

Will craned his face round into her vision and beamed at her. She shoved him away.

She laughed. 'No, no, not a wimp.'

There was a pause. A long pause. Bella was frowning. 'It's a bit tricky. He's very busy.'

'No, I'm not,' said Will.

The volume dipped again. Will tried to get closer to hear. Bella kept him at elbow's length.

'She is. You know what she's like.'

'It'll put him off and then she can play her sympathetic-but-not-at-all surprised part.'

'Mmm. You always say that. Possibly. I'll consider it. No promises. Yeah. Bye, Dads, bye.'

Will was standing with his arms folded.

'They want to meet me, don't they? You can't hide me from them for ever.'

'It's the other way round, silly. I'm protecting you from them. Her. We'll go if you insist, but don't blame me when it all goes horribly wrong.' She stomped upstairs. 'Can I run a bath?' calling back over her shoulder.

'You don't need to ask, for the 45th time. Only if I can come and molest you with my rubber duck.'

'Hmm? I've never heard it called that before.'

'I had such rude thoughts about you last night, you have no idea.' Will rested a glass of chilled rosé on Bella's tummy for a moment as she lay in the bath. The circle of cold sang against her skin.

'Tell me,' she said.

'Tell you my fantasy? You sure? It was pretty rude.' She nodded.

'It is a hot, hot day and I have been walking for hours across the downs. At last, I come to a meadow with long grass, rippling like water in the wind. Far off, on the other side, I see a splash of colour – an orange blanket spread out with a figure lying on it in a white dress. I weave a cautious path through the grasses, then stop a few yards away. I am very thirsty but now I notice nothing but you. Your hair allows me only a tantalizing glimpse of your face, your eyelids flickering as you dream. A gust of warm wind lifts your dress, sliding it higher up your legs. For one brief moment, I am treated to a flash of white cotton at the tops of your thighs, then your dress settles once more.

'I do not want to alarm you, but I am feeling so hot and flushed and I can see you have a cool-bag with you. Perhaps you have water. I start to sing quietly, to waken you gently: "...and when she passes, each one she passes goes 'Aaah...'" Your eyes flicker open, I reassure you, and you give me chilled water to drink, gesture to the ground by your side. Drowsy from the sun, we lean back on the blanket. Slowly, your hand strokes up my side and round to my chest. You start to unbutton my shirt, saying I must be very hot. You pour a little water into the well of your palm and rub it into my chest, cold against my skin.

'"I'm hot, too," you say. "You must cool me down." I kneel beside you and drizzle water from the bottle over your dress. The wet cloth clings to you, outlining your luscious curves, moulding itself to your shape. "Blow on me," you say, looking down. I begin at your feet, blowing cool breaths between your toes, over your insteps, around your ankles. Your murmurs mingle with the breeze, the whispering of the grasses.

'As I blow just above your knee, you tremble and your legs ease apart a little way. "More," I say, blowing along your thigh, "part for me." The V of your legs widens, welcoming me in. I blow softly, then, as I breathe in, I take in your scent. Intoxicating. I cannot resist. My tongue plays around your inner thigh, flicking higher and higher. My lips press against you. The softness of your skin is like silk against my cheek, my chin.

'I nudge my head forward beneath the white awning of your dress. I am so close to you now. I can see your knickers clinging to you damply. I want to pull them off, tug at them with my teeth... but first I must tease you a little more. My breath finds you again and your murmurs are deep, almost moans. At last, you arch towards me, pushing yourself against my mouth and I—

'Bella?'

She clambered out of the bath, sloshing water over the rim, and sat astride him, kissing him, her mouth hard on his. He scooped his hands under her and pulled her close.

'Sorry I'm getting you all wet.' Bella tugged at his belt. He slid his hand between her legs.

'You certainly are,' and he laid her out in front of him on the bathroom floor.

They talked late, murmuring into the early hours. Will asked if she'd mind leaving the bedside light on for a while.

'I want to see your face.'

His fingers stroked the length of her upper arm.

'It's funny,' Will said, 'sometimes I feel you're not really here. I want to say I miss you but it seems silly when I can see you in the room with me. Um, I'm sorry if I upset you earlier. About Patrick. I wish you'd told me before.'

'I'm sure you don't want to hear me droning on about my exes.'

'Hardly droning on. We've all got a past.'

'Really, Will. You wouldn't like it if I started making comparisons – "Oh, *Patrick* used to do that too – that aftershave smelt quite different on *Patrick* – *Patrick* loved being touched like this in bed—"'

'Thanks, Bella. Why do you do that? You know that's not what I meant.

You're just being – I don't know – thingy.'

'I'm just being thingy? Well, that makes everything so much clearer. I'm so glad we've sorted that out.'

'Now you've got your Snow Queen voice on. I always feel like I'm interrogating you if I dare to ask you anything, like you've sworn some blood oath never to divulge how you feel. I'd like to think you can tell me stuff.'

'There's nothing to tell.' He sighed.

'Can I just ask – I mean, you must miss him, right?'

In her mind, Patrick watches her, his face half in shadow, his expression veiled. He does not speak.

'It's not – you don't – you couldn't understand. I'm sorry.'

'I might. I lost my stepdad, remember? I'm not a bereavement virgin. Won't you even let me try? How do you know if you won't tell me?'

'Will. Please don't.' She closed her eyes, silently speaking to Patrick: 'Patrick. Please don't.'

'I'm sorry, Bella. I'm sorry. The last thing I want is to hurt you. I'm being selfish, I know – but I just want you to love me – as much as you obviously loved him.'

There was a barely discernible shake of her head, then her eyelids flickered and she was silent. She felt his soft kiss on her brow, the breath of his silent sigh.

He reached over to turn out the light and she heard his whisper in the darkness,

'I wish I could really know you.'

22

After a mere eight days rather than the promised five, the DAMP was done, the walls replastered and painted, and there was no excuse for her not to return home. Bella repacked her clothes into her holdall, took her dress, her tops down from the hangers in Will's wardrobe, retrieved her underwear from the drawer. She knew now that she shouldn't have stayed with him, how much worse it was bound to make her feel.

Will watched her as she retrieved her bits and pieces from the bathroom, as she zipped up her toilet bag with a final flourish.

'Come on, sweet pea. I feel like we're getting divorced or something. You don't have to take every little last thing with you. Leave some stuff. Here – ' He started shoving aside his own deodorant and shaving foam. 'Let me clear you some more space.'

She laid a hand on his arm.

'Thanks, Will. Really. But it's not necessary. I need to have my things around me at home.'

'I – well – I thought, maybe...'

She stretched up to reach him, silencing him with a kiss.

'Come and stay with me this weekend. I can spoil you for a

change. I want to paint you anyway. And you can help me unpack the dreaded boxes.'

He gathered her into a hug.

'If you really want to spoil me, will you do that duck thing again? With the sauce?'

'You're squishing me. Yes, you can have the duck thing, but you'll have to do extra box duty.'

'It's a deal. And don't forget your promise.'

'I won't. Which promise?'

'I knew you'd do that. About the galleries. You said you'd take in your pictures.'

'I will. At some point. There's no rush. Don't go on.'

'There is a rush. Life's short, you know.' He saw her eyes flicker. 'Sorry. But you must... otherwise I'll be forced to suck your toes until you beg for mercy.'

* * *

'So?' asked Will, manically raising and lowering his eyebrows at her when he met her from work on Friday evening.

'What?'

'Did you go and see any galleries?'

She kept it brief. Yes, she had, so could he please now stop nagging her about it. She had tried to arrange appointments but two places said just to turn up on the off chance; the third had said they weren't looking at any new artists at the moment. At the first gallery, the manageress had said they were certainly 'well-painted, very well-executed, but slightly disturbing'; they preferred still lifes, landscapes, more conventional interior scenes. At the second, the decision-making person had turned out to be away for a week and she couldn't see why they hadn't just told her that on the phone because she had dragged out of her way to go there; they said she was welcome to leave a couple of paintings for him to see on his return, but she had declined and said she would call again later.

'Did you go to that Mackie one, what's it called? The top one?'

'MacIntyre Arts. No, I didn't. What would be the point?'

Will shrugged.

'Can't see what you've got to lose. Don't be so negative. They've got to hang somebody's stuff on their walls – why not yours? We could go there now, just for a look.' He stopped in the street, blocking the narrow pavement.

'No we couldn't. Why have you stopped? Can't you walk and talk at the same time? Does it run down your batteries?'

'Yes it does. I stopped because I like to see your face when you talk. Can I see any of your paintings yet, by the way?'

'Nope.'

'Just one?'

'No.'

'A little, tiny one?'

'Good grief. What are you like? OK, but no smartarse comments.'

'But these are stunning.' He held a small canvas up to the light to see it more clearly.

'What's the "but" for? No need to sound quite so surprised.'

'Don't be annoying. I'm not surprised that they're so good, Paranoid Person. But I can't *believe* that anyone could produce anything so beautiful and – and powerful and want to keep them under wraps. I love the colours. I'm glad I nagged you to try the galleries now. You're bonkers.'

'Thank you for your support.'

'You have to try that top gallery. You know that, don't you? If you don't, and you exhibit in some ordinary, run-of-the-mill place, you'll always know you *settled,* that you didn't go for what you really wanted, never even tried to see if you could have it.'

'It doesn't bother me that much. Anywhere would be wonderful.' He blew a raspberry.

'Yes, dear. I believe you. Now look at this one—'

'Yes, I've seen it. I painted it.'

He ignored her.

'It's almost creepy – in a good way. It feels hushed, something about the light and this shadow over here. I feel I should whisper, the woman looks so sad. No, not sad exactly. *Bereft.*'

Will pointed to details.

'...and these flagstones, the dip there where it's been worn by footsteps. Is that the cathedral? Odd. Bits of it look like the cathedral, but it feels like somewhere else, like in a dream.'

'Full marks, boy. It's a fusion, innit? A synthesis of reality and imagination. All paintings are to a degree, anyway – because the way you see the world is never quite the same as the way it is.'

'You mean you can paint what you see inside your head?' She nodded.

* * *

Monday lunchtime. She stood looking in the window for a long time. Good stuff, very good: a first-rate portrait of a slightly cross-looking woman in oils, rather quirkily done; two small pastel nudes; a set of four woodcut landscapes – beautifully stylized, accomplished. She tried to look beyond the window, to see inside.

'Going in?' A tweedy, middle-aged man about to enter the gallery was holding open the door for her.

'No. I just—'

Why not? She was here now. Nothing to stop her from having a quick look.

. . .

She went from picture to picture, her mood swinging from elation – 'this is wonderful' – to depression – 'I haven't got a hope in hell.' She must bring Will here. 'Oh, look at this, and this, and this,' she wanted to say to him. A tiny ceramic enamelled piece caught her eye, glittering like a jewel. Even the pictures that weren't to her taste were at least well done. They would never take her work here. She couldn't possibly ask. They'd probably laugh and look embarrassed; they'd say, 'But you're *only* Bella. Perhaps you didn't understand: we only exhibit *proper* artists here.'

The tweedy man was standing by the desk, talking to the assistant.

'So.' He swung round towards her while looking through his post. 'Have you come to see me?' He nodded at her portfolio, her brown paper parcel.

'Let's have a look then.' He held out his hands.

Mr MacIntyre nodded as he looked through, without speaking. Oh, God, she thought, he couldn't even think of anything polite to say. This was awful, worse than being at school, standing there while teacher read through her story. Would she get a single red tick? A 'could try harder'? She focused all her attention on her toes, clenching and unclenching them inside her shoes. He hovered a long time, looking at the five cathedral paintings she had brought. Were there any others? he wanted to know. Yes, several, more than a dozen she thought, and some other watercolours. Was she planning to do more? She couldn't stop at the moment, she said.

He flicked through his calendar.

'We're booked solid for the next ten months or so, pretty much.'

He was letting her down gently. Good. Now she could zip up her folio and leave.

'But, but, but,' he said as she retaped the brown paper around the paintings. He ran his finger along the dates. 'It's decidedly tight time-wise, but we do have a mixed show in three months. Three artists. It was supposed to be four anyway, but one dropped out to have a nervous breakdown. You'd fit in.' He laughed. 'The show's called Visions, which covers anything we fancy really. But these...' He patted the parcel. 'These *are* visions.

'Have a think anyway. I'd understand if you wanted to hold out for a solo show – if that's the case, we'd be looking at next year, say early autumn and, obviously, we'd need quite a lot more. I'd like to come and see the others. Whereabouts is your studio? Give us a ring tomorrow if you can, Thursday at the latest, and we can talk about framing and so on.'

Did that mean he liked them? Had he said? Had he just offered her a joint exhibition or had she imagined it? Could she possibly ask? He'd think she was bonkers.

He smiled, his sober face suddenly bright and youthful.

'They're superb, by the way. Really.' He nodded to himself. 'Let's talk tomorrow.'

* * *

Bella was finally 'in conference' with Seline, i.e. having a chat but with the door shut. She had put off making a decision for as long as she reasonably could, but Seline had finally pressed her: was she interested in the possibility of a partnership next year or not?

'I really appreciate your asking me...'

'But you've decided against it? I'm sorry but I suppose it's not a huge surprise. Can I ask why?'

Bella explained about the exhibition and wanting to spend more time painting. Perhaps Seline would like to come? She'd love to.

'I don't think I'd really be able to put in more time here. In fact,' she heard herself say, 'I was wondering if you'd let me work part-time. Say, three days a week? So I'd have time to paint. Anthony could take more charge when I'm not here. He's got the experience. Or I could leave altogether if you think that would be better?'

'Don't you dare!' Seline clicked her pen against her teeth. 'We'll take whatever time you can offer. I guess we can get it to work as long as we don't have to lose you completely.'

Now that the words had been said aloud, Bella realized that the idea had been lodged in her head for months. Now it had been spoken, it was Out There, no longer safe in silence. She agreed to carry on full-time for the next couple of months while she trained Anthony in the small but vital matter of diplomacy when dealing with awkward clients.

Bella closed the door behind her. *Did I really say that?* Her knees seemed to be trembling slightly but her body felt lighter, clear and fizzy, as if her veins were flowing with lemonade – was it oh-shit-what-have-I-done nerves or something not unlike excitement? She bustled through to the office kitchen, fluttered to and fro wiping down the worktop, refilling the coffee machine, anchoring herself. Standing listening to the rhythmic drip-drip of the coffee, she caught sight of her distorted reflection in the shiny curve of the kettle: a new, unfamiliar Bella.

23

Will's sister Helen was coming over with her two children the following Sunday. Would Bella join them? Meet more of the Henderson tribe?

'Could be a bit tricky. Got lots to do.'

'Anything I can help with?'

'No, just, you know, stuff.'

'Oh, stuff. Right. Sounds important.' Will puffed out his cheeks. 'Do we have to go through this every time I want you to meet my family?'

'I'm working on a painting, Will. It's your fault. It was your idea to send me to the gallery in the first place.'

'*Send* you to the gallery? So it's my fault that you're in danger of being fulfilled and successful? What a bastard. I don't know how you put up with me.' He reached for her. 'Of course you must put your painting first, sweet pea. I only meant if you weren't doing anything special.'

'Perhaps I could pop in and say hello briefly at teatime?'

'Mmm. Do that. Offer me crumbs – old Will'll lick 'em up.'

'I don't have to come at all.' She started to turn away.

'Yes, you do have to come at all. Didn't you read the job description? Will's partner – Official Duties. Number 1: Love me hugely. Number 2: Have lots of sex with me. Number 3: Meet my family. It's not as if we're down to Number 54: Meet my boring cousins from Uxbridge, is it? This is actually important to me, for two of the people I love most in the world to get to know each other. Can you not understand that?'

'OK, OK. Remain calm. I said I'd come.'

'And the crowd went wild!' Will tore around the room. 'Will you grow up?'

'Too late for me now.'

* * *

Helen shifted her baby to balance him on her hip so she could shake Bella's hand.

"Scuse the sprog. I can't remember the last time I had both hands free. I always seem to be holding one or restraining one or hoiking one back from near-death.'

Bella looked at the baby. He looked back. 'Leo, is it?' she asked.

'That's right. The munchkin trying to scale Mount William over there is Abigail. Come and say hello, Abby.'

Abigail looked around, saw a New Person, and buried her face in Will's leg.

'Don't take it personally. She's going through a shy phase.'

'That's OK. I'm still waiting to grow out of mine.'

Abigail stretched out on the floor, surrounded by paper and crayons.

Bella took Leo's foot in her hand and gently squeezed it.

'Hello, Leo.' She puffed out her cheeks and blew her breath out in a raspberry. His little cheeks bulged into a smile.

'Here, cop hold of him a minute, will you? God, he's so heavy now. I'll just get some cups.'

He was heavier than he looked for such a small person. How was it possible for hands to be so tiny, yet still be hands? With fingernails in miniature, perfect replicas of the real thing, as if made by an apprentice craftsman practising before working full-size. He grabbed her outstretched finger with surprising strength.

'He's got quite a grip,' said Will. He held up his hand with one finger bent down. 'See, lost one last week.'

The baby's face crumpled in unknown distress. Bella started to sway smoothly, rocking from foot to foot as she cradled him. She dipped her face and sang quietly to him, her voice soft and low.

'Hush, little baby, a dum-dah-dah-dee. Can't remember the words, dah-dee, dah-dah dee...' Leo's face smoothed into a calm smile, near sleep. She looked up and her eyes met Will's. Neither spoke.

Helen swept back into the room with the cups.

'Just chuck him back if he gets too heavy. Oh, he likes you. Normally, he'd be bawling his fat little head off by now, wouldn't you, chubs?' She touched her baby softly on the nose.

Helen started pouring the tea.

'So, you planning to do all this nonsense? Do you look forward to the delights of Motherhood or are you sensibly relishing your peaceful existence while it lasts? It's great if you don't mind being wee'd on and getting so knackered you can't remember your own name.'

'I think I'd be a lousy mother.'

'No you wouldn't!' said Will. Helen gave a loud cackle and raised her eyebrows at Bella. 'Somebody sounds broody.'

He lowered his voice. 'Well, it's rubbish. You'd be brilliant. Why d'you say that?'

'I'd be bound to mess them up and they'd grow up resenting me

– they'd need decades of therapy and then send me the bill. Or I'd be too anxious and over-protective. They look so fragile. I couldn't bear it. I'd lie awake all night to check they were still breathing.'

'Believe me, after a few nights of no sleep, you'd find yourself dropping off in the middle of the supermarket. Anyway, babies are tougher than they look, but, yes, it's a worry. Mum says she still worries about us and look how old he is.' Helen nodded at Will. 'What about your lot – do they nose into your life·all the time or are you more the typically English family who meet up twice a year?'

'Dad can be a bit of a fusser. My mother likes to interfere but not to the point where I might think she actually cared one way or the other, so she treads a delicate line – takes years of practice to get as good as that. She'd love me to settle down only so she would no longer have the embarrassment of having this *spinster* daughter.'

Leo started to cry and Helen reclaimed him and held him close against her.

'Oh, come on,' said Will.

'It's true. As for worrying about me, the only reason she'd mind if I was squished by a truck tomorrow is because then she'd have to put up with pitying looks from the neighbours.'

'That's a horrible thing to say.' Will's voice was quiet. Helen was silent.

'I can't believe you said that.' Will looked glazed.

Bella shrugged. She had intended it as an amusing hyperbole, but said out loud it had suddenly seemed not very amusing, not very amusing at all.

'You sound very angry,' said Will.

'I didn't come here to be analysed. Don't patronize me, Will.' Helen topped up their cups.

'Well, it's none of my business,' she said, 'but I'd be angry if I thought *my* mother didn't care. So would you, Will. Course you would. Anyway, you can share our mum, Bella. She obviously thinks you're the best thing since sliced bread. Went on about you for hours after Will took you to see her. I felt quite jealous, I can tell you.'

Bella wondered how she had sounded. Was she really so angry? She didn't know any more. Her mother – Mum; it sounded odd, too aprony and cosy for Alessandra – had always been like that so she was more resigned to it than anything, she supposed. Whatever you grew up with, that was what was *normal* to you. You only questioned it when you came across something different.

* * *

She is at Sara's house, for tea. They have had egg sandwiches in white bread, soft and flannelly, with the crusts cut off. Now they each have a fairy cake, covered in hundreds-and-thousands, and a drink of orange barley water in a glass with red and yellow rings around it. As they eat their cakes, the hundreds-and-thousands keep falling off onto their plates, making a tiny pattering sound, multicoloured rain. Sara reaches across to try to steal some of Bella's windfall with a licked finger, laughing. Bella leans over to get to Sara's plate. As she stretches out, she knocks over her glass of orange barley. Sara squeals as it spills across the table and drips onto the floor.

Bella holds her breath. Sara's mum will call her clumsy, shout at her. She will be tipped off her chair and pushed out of the kitchen. She will have to go in the garden and hide behind the bush with the purple flowers where the butterflies play.

Sara's mum wipes the table with a stripy cloth.

'Oops-a-daisy,' she says. 'There we go.' She mixes up another glass of orange and gives it to Bella.

Bella looks at her, waiting, barely breathing. Any minute now. 'That cake nice, is it?' says Sara's mum.

Bella nods slowly and starts to pick off the hundreds-and-thousands to eat them one by one.

* * *

'I went to see my dad once. Our real dad. Remember, Will?' Helen said.

He nodded.

'I'd been pissed off at him for years. And I mean *years* – he made practically no effort to see us when we were growing up, after he'd left Mum. We had Hugh and he was great and all that but I wanted my real dad to want me, too. I went to see him when I was about eighteen, up in Yorkshire. Mum gave me the fare. I don't suppose she can have been keen on the idea, but she didn't try to dissuade me. I needed to see him, she knew that.'

'So, what was he like?' Bella asked.

'He was – a bit pathetic really. Ineffectual, not a real grown-up. It was such an anticlimax. He gave me this kind of awkward half-hug and I just felt, well, sorry for him. He didn't seem worth all that wasted energy of being angry all the time. I suddenly saw that *he* had missed out, by not knowing us. And he'd never get those years back. I couldn't be bothered to resent him any more. I send him a card now and then, but he's just like a distant uncle really. I miss Hugh much more.'

Leo had fallen asleep. His small face was completely calm, at rest. Helen carefully laid him between two cushions on the sofa and sat beside him.

'Have you ever tried to talk to your mum about how she is?' she asked. 'What would be the point? She's not going to change magically just because I ask her to.'

'No, she probably won't. That's not what I meant. But *you* might.

If you talked to her, you might start to understand why she's like that. What have you got to lose?'

Abigail came to whisper in Helen's ear.

'You don't have to whisper, sweetheart. What is it?' She whispered again.

'Just ask her. I'm sure she will.'

Abigail remained silent, but tugged at Helen's sleeve.

'Bella, would you mind looking at Abby's drawings? I think she wants a new fan.'

Bella and Abby lay on the floor, drawing with crayons while Helen fed Leo and Will washed up.

'What shall we draw now?' asked Bella. 'Me. Me. Draw me.'

A stylized Abby duly took shape on the page: springy, Will-like, brown hair, bright red dungarees, blue T-shirt.

'Shall we draw your baby brother in here, too?' Abby sucked her lip, considering.

'No,' she said. Bella laughed. 'Fair enough.'

Abby gave Bella a drawing as they were leaving – one she had done of Bella, with huge eyes and a red smile.

'Thank you very much. I'll put it up in my studio, and you must come to me for tea soon and we can do some more.'

'See, she's got your hair spot on,' said Will, pointing at Bella's head in the drawing, covered with a tangle of lines like unravelled knitting.

'Shut up, you.' She squeezed his arm. 'I'm glad I came. Thank you.'

'I knew you would be. Have you got to dash off to do "stuff" or do I get the good of you on my own for a while?'

She checked her watch.

'Hmm. I ought to be getting back.'

'Can't it wait?' He drew her towards the stairs. 'I've got something to show you... upstairs.'

'I bet you have. OK. On condition I can watch *Jane Eyre* here – starts in forty minutes.'

'Oh, you.' He towed her up the stairs. *Four* minutes will probably be sufficient. We don't need to bother with all that foreplay stuff now we've known each other all this time, do we?' He started unbuttoning her dress.

'Fine, dear. I'll just lie back and you take your pleasure.' Her dress fell to the floor.

'Forty minutes, hmm? Look, she gets him in the end – there, you don't need to watch it now.' He manoeuvred her towards the bathroom. 'Come and have a shower with me.'

Standing with Will in the shower, she watched the rivulets of water running down his chest, soaped her hands to lather his legs, his back, the curve of his bottom. He held her with one arm, pressing the cool bar of soap over her breasts, sliding his hands over her skin, cupping her tummy, dipping his finger into her navel. He turned her to clasp her from behind, reaching around her, his fingers roaming, slipping, tracing tingling paths over her flesh. Pushing back against him, she rested her head on his chest, her wet hair slicked to his skin. Curved her hand back to touch him. His sudden breath hot on her neck. His hand reaching lower. He guided her other hand between her own thighs.

'Carry on without me for a moment. I'll be right back.' Will jumped out of the shower. She heard him call through from the bedroom. The banging of drawers.

'Where are the bloody doo-dahs?'

'Under the pillow!'

He ran back into the bathroom.

'Enjoying yourself there? Can I join in at all?'

'Get in, you fool.' She pressed herself hard against him as he clambered back in.

'Now,' he said. 'Where were we?'

They were lying in his bed in a tangle of towels, pillows and duvet. 'Fat face?' Will turned towards her.

'Hmm?' She wriggled to face him. Raised her hand to his cheek.

'I —' he kissed her nose, 'love —' another kiss, 'you —' kiss, 'bigly.' Kiss.

'Bigly?' She snuggled closer to him, rubbing her face against his chest. 'Yes. Very bigly. I know this has all been – well – it has, really, hasn't it? – quite quick and intense, not just the sex – which is certainly intense but not too quick I hope – and anyway, the thing is—'

'You're wibbling, Will.'

'That's true. I am wibbling. I want to say something, but I don't want you to panic.'

'Don't panic, Mr Mainwaring, don't panic!' Bella slipped into the *Dad's Army* refrain.

'No,' he said, gently shaking her arm. 'Don't do that.'

'Oops. Have I got to be serious now?' She bit her cheeks. 'See? Being sensible.'

Will nodded.

'I don't want to scare you off. You know how I feel about you.'

He took her hand, looked down at her fingers as he squeezed them in his own, ran his thumb over her knuckles, her fingernails as if he had never seen them before, then looked up and straight into her eyes.

'I want to marry you.'

For a tiny fraction of time, she felt herself flooded with warmth.

Her face must be glowing. For one moment, light shone from her eyes. Tears pooled softly below the rims.

Yes, yes. *Love me, marry me. Yes.*

Then a wisp of cold blew down her neck. She shivered. Her skin was clammy, pale, her mouth dry. For a moment, her eyes closed. And there was Patrick, his back turned towards her. But she dared not reach out to him. What would she see in his eyes? She clenched and unclenched her fists, digging her fingernails into her palms.

'Er, does your silence mean you'd like some time to think about it? Or are you just gobsmacked? Or is that a yes but you're playing hard to get?'

'I wouldn't do that.'

'I sort of thought you might feel the same way. Shit, I knew I shouldn't have rushed. I'm such a dickhead. Forget I said it.'

'How could I? It's fine. Really. I'm flattered. I'm just not sure yet. Sorry.'

Why could she not say what she wanted to? *Yes, yes. Love me, marry me. Yes.*

He managed a smile.

'Will you think about it at least? At some point, as you would say.'

'At some point.' She smiled and kissed his cheek. 'Thank you.'

'Will you stop being so polite? Here, come and give us a cuddle. Consolation prize.'

* * *

She met up with Viv on Monday lunchtime. They sat on a park bench eating sandwiches.

'Oh-oh, you've got that strange mask look.' Viv's eyes narrowed. 'What's occurring? You've not had a fight with Will, have you?'

'Uh-uh.' Bella shook her head. 'Quite the contrary. He proposed.'

'Proposed? What, like marriage you mean?'

'No. He proposed we start drilling for oil in my back garden. Yes, of course marriage. Is that so ridiculous?'

'Of course not. But that's brilliant!' Viv clasped Bella in a big hug. 'I'm so pleased, you know I am. Oh, a wedding! I may have to cry.' She took a bite of her sandwich, then chewed slowly. 'Hang on – shouldn't you be looking a bit more ecstatic or something? You did say yes, babe?'

'Not as such.'

Viv stopped mid-chew. 'I'm not hearing this.'

'Well, it is quite quick. I thought you'd be all in sensible mode – now don't rush into anything – take your time – it's a big decision. All that. Look at you two for Chrissakes, you've been together what? Four? Five years? And still no sign of your personalized Viv 'n' Nick napkins with the little silver bells on.'

Viv flushed.

'Sorry,' said Bella. 'That was out of line.' Viv wouldn't marry Nick only because the wedding would inevitably be boycotted by one of her parents; some eighteen years after their acrimonious divorce, they still refused even to be in the same room together for five minutes.

A shrug from Viv.

'Never mind that now. Anyway, why did you turn him down?'

'Don't know, miss.' Bella picked at a bit of lettuce from her sandwich and kicked one of her shoes with the other.

'Bel? Is it...? Is it, well, because of Patrick? Oh, babe. I'm sorry.' Bella was shaking her head, her eyes scrunched tight.

'I don't know, I don't know. I just can't. I can't—'

* * *

'Bella, can I ask you a favour?' Will called up from her kitchen.

'Sure. Why so serious?' She ran down the stairs. 'You don't want to borrow my life savings, do you?'

'No. Now don't go ballistic on me, but is there any chance – would you mind moving those photos of Patrick from the pinboard, up to your studio say?'

'Really, Will. You can hardly be jealous of a dead person? I'd no idea you were so insecure.'

'Thanks. No. I'm not jealous. Not exactly. But every time I come into the kitchen I'm confronted by this picture of you in bed with someone else.'

'Will, we're wearing toy antlers. It's not exactly a writhing bodies shot, is it?'

'Now you're deliberately missing the point. To be honest, I would have thought you might have been sensitive enough to move it without my asking.'

'I think you're the one who's being rather insensitive.'

'Well, I'm sorry if I am, but I don't think it's unreasonable. It's not as if I'm asking you to chuck them out – couldn't you just keep them somewhere out of my sight?'

'I could burn them on a ritual bonfire if you want.'

'Why do you have to overreact? I don't think I ask for much. But, seeing as we're practically living together, I thought—'

'We're not living together.'

'Oh, aren't we? Forgive me. There must be some mistake. And what would you call spending every night together and every weekend and me having shirts in your wardrobe? That is my jacket out in your hallway, isn't it? My shredded wheat in the larder? My razor in the bathroom? Or is it Patrick's?'

'No need to shout. Now you're just being offensive.'

'I'm sorry. I didn't mean that.'

She shrugged. 'No big deal. I meant to take them down anyway.'

'No. Leave them. It's OK.'

She shook her head. Carefully prised out the drawing-pins and took the photographs upstairs. Standing in her studio, she hovered between her desk drawer and the mantelpiece above the fireplace. She looked down at the photographs, the one of the two of them together and the one of Patrick on that Scottish holiday soaked to the skin. How peculiar it was to have a photograph of someone who no longer existed. It was like a lie in a way, a fiction, as if he were an actor in a film only now it was over and the lights had gone up in the cinema. Perhaps she should go back, she thought, say goodbye to him properly at his graveside, then at once dismissed the idea as self-dramatizing, embarrassingly self-conscious. That didn't feel like him anyway; she felt closer to him when she ordered a Chinese take-away. Still, she felt a flush of guilt as she realized how long it had been since she had last visited his grave. Just after the head-stone was erected.

* * *

Now that she is here, she feels like a bit of a twit. She has seen this scene in films and drama serials so she knows how it's supposed to go. Bella stands looking down at the grave and tries to clear her head from the array of mixed-up, irrelevant thoughts that keep bumping into her mind like so much flotsam and jetsam. The grave is bordered by a concrete kerb, the plot filled in with small stone chips. The sort used in driveways, she thinks. Patrick used to say you could tell how rich someone was by the relative crunchiness of their drive when you drove up it. This is the moment where she's meant to say something serious and important, she reminds herself. She's meant to say how life can never be the same again, but she will struggle on and be guided by his memory like a beacon. She can hardly say all that to a stupid driveway. And what would be the point of saying it out loud? He can't hear, can he? He didn't listen half the time when he was alive.

And anyway, that's not it, not it at all. She is not even sure if there are words for how she feels.

The headstone is arched at the top, like a church window, with a bas-relief angel, fortunately not too naff. Patrick would have thought it 'acceptable', one of his favourite words as in 'This wine's certainly very acceptable' or, to wind her up, 'You're looking most acceptable tonight.'

She focuses on the inscription:

Here lies
   PATRICK DERMOT HUGHES

Streuth. She'd forgotten about the Dermot bit. He hated it, would be well pissed-off about that. 'You won't believe this,' he'd say, 'they actually paidextra for those bloody six letters!'

Beneath his name are inscribed his birth and death dates, the too-brief gap between the years more eloquent than any 'Suddenly taken from us' or 'Snatched in his prime' could be. Below that:

MUCH LOVED, MUCH MISSED ALWAYS IN OUR THOUGHTS
   R.I.P.

Rest in Peace. R.I.P. *RIP.* An oddly violent word when you looked at it like that, not peaceful at all. But that was right, wasn't it? That was what death did to all those it touched. Rip your lives apart, leaving them in shreds. Ripped you open, too, so you felt as if your skin had been flayed, your muscles and tissues torn, your insides soft, exposed. Ripped you naked, spread out like a pinned butterfly, your fragility on display to be battered by the slightest breeze. R.I.P. What else could it stand for? Really In Pain? Rather

Inconvenient, Patrick? Ruddy Irritating Pillock? The dead person got the cushy end of the bargain, the free lunch. All he had to do was lie there. It was those left behind that were stuck holding the bill.

Awkwardly, she dips to lay the small bunch of tight pink rose-buds she has brought. She feels like an actress, as if there is a camera behind her shoulder, zooming in on the flowers. Focus on a single bloom, she thinks, one perfect teardrop balanced on the rim of a petal. Cut to a close-up of her face, looking sad. Patrick would think this all too stupid for words. 'Don't waste money on flowers, Bel. Go and have one for me at the pub.'

* * *

She looked again at the photographs in her hands, then propped them up on the mantelpiece.

24

'I just know I'm going to regret this.' Bella put down the phone and scrunched her forehead into exaggerated furrows. Will kissed it and cupped the back of her neck in his palm.

'Stop worrying so much. Everyone's embarrassed by their parents. That's what parents are for. They have to have some sense of purpose in life, don't they? You met my mother and survived, didn't you – and she's pretty odd.'

'On your own head be it. Just remember that it was your idea.'

'You want it to be hideous, don't you – then you can get to be right. Come on. How bad can it be?'

How bad can it be? How bad can it be? Was he kidding? Bella recalled the first time she'd taken Patrick to stay for the weekend.

* * *

'Very smart. Did you have a meeting today?' Bella says, looking at Patrick's Prince of Wales check suit, crisply ironed shirt and silk tie. 'There's time to change before we go if you want.'

'I just have.' Patrick plucks an invisible fragment of lint from his sleeve.

'Whatever for? You're not asking for my hand or anything. You don't have to impress them.'

He sets his jaw.

'To be honest, you seemed so anxious about my meeting them that I thought I'd make a bit of an effort. Didn't want to let you down.'

It was sweet of him, she reminded herself. But what mileage would her mother manage to get out of the suit? *I do hope Bella didn't make you dress up on our account.* Or I *was expecting you to be wearing overalls, Patrick. Bella says you're something to do with buildings.* Perhaps she should dress down a bit herself, even things out a bit? She is wearing a chic grey trouser suit, black suede shoes. Her hair is held off her face by a heavy twisted silver clip, matching spiral earrings that catch the light as she moves. She takes off the earrings, replaces the jacket with a chunky brown wool one and swaps the suede shoes for a pair of old burgundy loafers.

Alessandra eyes Patrick's suit.

'I feel we should all change for dinner, Patrick. You quite put us to shame with this elegant suit.' She feels his lapel between her finger and thumb as if she is a professional couturier and smiles. 'Will you not put on a skirt, Bella? You don't want to let down your escort.'

'Escort!' Bella says under her breath. 'As if I'd hired him!'

'Normally, I'm a complete scruff,' Patrick protests. 'It's just I had this meeting...'

'Well, you menfolk must think of your promotion prospects, mustn't you? All part of the world of business.'

'He's not in the world of business. He's a surveyor. And he's not looking for promotion because he's already a partner in the firm.'

Patrick scowls at her and turns to admire a framed engraving on the wall.

* * *

The drive was punctuated by Bella's explanations of the various idiosyncrasies of the house and her parents.

'And in the downstairs loo, people can hear you if they're near the back door so you might want to sing or hum loudly but sort of casually, as if you always do that.'

'Rightio. Note 312b: downstairs cloakroom – HUM. Got that. Is "Fascinatin' Rhythm" OK or is there a list of prescribed melodies posted up on the wall?'

'Oh, oh, I forgot – most important of all, don't forget to be nice about my mother's cooking. That should be easy because she's an exquisite cook—'

'Do you know, I think that's the first time I've heard you say anything complimentary about her?'

Bella shrugged. 'Have you been taking notes? Haven't you got better things to worry about?'

'Strangely enough, I do actually spend quite a lot of time thinking about you.'

'Right. But you have to be specific. About the cooking. Don't just say, "That was lovely" or she'll think you've been coached. And ask her questions – give her a chance to show off.'

'I should have come in black tie. Then I could have written notes on my stiff cuffs.

'What should I call your mother anyway?' Will unwound a tube of fruit pastilles to find the one he wanted.

'Will you not pinch all the red ones, pig? You may call her "O Perfect One" as this is a fairly informal occasion.'

'Fine. Did I mention that I prefer to be addressed as "Divine Sex

God"? That's just to my close personal friends, of course, but seeing as they're practically family...'

Bella scanned his expression. *Practically family*. He touched her cheek with the back of his hand.

'So, do I call them by their first names or what?'

'Dad's Gerald. He'd find "Mr Kreuzer" just puzzling and you'll see he doesn't look like a Gerry: he has these little half-moon spectacles for doing the crossword and he looks a bit vague, as if he's just been set down on the planet but he's not quite sure what he's doing here. Gerry's more of a dynamic, striped-shirt, espresso-quaffing, marketing-person sort of name.'

Will gazed at her.

'I've never met anyone who could read so much into the tiniest detail. Completely extraordinary. What about Will? What can you tell from that – as opposed to William, say?'

'Well, William's more what your financial advisor might be called, or the boy at primary school who wears hand-knitted jumpers that are too big. Trustworthy, stable. A tad wet maybe. The kind of boy who always has a small trail of slime descending from one nostril. Not sexy. Bill sounds too short to be a proper name – and a bit suspiciously genial, like an uncle who smiles a lot but you wouldn't want to sit on his lap.'

'But Will's the same length as Bill. Be gentle with me...' Bella cocked her head on one side, assessing.

'Yes, but it doesn't feel so truncated. It's more confident but relaxed.

You feel safe with a Will. Reliable but not dull. Enough edge to be sexy.'

'Sexy, yes. That'll be me then. Anyway, back to the Aged Ps. No Gerry.

What about Old-timer or Pops?'

She slapped his thigh.

'It might be a thought to call Mum Mrs Kreuzer. I know it seems absurd but it will allow her to play Lady Bountiful for a few moments as she graciously insists that you call her Alessandra. Don't, whatever you do, shorten it to Sandra, which she considers a horrid, flock-wallpaper type of name, or she'll feed your entrails to Hund before you've even taken off your coat.'

'What's a Hund? Fire-breathing dragon? Mad aunt kept locked in the attic?'

'Dad's golden retriever, though I don't think he's ever retrieved anything more energetic than a chocolate biscuit. Hund's German for dog, as you no doubt know. It's Dad's idea of a joke.'

They turned into the driveway through a white, five-barred gate; the tyres crunched on the gravel, signalling their arrival. Hund lolloped around the corner of the house to greet them. Bella bent down to hug him.

'Hello, Hund.' She fondled his ears. 'You lovable old thing.' Will looked at her and whimpered, dog-like, for attention. 'Oh, you,' she said.

He hunched down to check his hair in the wing mirror and pressed it with the flat of his hand to smooth it down. It bounced back.

'C'mon, Springy Hair. Into the lion's den.'

* * *

Alessandra smiled and extended her hand.

'You must be William. Do come in. We've heard so *little* about you.' Will joined in as she laughed at her jest.

Bella dipped forward to exchange dual cheek kisses with Alessandra. 'It's Will,' Bella said. 'Not William.'

'Whatever.' Will waved his hand.

'Perhaps you'd like a sherry?' Alessandra ushered him by the elbow towards the drawing room. 'Bella's *last* boyfriend was *very* fond of a glass of fino, wasn't he?'

Surely any man would be driven to drink by living with Bella? She made him sound like an alcoholic. Who wouldn't want a glass of fino? A bottle, for that matter? A Quaker would be tipping meths into his cocoa to get through a weekend with her mother.

'Well, a little—' Will started.

'Of course, we rarely drink this early ourselves, but we're rather green when it comes to sophisticated city habits. Perhaps you'd prefer coffee?'

'Yes, whatever you're making. Coffee, of course.'

Gerald came in from the garden and shook Will's hand and patted him on the arm.

'So you're Will. Good, good. We're very pleased to see you here.'

There was a promising clinking as Gerald delved into a cupboard. 'Say you'll join me in a Scotch. Or would you prefer gin and tonic? Bourbon?'

'Just a small Scotch, then. Thank you. This is a beautiful room, Mrs Kreuzer.' Will crossed to the corner cabinet. 'Is this eighteenth-century?'

'It is. I do hope Bella hasn't schooled you to be so formal, William—'

Will,' said Bella.

'—Gerald and I are very easy come, easy go, aren't we darling?'

'Hmm?' said Gerald.

'Please do call me...' She took a breath as if about to launch into an aria. '...Alessandra.'

To Bella's surprise, they were shown to the guest bedroom, rather than being segregated.

'I dare say you'll want to *share,* will you?' Alessandra said, giving a little, indulgent laugh, making it sound like a perversion.

'It is pretty normal for people in their thirties.'

'I daresay it is, Bella dear.' Alessandra closed the curtains and moved a vase of spiny sea holly slightly. 'I'm sure I'm hopelessly out of touch.' She straightened the guest towels by the washbasin. 'Towels. Soap. Yes. Wait until you have children and they start telling you off every time you open your mouth.'

Bella started to unpack her holdall.

'I'm *not* telling you off,' she said at her washbag. 'I'm just *saying* – it'd be abnormal if we slept in separate rooms at our age.'

'Well there's no problem then, is there?' Alessandra paused by the door. 'You're not in separate rooms.' She smiled at Will. 'Do just say if you need more towels.' The door closed behind her.

'For God's sake! *I daresay it is Bella dear.* And *more* towels!' Bella thumped a plumpfy pile of them laid on a chair. 'Whatever for? What *does* she think we'd be doing in here? Having babies? Covering ourselves in maple syrup? What?'

'Oh, keep calm.' Will looped his arms around her. 'Now, about this maple syrup...'

'I can see where Bella gets her culinary finesse from,' Will said at supper, grinning as if he'd had a whole bowlful of manna. 'This is superb.'

Bella mouthed 'Crawler' at him.

Back in their room, Will sat on the bed and asked Bella what was the matter.

'I can see where Bella gets her culinary *finesse* from,' she parroted. 'Culinary finesse? Whatever happened to good old cooking skills, Mr Lover-of-Plain-English?'

'Why are you having a go at me? I'm not your mother.'

'Very funny. I'm not, anyway.'

'Yes you are. I thought you wanted me to praise her cooking. That's what it said in the manual: Bella's Parents – A Visitor's Guide.'

She could see the corners of his mouth curving, expecting her to laugh with him.

'It didn't say be a slimy, goody-goody, suck-up sycophant, did it?'

'Oh, charming. I love you too.'

'I just think it would be appropriate if you were to show me some support while you're here.'

'Appropriate? What? I'm not *not* showing you support by being nice to your mum. It's a common custom when you're a guest. It's called Getting On with People. You should try it sometime.'

'Ssh! Will you keep your voice down. And I don't Get On with People, I suppose?'

'Well, you could try the revolutionary new tactic of being pleasant to your mother. It wouldn't kill you, would it?'

Bella fiddled with the stiff latch and opened the window. 'I knew you wouldn't see what she's really like.'

He crossed to her and put his hand on her shoulder but she shrugged it off.

'I can see that she's awkward with you. Not relaxed. I've no idea why.

But you're making it worse, can't you see that? She looks nervous around you, almost as if she thinks you might hit her.'

Her nervous around *me*. Hah!' Will nodded, serious.

'Yes, that's how it looks. Like you've both got stuck in some stupid – deadlock. Why don't you make the first move, like Helen said?'

'Why should I? She's the mother, that's her job.'

'Excuse me? Hello? "Sir, sir, she pushed me first" – that's certainly going to get you good results.'

'I do try actually.' Bella folded her arms, holding herself. 'You've got no idea. You don't know anything about it.'

'Yes, well, I wouldn't, would I?' His voice became brisk. 'Because you haven't told me. If something's difficult, painful, you don't talk about it. You just turn away or change the subject or make it into a joke – that's your solution to everything. Except it hasn't actually *solved* anything, has it?'

Bella wanted to speak, to protest, retaliate. But she couldn't swallow. She tried to concentrate on moving the muscles in her windpipe so she could take in some air.

'No,' Will continued. 'But then what would I know? I'm just an outsider. I guess it's none of my bloody business.' If she had turned from the window, she would have seen that he looked suddenly smaller, somehow defeated.

'Guess not,' she said, staring straight ahead. 'So it's really not your worry.'

She heard him let out a breath as if his whole body were sighing, then the quiet click as he closed the door behind him. She stayed completely still, seeing herself as if she were in one of her own paintings, leaning on the window ledge, looking out to the garden in a dream.

* * *

Through the bars in the back of the bench, she watches them sitting over there under the almond tree. From where she lies, here in the long grass, pressing herself close to the ground, she can see stripes of people through the bench – neat segments at once unfamiliar yet recognizable: Daddy's Sunday jacket, green and scratchy like dried-out moss; Mrs Mellors's 'strawberry-blonde' hair, not like strawberries at all ('It's not *dyed* – just a rinse to bring out my natural highlights'). Patterns of sound reach her, shifts in tone and pitch going up and down like the temperature chart she did at school, as each grown-up speaks. Then, out of the pattern, words suddenly take on shape, sharp and clear in the sunlight.

'—finds it hard to mix with other...' says her mother. '...really very...'

'...more of an effort?' says Mrs Mellors.

Then Daddy's voice, low and gentle, tantalizingly beyond grasp. Suddenly, a loud 'Ssh!' and silence. She flattens her face into the smell of greenness, but it is too late.

'Bella!' Her mother's voice, careful and distinct. 'We didn't see you there, darling. Don't skulk in that damp grass. Come and say hello to Mrs Mellors.' Bella gets up and rubs her grassy knees hard with the heel of her hand, tucks her hair back behind her ears.

'There's *panettone*,' adds her mother, briskly brushing bits of grass from Bella's front, 'for good little girls who come and sit down nicely.'

25

By Sunday lunchtime, Alessandra was patting Will's arm and laughing at everything he said. Gerald took him on a tour of the garden and pronounced him 'a breath of fresh air and robust enough to stand up to Bella'. He laughed when he said it, so Bella was sure he must have been joking. Will found Bella in the sitting-room after lunch, curled up in an armchair reading a book. Was she coming to join them, he asked; there was fresh coffee.

'No thanks.'

'Would Madam like a cup brought through before the staff go off duty?' He smiled and leant down to see her face.

'I'm fine, thanks.'

'What's up?'

'Nothing. I'm reading.'

'Rightio. You're reading. Of course. We trail miles across country so that you can introduce me to your parents then you spend the entire time skulking in corners like some snotty adolescent. Do you always visit people then ignore them when you get there?'

Bella continued to stare at her book.

'I think it's very rude. To me as well as your parents. I'm here only because of you but you've practically abandoned me.'

'You seem to be managing very well without me.'

'I'm trying to be sociable enough for two people to compensate for you.'

'Please don't bother on my account. They're used to it. I'm "difficult" apparently – surely my mother mentioned it?'

'Come on. Will you please at least look at me?'

Bella raised her eyes from the page. They were like glass.

'I hate it when you do that.'

She raised her eyebrows and remained silent. 'Aren't you going to ask me what?'

'I daresay you'll tell me anyway.'

'God, you can be infuriating.' He shoved his hands down deep into his pockets. 'I hate it when you shut me out like that. Go all icy. I don't know how to get through it.'

'Better not waste your energy then.'

'What is all this? What's the matter?' Will moved towards her and laid a hand on her hair.

'Don't do that. Flattens it.' She flicked her head. His hand dropped back to his side.

'Come through when you're planning to rejoin the human race, why don't you?'

Bella deposited a single kiss on Alessandra's right cheek and promptly stepped backwards, stranding her mid-ritual. Alessandra hovered, then tugged at her silk cardigan draped over her shoulders and crossed her arms. A hug and kiss for Gerald, then Bella squatted to clasp Hund in a warm embrace. She heard Will kissing Alessandra and her light laugh, heard Gerald clapping Will affectionately on the back. She kissed the top of Hund's head again and showered him with extra pats.

'You must come and see us again, dear Will. Don't wait for Bella to bring you – we'll be quite old and grey by then!' Alessandra laughed.

Will got into the front passenger seat and balanced a tin of home-made biscuits on his lap. A jar of cherries macerated in brandy was wedged between his feet.

'Enough going-home presents there, have you, *dear* Will?' Bella turned the car and gave a cursory wave out the window, a perfunctory goodbye toot of the horn.

'I thought it was very kind of her. She was only trying to make me feel welcome.'

'Welcome? She practically offered to adopt you. I'm surprised she didn't just swap me for you, old for new: "Don't throw that old, unlovable child away. Trade it in for an easier, more adorable one."'

'I've told you a million times, don't exaggerate.'

'Is that the best you can do? Time to splash out and invest in a few new jokes, I think.'

'You *are* angry, aren't you?'

'As you well know, nothing is more guaranteed to make a perfectly calm person angry than telling them they're angry. You're so – so *fucking* smug sometimes.'

'I'm afraid you've lost me. I really don't understand why you're so upset.'

'Don't you? Don't you really? You've just spent all weekend forming a cosy little mutual fan club with my parents, especially my mother, and you've no idea why that would upset me?'

'Not really, no. Well, I could hazard a guess.'

'And what would that be, Mr Smug?'

'Cut it out. Don't push it, Bella.'

'Bella. Oh, you do know my name then? But only when you're

telling me off? The rest of the time it's "sweet pea" or "pumpkin" or some other type of vegetable matter.'

Will was silent for a minute.

'That's just me being affectionate, you know it is. Why didn't you say if it annoyed you? I thought you liked it.'

I do like it. She felt as if she were at the bottom of a pit and could see no way to scale the walls; what could she do but dig deeper?

She exhaled shortly through her nose. Will ignored it.

'I think you're pissed off because I got on OK with your mum and that's blown your guiding theory of life out of the water – that she's the Wicked Witch of the West and you're sweet little Dorothy.'

Bella raised one eyebrow.

'Oh, the famous Kreuzer look. I *am* scared. I think you'd actually rather be right than happy, wouldn't you?'

'That does sound likely, doesn't it?'

'OK. Why are you so upset then?'

'I'm not "upset" – I might be justifiably pissed off that you smarmed up to *Alessandra,*' her voice quivered dramatically. 'So that I was made to look like the bad one, a naughty misfit schoolkid.'

'You were acting like a stroppy brat, so what do you expect?'

'I really fail to see the point of this conversation.'

Will rested his hand on her leg.

'C'mon, you.' He moved her leg to and fro playfully. 'Let's not fight, eh?'

Bella reached to change gear and nudged his hand away. ''Scuse me. Could you...? Thanks.'

He withdrew it and clucked a quiet rhythm to himself for a minute, then he turned to look out of the window.

The rest of the journey passed in near-silence.

Will pulled out a tape.

'OK if we have some music?'

'Mmm-mm.'

'I'll take that as a yes then, as you would say.' He hummed along without enthusiasm.

'Got a busy day tomorrow,' he said. 'Hmm?'

'Yes, indeedy. Busy day. Busy, busy day.'

'Oh, right.'

Will turned to look out of the window once more.

Bella stopped the car outside Will's house and kept the engine running while he unloaded his bag from the boot.

'Well then,' she said.

'Bella? Could you park the car and come in for a minute?'

'I'm really tired.'

'Aren't we all? Just for a minute. I want to talk to you.'

'Why? Not if you're going to tell me off. You're doing your schoolmaster voice.'

'Give it a rest.' Will let out a breath. 'Right.' He got back into the car and slammed the door.

Bella sat facing straight ahead like a passenger on a bus, feeling his eyes on her.

'Hello?' Will ducked his head from side to side to try to make eye contact. 'Hello? Am I going to get any response or what? It's like you're not even *here*. You've gone off to Kreuzer Dreamworld again, haven't you?'

Anger rose inside her, bubbling up through her body like boiling milk, threatening to spill over in a hiss of scalding steam and acrid smells. How could he? How dare he? She wanted to let it out, scream at him, rage at him, punch him as hard as she could. She dug her fingernails into her hands, felt her fury wind tight as a spring, coiling around her in wiry bands; she clung onto it, buckling it around her so it would hold her together.

'Just don't.' She raised her hand in front of her face as if he were about to strike her.

'Have you any idea how cold you seem when you do that? How on earth is anyone ever supposed to get close to you if you keep shutting them out?'

'I don't imagine anyone is *supposed* to get close to anyone else. You either are or you aren't.'

'Fine. And I never have been?' Bella shrugged and folded her arms.

'Right. No need to put up a placard. I think even thicko Will has finally got the message.' He fumbled for the door-handle. 'I love you to pieces. You know I do. But I can't—'

She could see him trying to swallow.

'Whatever.' He clenched and unclenched his hands. 'Why didn't you just say you didn't love me? Is it so hard? Will, I don't love you, please go away. There. I feel like – I don't know. Jesus. I—' He ran his fingers through his hair and was silent for a moment. 'It's Patrick, isn't it? You're still in love with him. And how the *fuck* is anyone supposed to compete with a *dead* guy on a fucking ginormous pedestal?'

Bella held herself still as he opened the car door. A wall of cold air hit her, surrounding her. She felt it was coating her, pouring over her like chilled liquid glass, sealing her in.

'I do love you,' she spoke quietly.

'Well, feel free to have mentioned it before now. Or had you signed the Official Secrets Act?'

The touch of his lips briefly brushing her hair.

'Take care of yourself,' he said, without turning round.

The door clunked firmly behind him. And then there was nothing, only the almost-silence of air prickling in her ears and his footsteps walking away.

26

Bella took from the dresser a fine china cup and saucer, one patterned with tiny shamrock leaves and edged with gold. Decanted some milk into a small matching china jug. She needed proper tea, more for the predictable complexity of the ritual than for the flavour. Real tea, English Breakfast. Warmed the hand-painted teapot, losing herself in its swirls of colour: citrus, sky and seaweed. One and a half spoons of tea, using the smooth wooden caddy spoon Patrick had given her in her stocking one Christmas, carved from a cherry tree; a tiny bit more to make it just so.

If only tea were harder to make, then she could really put 100 per cent of her mind to it, lean on it, let it hold her together, perhaps that was what the Japanese Tea Ceremony was all about, the quest for order, for pattern in the untidiness of life. Then she could sink herself absolutely into the perfect execution of the elaborate process, keeping those other thoughts at bay – those thoughts that now nestled in the tea tin, waiting for her when she eased off the tightly-fitting lid, that poured creamy-white from the milk jug, clouding the clear tea in her cup, that breathed hotly on her upper lip as she dipped her head to drink.

She cradled the cup in her hands, concentrating on the slight
burning of her fingers through the thin china, and examined the
floor. That rug was really very pleasing in here, she thought,
wonderful colours, but a bit slippy on the floorboards; perhaps she
should get one of those mat thingies to go underneath. Or, she had
a sudden thought, she could get rid of it and *paint* a rug on the floor.
An image came to her of the entire house emptied of objects, with
trompe-l'oeil furniture painted on the walls, lamps on the ceilings, a
stage set in distorted perspective; the cushions would never be
creased nor the rug ruckled; nothing would wear out, nothing
would get broken, nothing would change.

Of course, it was impossible NOT to think about a particular
person or a particular thing just by deciding to. The very act of
NOT thinking about – brought his face bright and alive before her.
She would not name him to herself as if even the letters, the sound
of them in her head, held the power of a spell. His scent seemed to
hover in the air, catching her unawares when she entered the
bedroom. She felt she could see the imprint of his footsteps on the
floors, the whorls of his fingerprints on furniture, objects, as if she
had infrared vision. She must fill her head with something else,
anything else, to oust him. Flush out all thoughts of him as if they
were no more than niggling grains of sand stubbornly stuck
between her toes. Soon he would be uprooted from her mind, and
his face nothing but a fragile, gauzy image, a fleeting fragment of a
distant dream.

Thank God she had her painting to focus on. The date of the
exhibition private view gleamed in red pen in her diary; she forced
herself to keep it in her sights, a brilliant buoy in a dark ocean.
When she got home from work, she dumped her bag on the floor,
clunking her keys on the table, sloughing off her jacket like a snake
eager to slither from its old skin. She ate standing at the cluttered
kitchen worktop, shoving aside coffee-cups and old newspapers,

hunched over a dish of pasta – forking it rhythmically into her mouth as if fuelling a boiler, not bothering to chop onions, crush garlic for a sauce, bored with cooking, bored with eating, bored with herself. Then she climbed the stairs to her studio and sank into her paintings, losing herself in colour and shadow, letting the smell of paint and turpentine fill her head, her brush jabbing into the paint, swirling onto canvas, blotting him out.

She stood under the shower, an automaton washing herself by rote. Felt like a gerbil in an exercise wheel, running nowhere, endlessly watching the same scenery. Wash, dress, teeth, work. Eat, undress, wash, teeth. Again and again. Year in, year out. And a relationship was no different. Meet, date, talk, kiss, fuck, row. Again and again. What a waste of time. At least with painting, once the brush touched the canvas, the board, the paper, the mark was there. It existed without her having to redo it over and over again. Even if she were to paint over it, she knew the original brushstroke remained beneath, hidden yet real.

Bella started getting into work crisply at nine instead of breezing in towards ten with the rest of them, paring down the hours to be endured alone at home. Work was dull but safe and she was grateful for the routine and the office banter. She shunned socializing, pleading the need to prepare for her exhibition when the others sloped off to the pub, even avoiding Viv. She stayed late one Friday evening to excavate the office fridge, a task that had been left so long that Anthony said she should wear protective clothing and evacuate the building. Seline had agreed that it would be worth attempting to train Anthony as Bella's deputy if she could get him to act a little more responsibly and not refer to his pierced nipple in front of clients. Bella concentrated on 'grooming him for stardom' as he put it.

'Other boys wanted to be astronauts, footballers,' he said, 'but I dreamed of becoming a megalomaniac.'

'All in good time,' she said. 'Don't let them see the power-crazed glint in your eye until it's too late.'

* * *

She closed the door from Seline's office with a too-loud clunk, after yet another meeting that had once again been sidetracked from the insignificant issue of future projects and which ones Bella might be involved with on a freelance basis to the far more important one of the redecoration of Seline's house, involving the serious considera-tion of two thousand shade cards with tiny squares of infinitesi-mally differing tones of what used to be known as beige but now seemed to be called 'Cappuccino', 'Sahara' and 'Antique Gold'.

Two yellow stickies on her phone: 'Your dad called. Have you remembered your mum's birthday? Please call back.' Another Duty Visit, that would be fun; she flicked through her desk diary – it was a Friday, she'd have to book a day off. And a message from Viv, saying hello and goodbye before she went off to work at head office in Birmingham for three weeks. It was too late to ring her back anyway – she'd have gone by now. Viv had been strangely unsym-pathetic when Bella told her about Will – 'You're a bloody idiot if you've shoved him away, Bel. That man is a gem.'

* * *

A series of sketches were spread out on her studio floor and she was about to start painting when the phone rang. It was Fran's voice on the answerphone; Bella stood at the top of the stairs, wanting to run down and pick up the phone. Fran went on at length – she was ringing to see how Bella was, to tell her she was still very welcome, she didn't have to come with Will. Bella crept downstairs as if Fran could detect her presence, and rested her hand on the phone.

'I know I can be a bit of a nosy old bag, but I promise not to interfere. I'd just love to see you. I'm so fond of you and I hate it when people lose touch – life's too short. Besides, I have an ulterior motive...'

She'd just said she wouldn't interfere; surely Fran wasn't going to lecture her about Will?

'...I'd love some more of that flan you made. The upside-downy one...'

The tarte Tatin?

'I even dreamt about it the other night. That's what being past the menopause does for you. No more fantasizing about muscular chappies whisking you off into the sunset.'

Bella thought about standing in Fran's kitchen, rolling out pastry while Will peeled the apples, dipping a piece into the bag of sugar before slipping it into her mouth; his look of childlike wonder when she had turned the tin upside down and there was the tart, warm and brown and smelling of caramel; his face as he smiled at her across the kitchen table.

'I daresay you must be up to your eyes preparing for your exhibition. Will told me – he sounded so proud of you...' Should she pick up?

'Anyway, sorry to blether on, hope I haven't used up your tape. Do ring me any time you want to come. Don't wait to be asked. It's always open house here for you.'

And then she was gone.

Donald MacIntyre phoned from the gallery. How were things progressing, he wanted to know, and could she supply a brief biography of herself. She sat slumped on the stairs, lulled by the rich maleness of his voice.

'...you'll need to have them here by then at the latest so they can go to the framers... or would you like us to pick them up? We can do that.'

'I think – there – might – I think there could be a bit of a problem.'

'Oh?' His tone was cool.

'Um, yes. I'm not sure if they're – well, I might not be ready for the exhibition. I think perhaps you should just count me out.'

'No.' He spoke with authority. 'Sounds like classic pre-exhibition jitters to me. Let me come and see what you've done.'

'I'd rather you didn't.'

'I'm afraid I think I'll have to. Say this evening? Around eight?'

* * *

Donald MacIntyre was taller than she had remembered, filling the sitting-room with his presence. His smart suit made her suddenly self-conscious about her appearance – her hair hauled back roughly into a clip, her faded leggings and slipped-down socks. She saw his gaze sweep the room, noticing the half-drunk mugs of coffee dotted around on every flat surface, long-dry washing draped over the radiators.

'They're upstairs.' Bella led the way.

She was sure he would hate them, anticipated his embarrassed look of disappointment, the shrug of his shoulders as he searched for the most tactful phrases. Best get it over with.

'There are just a few water-colours.' She gestured. 'Some line drawings as well. The rest are oils, as before.'

He squatted, incongruous in his beautiful tailoring among the oily rags and half-squished tubes of paint.

'Careful! Those ones aren't quite dry yet.'

He paused by a large painting, the one based on her very first sketch of Will.

'This.' He nodded. 'For the window.'

'No!' She coughed apologetically. 'It's not for sale.' He laughed drily to himself and shook his head.

'We can fight about that later. Anyway, what was all this nonsense about your not being ready?'

Bella shrugged.

'With the others you brought, there's more than we have space for anyway. However...'

Here it comes, she thought, he hates them.

'These are better than a couple of the other ones, so we might have a bit of a swap round before they go to the framers, OK?' He straightened up with a creak. 'Getting old.' He tutted at himself, then looked at her. 'Is there a problem?'

'No. Yes. Are they – all right then?'

And then he laughed. A great big, generous, booming laugh. Bella giggled nervously, unsure why he was laughing, surprised that such a sound could emanate from this quiet, elegant man.

'I do apologize,' he said. 'Forgive me. Do you think for one second that I would exhibit them if I didn't think they were "all right"? Why would I? I'm not running a charity for unemployed artists. All right? No, they're not all right. They're bloody good. Really. Consider yourself told.' He shook his head, laughing again. 'I love this business,' he said. 'If only I didn't have to deal with artists.'

27

'You'll bring Will of course, won't you?' Gerald said on the phone when Bella finally returned his call about Alessandra's birthday.

'Hmm. Possibly not.'

'Oh? How's it going with him?'

'Going, going, gone, since you ask.'

And, no, she didn't want to talk about it and please would he not tell Alessandra, because she wasn't feeling up to that stoic, 'my-daughter-is-the-cross-I-bear' look.

She had already bought Alessandra's present – an antique serving platter, its edge patterned with clusters of deep pink rosebuds and touches of gold, but she spent almost as long hunting for the perfect wrapping paper to go with it. Although she usually gave her own hand-made cards to friends, she had long since switched to shop-bought ones for her mother. It was easier, none of that 'how charming, so lovely to have a home-made one' insincere bollocks, and she was very busy anyway what with trying to fit in some painting most evenings and sorting out her contacts book for freelance work. Friday, the birthday itself, was booked off, so she loaded the car late on Thursday evening – her clothes, the present plus a graceful weeping-fig plant as an extra, a new thriller (unbirthday present for Dad), a bottle of decent claret – and set off.

* * *

She slept in her old room once more, but stole quietly into the proper guest room where she had stayed with Will on her last visit. Here was where they had had that stupid row, with Will trying to give her a lesson in Happy Families, what a smug git he could be. She curled her lip, determined to be angry with him. That night, she had turned away from him, pretended to be asleep when he had touched her shoulder, curled his arm over her waist, whispered her name. If only she didn't miss him so much, didn't have this horrible ache in the pit of her stomach most of the time. Picking up her holdall once more, she strode through to her own room and closed the door firmly behind her. It was better this way.

Still wearing the baggy T-shirt she had worn in bed, Bella quickly pulled on her jeans and thick socks to come downstairs. She let out Hund from his preferred sleeping-place in the utility room, squatted to loop her arms around his neck, remembering Will's playful whimpering when he had watched her lavish her affection on the dog. Aside from the clicking patter of Hund's paws on the floor, the house was hushed and still, with the particular quietness of the hour before anyone else is up. It seemed to be holding its breath, waiting for the shuffle of slippers on the stairs, the clatter of cups, the muffled whoomph of the boiler, the clinking of milk bottles as the fridge door was opened.

The kitchen, as always, was pristine, with the slight chill of a very tidy room. She was glad of the socks – even through them she could feel the cold hardness of the quarry-tiled floor. She pulled out the prettiest cups and saucers from the glass-fronted cupboard, filled a milk jug, foraged in the cutlery drawer for the best tea strainer. Now, tray? And a cloth. She found a fresh linen napkin and laid that on the tray and set out the cups on it, pilfered a single bloom and a frond of foliage from the arrangement in the hall to add to a tiny vase.

She heard soft footsteps on the stairs, then Gerald came in.

'Morning, Dads. Back to bed with you. Go on. I'm bringing you both up some tea.'

He spotted the tray.

'What a treat, to have it made. Did you find everything you needed?' He paused at the door. 'Oh, did you know, your mother will only drink Earl Grey in the morning now? I prefer the ordinary, but don't worry.'

'No, no. That's fine. I'll just find a second pot.'

Balancing the tray on her raised knee and steadying it with one hand, she knocked on their bedroom door.

'Birthday tea in bed, madam?' Bella bent down to kiss her mother's cheek. 'Happy birthday. Your present's in the car; I'll go and fetch it in a minute. Your hair's looking nice.' Even first thing in the morning, it was already pinned up neatly.

'Thank you, Bella darling. How lovely. Pretty anemone – I have some just like it in the hall. Is this Earl Grey?' Alessandra peered at the tray.

'Yes, Dad warned me. Shall I pour?'

'Best leave it for a minute. Oh, could you not find the tray-cloths?

They're in the drawer.'

'No.' Bella turned her back to busy herself with pouring the tea, placing the strainer on each cup with infinite care, remembering to put the milk in last as was correct, carrying the cups over to the bed like a child, her brow furrowed in her eagerness to please.

'Marvellous,' said Alessandra. 'Perhaps I could have just a drop more milk?' Bella followed instructions with the milk jug then turned to go.

'No Will this time?'

'No.'

'Oh. Everything all right?'

'Fine, thanks. Why shouldn't it be?'

'Sorry. I didn't mean— Give him our best won't you?'

'Hmm-mm.'

They spent the morning in town, where Alessandra wanted to find a scarf to offset the beautiful amber brooch Gerald had given her.

'He says it reminded him of the flecks in my eyes. Really, your father's a hopeless old romantic.' She smiled indulgently.

They met up with Gerald for lunch, and he duly admired the new scarf. 'And Bella darling, do let me treat you to something nice to wear,'

Alessandra said. 'You must have had those trousers for ages.'

'They're comfortable. I do have smart clothes for work, you know.' Her mother nodded.

'Well, of course, I can't keep up with what's in fashion now.' She tweaked at the edge of the deep cuff of her silver-grey crêpe-de-Chine blouse. 'I just stick to the classics.'

* * *

Bella had insisted on cooking the birthday banquet. They started with hard-boiled quails' eggs, sitting on a salad of mixed leaves, fresh rocket, shreds of purplered radicchio, blanched sugar snap peas, strips of grilled red and yellow peppers, with a warm sesame oil dressing.

Alessandra had 'just popped in for something' while Bella was cooking. 'Mmm. Wonderful colours. Your father won't eat peppers, you know.'

'Is this from that cookery book I gave you at Christmas?' asked Alessandra at supper, cocking her head to one side, assessing.

'No, actually, I just made it up. What do you think?'

'Delicious!' said Bella's father. 'The peppers are lovely cooked like this.'

'It's very good. But the *rucola* must have been expensive,' said Alessandra.

The main course was poached salmon, served warm with a watercress sauce, pommes Anna, layered with translucent slivers of onion and moistened with milk, and fine French beans with glazed carrots. Nothing innovative, nothing risky, nothing with too much how-interesting-I-never-cook-it-that-way potential.

'And there should be some left over for having cold tomorrow,' said Bella.

'Oh, but I've plenty of food in for tomorrow already.'

'You still haven't opened your present from me yet. It's in the hall. I'll go and get it.' Bella rose from her chair.

'Please don't bother, Bella darling. I'll open it later.'

'Please open it now.'

Bella cleared the plates and placed the present in front of Alessandra. 'Well, isn't this wonderfully wrapped? What pretty paper.'

'I hope you like it.' Bella straightened the salt and pepper in front of her, brushed crumbs from the cloth into her palm. 'I'm afraid I can't take it back.'

'Of course you won't need to take it back.' Alessandra delicately picked off the sticky tape. 'Well now.' The platter lay exposed in its nest of pale pink tissue and rose-covered wrapping paper. 'That's really very charming, Bella. Thank you.'

'We must give it pride of place,' said Gerald. 'Why don't we move that boring green one and put it in the middle of the big dresser?'

'But Gerald darling, that was Mamma's. Perhaps we could fit this one on the dresser in the hall.'

Bella went into the kitchen to get the dessert.

'I hope you'll use it sometimes,' she called through as she looked for the silver cake slice.

'Well, of course we don't entertain as much as we used to, Bella, not like I did when I was your age. It's a bit big just for the two of us.'

Bella appeared bearing her chilled lemon mousse cake, circled by a red moat of raspberry coulis. The perfect, smooth surface was piped with a large A in curlicued chocolate script.

'Dah-dah,' said Bella, flatly, a token fanfare.

'That looks simply delicious, but you know I don't think I could manage another mouthful just now. You and Dad have some.'

'It's very light,' said Bella. 'It's mostly air.'

Alessandra smiled, gestured gracefully with her hand in refusal, and wiped her lips conclusively with her napkin.

'Now, *I'll* make the coffee,' she said, getting up from the table.

Bella looked down at the mousse cake. There seemed to be a large drop of water on one twirl of the A. Another. Her tears fell as she stood, poised with the cake slice.

'Oh, Bella, sweetheart, don't,' said her father. 'It's all right. She can't help it.'

She was gulping now, her breaths coming in great waves, pulling at her ribcage.

'She – never—' Bella slapped at the top of the cake with the flat of the cake slice, hitting it as she gulped in air. 'Says – anything – nice.'

'Hush, now.' He put his arm around her stiff shoulders. 'That was a delicious meal you made. Of course she liked it.'

'She – *hates* – me.'

Alessandra swept in with the tray of coffee.

'Oh, have I interrupted something? What happened to that lovely-looking cake? I was just about to have a piece.'

Gerald silenced her with a look.

'Well, I'm sure I don't know why she's crying. It ought to be me. I'm the one who's a year older.'

'Ali! That's enough now.' She sighed and shrugged. 'All this fuss...'

Bella turned on her, shouting, choking out words:

'Yes, all this *fucking* fuss. Nothing's ever good enough for you, is it? No matter what I do, it's just wrong because it's me.'

Bella looked down at the cake slice clutched tight in her hand; it felt hard, solid – comforting. The cold glint of metal. She couldn't seem to let it go.

'What do you *want* from me? What can I do that would be *right*? You don't even like me, never mind love me. Why did you bother to have me? *Why?* You've never wanted me, have you? *Have* you?' Bella screamed into her mother's face.

Alessandra's eyes looked huge, flecked with shock and fear; she recoiled in tiny flinches as the words struck her.

Bella raised the silver cake slice high and slammed it down hard into the middle of the cake, splattering great gobbets of mousse across the table. Raspberry coulis spurted blood-like over the crisp white cloth.

Gerald folded his hand around hers, firmly guiding it down to the table, releasing her fingers.

'No,' said Bella, wiping her nose with the back of her hand, and laughed. It seemed so obvious. 'You never have. It's as simple as that.' She looked down at the smashed cake, the silver slice, the white cloth with its splatters of violent red.

She was too weary to drive back now. She'd go in the morning, as soon as it was light. Now, all she wanted was a long, hot bath and some sleep. Her ribs seemed to hurt from crying, but there were no tears now. She was calm. The unsayable had been said, and it was a release.

Gerald came up to her room as she was getting ready for her bath.

'Your mother wants to talk to you. She wants to explain. Just talk to her. Please.'

'I'm sorry, Dad. I've had enough. I'm not in the mood to hear her justifying the way she is.'

'I know it's hard. She does try. She can't help it really.'

'*Dad*. Let's just leave it, OK?'

'All right.' His shoulders sagged and he looked tired. 'Maybe in the morning though, hmm?'

'Maybe.' She smiled, and gave him a hug. 'I'm sorry about the mess.' He shooed away her apology with a wave of his hand.

'Forget it. Still – mostly air, indeed!' He patted her cheek.

* * *

She is sitting on the floor, clutching her knees close to her chest, in the big cupboard under the stairs. If she stands on tippy-toes, she can just reach the light-switch, so sometimes she comes in here with Fernando, her fluffy toy frog, and some paper and her best felt-tips. She draws princesses, herself as Chief Princess of course, attended by her friends as smaller, minor princesses, all wearing long dresses and yellow crowns studded with painstakingly drawn over-large jewels.

So far, she has never been discovered in her secret hideaway, partly because she is careful not to stay too long and her mother is by now resigned to her habit of disappearing into thin air, and partly because, with the ironing board propped against the wall and Daddy's big winter coat and fishing things hanging from the coat hooks, she can't be seen by a casual glance. But today she does not have her paper or felt-tips. There was no time to get them.

This morning, she had been in the garden, pulling up the little weeds that Daddy had pointed out to her and picking raspberries from under the great green tent of the fruit cage. Mummy wants them to make into a special dessert. She eats as she picks, counting as a ritual: one, two, three plop into the bowl, and one is pushed into her mouth. When the bowl is full, she takes it into the house, trailing her hand dreamily along the wall as she goes. Mummy says thank you for being such a good girl and she hoped she hadn't eaten too many while she was picking because it would spoil her appetite for lunch. Mummy swishes through to the dining room.

'Bella!'

She freezes in the kitchen, her hand poised to take another raspberry, then starts to creep towards the other door, the hall, the front door and safety. Alessandra is screaming for Gerald to come and see what that impossible child has done now.

'Raspberry finger marks all over the wallpaper. Bella! Come here!' She is almost at the front door when she feels herself grabbed by the arm and whirled round.

'You did it to spite me, didn't you? Didn't you?' Her mother's face is only inches from hers; she can smell the sweet soapiness of face powder and jasmine bath oil. Her mother's eyes look huge, bright and flecked with fire, like a tiger's.

'I didn't,' she whispers. 'I didn't.'

'Yes, you did. Don't lie to me.' A sharp volley of slaps stings the backs of her legs. 'Now go to your room and stay out of my sight for the rest of the day.'

She is biting her lip, concentrating on not crying. She won't let *her* see her cry, she won't.

She starts to climb the stairs to her room, then hears voices in the kitchen so creeps back down and slides soundlessly into the cupboard. From the far end, behind the soft bulk of Daddy's coat, she strains to hear what they are saying, but she is not sure what it means.

'...enough,' says her father. '...didn't mean it.'

'...take her side.'

'...no sides ...the same side.'

'...try so hard.'

'...to help you... punishing her won't bring—'

'Don't, Gerald. Please.'

The sound of light footsteps, running upstairs. The click of the bathroom lock.

She opens the cupboard door a crack. She sees a narrow slice of hallway, a strip of the kitchen door – open. She treads carefully across the hall to peer in. Her father is standing at the sink, with his back to her, looking out of the window. He is washing up. The green and white china cup looks so small in his hands, like part of her dolls' teaset. It must be very dirty because he turns it around and around, scouring at the inside. He must have thought of a good joke because his shoulders are shaking the way they do sometimes when he laughs. She would like to know the joke, too, but she feels

strange and sick and afraid, so she sneaks back past the raspberry-
printed walls and out of the French windows into the garden to
squeeze out through the gap in the fence to the field and the long,
long grass beyond.

* * *

And in the morning, when her father knocked on her door with a
cup of tea, she was gone.

28

The light on her answerphone flashed manically, the tape full of unreturned calls. Her father phoned most of all, leaving weary messages. She didn't want to phone in case her mother answered and she couldn't see the point of talking to Dad either. He'd only try to do his UN diplomat act, coaxing her into coming for a visit, assuring her it would be different this time, apologizing for Alessandra at the same time as justifying her, defending her.

* * *

Anthony had just chucked the office sponge basketball at her head when her phone rang. She hurled it back, hitting his coffee mug.

'Ant, I'm NOT in the mood.' She ignored his making faces at her. It was Gerald.

'Hi, Dad,' she said, without enthusiasm. 'How are you?' Great, trap me at work, why don't you?

The basketball bounced once in the middle of her desk; she punched it over towards the photocopier and mouthed 'Bugger off!'

'Please tell me you're not ringing for the reason I think you're ringing.' She delivered a series of 'hmms' and 'uh-uhs'.

'If she's so sorry and wants to explain, why is she unable to pick up a telephone herself, may I ask?'

She sensed Anthony trying to eavesdrop and gave him the Kreuzer Raised Eyebrow, guaranteed to turn most men to stone at fifty paces. He switched on the radio for discreet, camouflaging music.

'Course I'd have bloody listened,' she dropped her voice. 'She's damned me without giving me a chance – as usual, I might add. What's she got to be afraid of? That's ridiculous.'

'I've absolutely no idea. Why should I have? I haven't seen him. You two are so fucking fond of him, you ring him up. Then you can all play Happy Families together. Won't that be *so* sweet? Why not take a picture of you all grouped around the fireplace for your next Christmas card?'

'Being like what? Dad, I really can't see the point of this. I'd be very happy to see you, on your own, if you want to come over some time, but not to talk about this fairy-tale she-loves-you-really-she-just-can't-show-it *bollocks*. Anyway, I have to go now. Got a meeting. Yes, right now. Goodbye. Yup, 'bye.'

A mug of fresh coffee appeared on her desk and two fingers of Kit-Kat. 'Thanks, Ant.'

'No sweat. Sorry about the ball, miss.'

'Class detention tonight.'

* * *

When she got home from work, she plonked herself in front of the TV, letting the stream of fleeting images wash over her without absorbing them: game shows with audiences apparently all on Ecstasy, soaps where she didn't know the storyline or the characters, even sports programmes where she didn't care who won or understand any of the rules. Sometimes, she forced herself to go into her studio, pushing open the door against stacks of paintings, blank prepared canvases, old sketch-books. The brush in her hand felt awkward, as clumsy as a trowel. Pictures lumbered into her head as if wading through molten lead, then merged into muddy pools as soon as she tried to capture them. Downstairs again, she stared at the brush still in her grasp as if it were an alien object, its purpose a mystery.

* * *

The post plopped onto the mat. Bound to be nothing but bills and circulars, she thought, but a postcard on the top caught her eye. She picked it up, with a few envelopes beneath it.

The postcard was from Viv, still in Birmingham spending some time at head office – 'Hello, snotface. Hope you're OK and not brooding too much about Will. Sorry if I was bit of an insensitive so-and-so – it was only because I thought you two were so right for each other. Now I suppose I've only gone and made it worse. Sorry, sorry again. Do go and see Nick if you need cheering up (he'll need it if you don't and he loves your spicy prawn thing). Back next week.' Estimate for replacing broken sash-cords on three windows. Creditcard bill – open that later. Flyers advertising a new restaurant and a beauty salon with 'Special Offer: Half Price Eyelash And Eyebrow Tinting!' Was that two eyes for the price of one? And why did they capitalize each word? Was it supposed to make you think they were Telling You Something Important? That was one thing she didn't need, she thought, furrowing her straight, dark brows at herself in the hall mirror.

Oh, hello, she hadn't seen that elegant script for quite a long time: Letter from Her Mother (that did merit capitals). What beautiful handwriting she had, with elongated ascenders and descenders like elaborate scrolls of icing on a wedding cake; no doubt the letter within was packed with poison, a razor-sharp dagger in a jewelled scabbard.

Don't say Alessandra had actually written to apologize? She'd better phone up the Vatican to report a Modern Day Miracle. No, more likely it would be a justification, an implied blaming of Bella. This should be entertaining.

She hotted up her coffee with water from the kettle and opened the letter.

Dear Bella

I'm surprised she didn't put the Dear in quote marks.

I am unaccustomed to writing, or indeed talking, about my emotions so you may appreciate how difficult it must be for me.

Indeed? How difficult it all is – poor Alessandra, got at by nasty Bella.

I think we are so alike in so many ways.

Alike! Ha! Bollocks we are. We're completely different.

I know we both tend to shut ourselves off from those we love most when we feel hurt or vulnerable.

I do not. I'm very open.

Will's face came into her mind, his voice: 'I wish I could really know you.' She saw flashes of herself: her own averted face, her pinched-shut lips, her swift exits through doorways, leaving awkward conversations behind.

I apologize...

Couldn't she actually say 'I'm sorry'? Did she have to be so formal all the time?

...if you feel let down by me or that I have not shown you as much love or warmth as you would have liked.

This could have been worded by a lawyer. Wouldn't she take some responsibility for being so cold? Some – some blame? (Will's voice echoed through her: 'She's the Wicked Witch of the West and you're sweet little Dorothy.')

I do not believe that I have been such a bad mother.

Ha! You wouldn't, would you?

I wish I could have been a better one. Perhaps all mothers do. We both did our best to feed and clothe you, provide a safe and stable home for you. We always welcomed your friends, encouraged you to develop your talents, allowed you a great degree of independence.

Hmm. Only because you didn't give a toss.

All I can say is that I did the best I could – being the person I am. I would never deliberately upset you. I dare say I could have been a 'better' mother...

Ah-ha. Interesting you put that in quotes – definitely an alien concept.

...and I will try my hardest. I do not want to justify myself or feel that I ought to...

But you will anyway.

...my own upbringing was very different. We had very little money, as is often the case with immigrants, so perhaps I gave too much importance to providing for you rather than giving you the attention you feel you needed. Later, there were other problems too that affected me very badly. Perhaps, one day, I will tell you about them.

Oh, a cliffhanger? Very slick. Problems, such as? Lost a lipstick when you were twenty? Curdled the hol-landaise once fifteen years ago? Won't specify because you know it would sound feeble?

You are wrong in thinking I don't love you. Very wrong. I'm sorry if I do not show it as much as you would like – or as much as I would like.

Why couldn't you put you do love me? I love you. Is that really so hard to say, to write? (She thought of Will: 'You can't say it, can you?' and her response, 'What? The "L" word?') But surely only her mother could manage to phrase it so that it actually appeared on the page in the negative.

A quiet voice in her head asked: 'And have you ever told her you loved her?'

I hope we can both try to be better friends to one another.
With much love, Mum.

Bella peered at the signature. She could see where her mother had started to write 'Alessandra'. The down-stroke of the A had been carefully turned into the too-deep central valley of the M instead. *Oh please. Mum. Very convincing. Why didn't you send a coconut cake along with it? That would prove you were a good Mum'.*

She refolded the letter to put it back in the envelope. There was something else in there; she shook out the envelope. Two photographs fell onto the table. She had never seen them before, nor any like them. Most of the family photos were slightly formal, awkward poses or ones of Alessandra looking glamorous or a few of Bella on her own or playing with a friend. Her father had taken most of them, so was hardly in any himself. But these were different. One of them was slightly out of focus: in it, Alessandra stood, looking pretty and relaxed in a summer dress with her hair loose; she was carrying Bella on one hip, apparently tickling her under her chin; little Bella was laughing. When had it been taken? Bella turned it over. No date. She looked about two, maybe three.

The other photograph was sharper, clearer. It was a beach. Alessandra was kneeling on the sand, holding her hair out of her face and watching Bella, who was just sticking in a flag on top of a large sandcastle that reached up to her shoulders. It had turrets studded with shells, and a moat. Again, there was no date, but Bella thought she couldn't have been more than three. Looking at it more closely, she recognized the little swimsuit she was wearing in the picture. It had been navy, she remembered now, with a little white skirt and a stripy, V-shaped bit at the top. She'd forgotten all about it until now, although she'd been absolutely thrilled when her mother had bought it for her. It had been so grown-up, her first proper swimsuit, instead of wearing just her pants with no top as if she was a baby. Perhaps she would ring Dad and ask him if he knew the date and where it had been taken. Bella stared deep into the first photograph. What was so odd about it? It was like a thousand family photographs. It was delightful, but ordinary. She looked more closely at her mother's face. There, that was it. Although it was slightly blurred, she could see that Alessandra was looking at the young Bella with rapt attention. The photograph was a whole little world, with only Alessandra and Bella in it, mother and child completely absorbed in each other. She shut her eyes as if she might recapture it.

Warm arms around her. The smell of jasmine and face powder and sea. Rubbing noses.

She looked down at the photos in her hand, then propped them up on the mantelpiece.

* * *

Bella went round the supermarket in a daze, gliding up and down the aisles as if guided by remote control. She picked up packets and tins in a trance, mechanically transferred vegetables from their heaped displays into bags, dropping them into her trolley. What did she need? Why was she here? She picked up a pot of yoghurt and stood staring at the label, biting her lip as if considering her selection; another careful shopper expertly assessing the list of ingredients, the price, the weight, the nutritional analysis. Modified starch, she read, citric acid; 104 kcal per 100g, 208 kcal per pot. Was that good? Did that mean she should have it or not?

Again and again, Will filled her thoughts, her vision. She saw him asleep, his irrepressible hair curling against the pillow; out walking, stopping frequently when he got excited by their conversation. 'Can't you walk and talk at the same time?' she'd say. 'No,' he'd catch her arm and hold her so he could talk face to face, see her reaction; in the shower, letting the water stream over his face, running down his chest, washing the lather down his legs; even here in the supermarket, skidding down the aisles with the trolley at breakneck speed, making car-chase screeching noises as he sharply rounded a corner; in bed, his face relaxed, his eyes shining as he looked at her, wound his finger into a lock of her hair – 'See? We're entangled. You'll never get shot of me now.'

She tried to push the thoughts away, as solid as if they were boulders. Then the photos flashed into her mind, the ones of her and her mother. Impatient with herself, she concentrated on the chill cabinet in front of her. What else did she need? She stared at a carton of orange juice as if the answer might be written on its side.

At the till, she signed to pay. 'Jawan-kashba?' She felt like a foreigner, an alien in her own land. 'D'ya want cashback?' the cashier repeated. She nodded automatically and remained silent. 'How *much?*' Emphatic now, impatient. Her gaze fell on the sign by the till: You may withdraw up to £50 cash back when you pay by any of the following debit cards. 'Fifty,' she parroted. Mindlessly, she unloaded the trolley, packing the goods into the boot of her car, wedging the eggs in snugly as if she cared whether or not they made it safely home unbroken.

She manoeuvred around the one-way system of the car park, driving at a snail's pace, forcing herself to notice people backing out, shoppers with uncontrollable trolleys, below-eye-level children. She saw his face clear in her head, his half-smile as he listened, his eyebrows straightening as he thought. She blinked hard and swallowed. She didn't have to think of him. Wouldn't. Anything else. Anything.

Then, as if through mist, she thought she saw Patrick ahead of her, walking away. He half-turns as if he senses her behind him, but still she cannot see if it is him. As she breathes in, her nostrils flinch at the smell of damp, a sly odour of mould. The hairs rise on the back of her neck, goose bumps freckle her arms. Perhaps he will turn around, beckon her so she can follow him. Surely he will call her? Chill and dank, fear crawls over her, creeping across her shoulders, scuttling down her spine, sliding towards her knees. Patrick! she wants to shout after him. Patrick!

A sudden bang. The crunch of metal. The sickening screech of rubber on road. She was jerked forward and left, then jolted back as her seatbelt held her fast.

'You fucking *stupid* cow! What the *fuck* do you think you're doing? You must have *seen* me!'

A man was bellowing at her through her window, standing so close she could see right into his mouth. Was this how a dentist saw the world, she wondered. A gold crown glinted near the front of his teeth, incongruous against the angry dark square of his mouth.

She could see that he was still shouting. His lips were moving quickly, his mouth changing from shape to shape; he was pointing. There was a bang as he slammed his hand down at the side of her bonnet. If she could just hold onto the steering wheel everything would be all right. Her hands felt numb. A glance at the steering-wheel to check that it was still there, confirm that her hands were clenching it tight; beneath the wheel, her legs shook uncontrollably.

A policeman was talking to the bellowing man, laying a hand on his arm, drawing him firmly to one side. A tapping on her window. Another policeman was making a little circling motion with one finger and pointing. How sweet. Was it a game?

'Open your window,' he was saying through the glass.

Open your window. She could almost hear the cogs in her mind slowly whirring, then meshing into place. She watched her arm move through the air as if wading through water; it stretched out for the handle, grasped the knob.

'Switch off the ignition and get out of the vehicle please.'

Bella looked back at him. His expression shifted and he reached across her to turn the key. The door was opened.

'Are you injured, miss? Hang on. Don't move. Stay there.'

Someone else was squatting down beside her, asking her questions. Had she any pain anywhere? How did her neck feel? Could she move her legs? Her feet? What was her name? Did she know what day it was?

'Okey-dokey. Let's get you out of there. You're going to be absolutely fine.'

A soft spongy collar was carefully placed around her neck. A click as her seat belt was unfastened.

She took uncertain steps, a newborn creature testing its legs. The ground felt unfamiliar; her feet were weighted, too heavy to lift. She could not stop shaking. It was very cold. Something warm and heavy was placed around her shoulders, someone's padded jacket. There was an arm holding her. She was not alone.

'...badly in shock,' a voice said.

The policeman spoke to her slowly.

'Is there someone you need us to call?'

Will. I want Will. Someone pressed a wad of tissues into her hand.

She couldn't call Will. Mummy and Daddy ought to come and fetch her. They would make everything all right again. No. No, they wouldn't. Wouldn't want to see her now. She shook her head. A policeman gave her a small tube to blow into; a little green light glowed and he said she was 'all clear'.

'We'll have to ask you some questions,' said the policeman, but you need to be checked over first. OK?'

Yes, she nodded. She understood. There were questions to be asked. She needed to be checked.

First she was to climb these steps into the ambulance. Had someone been hurt? As she was helped up the steps, she looked back at her car and saw that a small white van was embedded in the front right wing: Fiona's Flowers – Something for Every Occasion.

That is her car. She was in that car. Her whole body started to tremble, as if a tremor were shaking the earth beneath her feet.

The paramedic asked her if she'd feel better lying down. Why would she want to lie down? She wasn't a bit sleepy. She was guided into a chair, with a blanket tucked around her.

At the hospital, she was given the all-clear.

'You really ought to have someone fetch you,' the nursing sister said. 'Is there someone you can call?'

'It's fine. Really. Thank you. I'll just phone a taxi.' The sister points to the payphone.

'There's a number on the wall there. Will anyone be in when you get home? You shouldn't really be on your own when you're in shock.'

'No. Yes. My— there'll be someone there when I get in.' Nodding now, backing away. 'I'm fine. Honestly. I'm fine.'

Ignored, the pile of post by the front door spread into the hall like unstuck tiles; unnoticed, sticky glasses and crusted dishes crowded the worktop; unseen, the garden grew on, its glory shut out behind the curtains.

There was a strange ringing sound. Bella flapped vaguely at the side of her head to make it go away. No. There it was again. A ringing. Definitely a ringing. And now banging. Bloody neighbours. Noisy people. It was very noisy around here. What was the point of moving away from London and going without proper olives if there was still so much noise? They should sssh. Someone should complain. Yes. She would write to them. To the people. The people you complain to. That's what she would do. More ringing. She stretched out for her alarm clock and hit it. The button was already down. Still ringing.

Bella swivelled her body around and slowly lowered her legs to the floor. Shoes. She should find some shoes. Looked down at her feet. In shoes. That was handy. Banging again now. Right. She would go and sort them out. She pushed herself to her feet. Wandered out to the landing. Noisy people.

'Sssh!'

She stood at the top of the stairs. Below her, the stairway stretched, elongating itself so that it seemed as deep as the Grand Canyon. She wondered if there would be an echo.

'Hell-o-o-o,' she called.

'Hello?' returned from below. Brilliant. There was an echo. 'Hel-loo-oo-o-oo-oooo-o-oo,' she called again.

'Bella? Hello! It's me!'

That wasn't such a good echo. Wasn't it supposed to say the same thing? It seemed an awfully long way to the bottom. She sat down abruptly on the top step and started to make her way down on her bum, step by step.

Near the bottom, she was confronted by a pair of eyes looking at her through the letter slot.

Bella waved.

'Bella! Thank God.' Viv's eyes widened. 'What *are* you doing?'

'Why are you in my letter box?'

'I'm not in your letter box, you idiot. I'm trying to look through to see if you're there.'

Bella looked around. 'But I am here.'

'Yes, I can see that now.' Bella seemed to be thinking. 'There was a ringing.'

'Yes. It was me. I've been leaning on your bell for ten minutes. Babe – it's bloody cold out here.'

'I could give you a little drinkie to keep you warm.' Bella pulled herself up by the banister. 'I've got a funnel.'

'No. That's not what I meant. Could you let me in, d'you think? I'm getting cramp.'

'You should take salt for that. And not be getting into people's letter boxes. Will you stop ringing if I let you in?'

'I'm *not* ringing.'

'Oh. It's stopped.'

As Bella opened the door, Viv practically fell inside onto the mat.

'Gone numb,' she said. 'I've been kneeling on your doorstep. What the hell's the matter with you? Why haven't you been answering your phone? Your answer-phone tape's full.'

'Do you still want a funnel?'

'No, I don't want a bloody funnel. Bel? You haven't —' Viv suddenly grabbed her by the shoulders '— *had* anything, have you?'

'Yes, thank you. Do you want some?'

'What? What?'

'What?'

'Yes, WHAT, you idiot. What have you had?'

'No thank you. I've had enough now.'

Viv shook her.

'Bella. I'm serious now. Tell me – exactly – what you have eaten or drunk.'

Bella thought for a minute.

'Bikkits. Jaffa cakes.' She held up three fingers.

'Three jaffa cakes?'

Bella shook her head. 'Three packets.'

'They've never had this effect on me. What else?'

'More—'

'More what? Come on.'

'More-teezers.' She giggled. 'Family-size packet. Bella-size packet.'

'And? What else? Tablets, was it?'

'No, no. 'm not ill. No tablets. Maltesers.'

'Yes, you said those.'

'Mmm.' She nodded. 'Wine... and some Bailey's... and a fuck of a lot of vodka.'

Bella sat on the stairs, watching Viv dash from room to room, listening to her babble on: why hadn't Bella phoned someone? Nick would have come round – could have given her the number in Birmingham – was this all about Will – what on earth was going on – unbelievable – all this mess – pile of mail – her office said – phoned in sick – she'd been frantic – she'd no idea – how long had Bella been – water – drink loads of water – how could Bella have been so stupid –.

It was very bad to be rushing all the time, like that. Gives you indigestion. And that other thing you're not supposed to have. Stress.

Viv squeezed past her to run upstairs, opening drawers and cupboards.

Reappeared stuffing clothes into a bag.

'You're coming to stay with us for a few days. No arguments.' She swept through to the bathroom and scooped up Bella's toothbrush and flannel. 'You had me shit-scared, you know. I just got back to discover you'd disappeared off the face of the earth.' Viv hugged her. 'You've got no idea, have you?'

'What?' said Bella.

* * *

She was lying in Viv and Nick's spare room, swaddled in Viv's fluffy dressing-gown. There was a glass of water by the bed. And a bucket. She could hear their voices, hushed outside the bedroom door. The reassuring whisper of grown-ups. The door opened a peep.

'Bel? You asleep yet?'

'Mmm-mm. Viv?'

Viv came in and perched on the edge of the bed. 'What is it, babe?'

'I'm sorry.'

'For what? You don't have to be sorry.'

'For being a daft bugger. Thank you for being so nice.'

'Night-night, you old silly. Sleep tight.'

The police were very polite. She had been on the main road, the other driver turning out of a side street. He thought she had stopped, he said, she was obviously letting him go, any idiot could see that; then she'd suddenly moved forward so he'd gone straight into her. Anyone would have done, he said, she must be a loony. Eyewitness reports conflicted. One thought she had almost come to a halt. Another said the van had swung out way too fast, she couldn't have avoided it. And it had been indisputably her right of way.

* * *

Viv drove her to the pound where her car had been taken after the accident. The other driver's insurance company had sent someone to inspect it; pronounced it a write-off. She could remove any belongings before it was taken to the wrecker's yard.

'Holy shit, Bel.' Viv looked at the car and laid a hand on Bella's shoulder. 'Christ, you were lucky.'

Viv started to empty the glove compartment while Bella went round the back to open the boot, keeping her eyes averted from the front and side of the car.

The stench was appalling. A dead smell, fleshy, of rot and decay. She retched and backed away. What on earth was it? Realization flashed through her. The shopping. Viv started to come near, then the smell hit her. She covered her face with her hands.

'What is it?'

'I don't know – chicken, prawns – everything. I feel sick.'

'OK. I'm going in.' Viv held her nose and plunged in, scooping up the two squelchy-looking bags and cramming them in another carrier, knotting the ends to seal it tight. She ran off, holding it at arm's length, to find a suitable bin.

Her breathing was tight, shallow. She felt sick, faint. That stench. And the car. She was in that car.

I have to make myself look. I have to.

The front and part of the right wing were crushed, as casually crumpled as a scrap of paper. Her fingers ran over the metal, feeling the ridges, the dents. Both headlamps were broken, shards of glass still clinging to the metal rims, as shocking as a pair of stamped-on spectacles. The wing, just in front of the driver's seat, dipped into a ragged valley, as if punched by a maniac.

Now, a cramp clenches her stomach and nausea swells into her throat. She flails her arm to clutch at the crushed metal for support and lurches forward, bent double, vomit splashing onto the tarmac. A dry inhalation of breath. Again she heaves, her whole body wrenched by spasms, and again.

A hand holds her hair back from her face, cool on her forehead. A quiet voice, soothing. An arm around her shoulders, steadying her, holding her. Viv.

Back at Viv and Nick's, they cup their hands round mugs of tea like shipwreck survivors.

'That gave me a hell of a fright, seeing your car. I suddenly realized – what if?' Viv stares down into her tea. 'You must take care of yourself. Who else would make me laugh and cook me lemon chicken?'

Viv asks if Bella has told Will.

'Why would I? Why would he care?'

'God, you can be irritating. Because he's probably still mad about you, that's why. I've never seen anyone so in love.'

'Oh, doyou think so?' A polite request. Bella's voice is flat, expressionless.

'You know he was. And so were you. You were sickening to watch, the two of you, like cute puppies falling over each other. Bleugh.'

Bella opens her mouth to speak.

'And don't even think about denying it.' Viv cuts her off. 'I've never seen you so happy. Sorry to say this, but not even with Patrick – nothing like. You had this incredible sort of – radiance. Your skin glowed.'

'Too much blusher.'

'Shut up. You always do that. Joke about stuff that really matters to you. Just stop it for once.' Viv drains the last of her tea. 'Don't you remember Nick teasing you because you wouldn't stop talking about Will? Don't you remember him saying: "So, what would Will say to that? Tell us Will's favourite colour, Bella. It's only midnight. We've got all night. Tell us more about how much he makes you laugh but how he can be serious too. Tell us again why his eyebrows are so adorable." How can you forget?'

'I know. I haven't forgotten.'

'Can't you, well, ring him up or something?' Bella shakes her head.

'It's too late.'

He won't want me now. And I don't know how. I haven't the words.

'How you doing there, babe?'

'Marvellous. Loving every second.' Bella closes her eyes and starts to cry. 'Peculiar. Crap. Shaky. Glad to be in one piece. Can I have a hug?' she says.

Viv holds her tight.

'And don't you dare scare me like that again – or I'll have to shoot you.' They laugh together, tears streaming down their cheeks.

30

'Of course you can. I told you – any time.' Fran sounds genuinely pleased.

Bella explains about her knock in the car.

'I still feel a bit shaky, but I know I have to drive soon or I won't be able to do it.'

The insurance company are processing the claim; they will decide on the value of her car and, eventually, send a cheque. She intends to start looking at second-hand cars in a week or so, when she feels a bit more robust. In the meantime, she is planning to hire one for the weekend.

'Thank you for not, well, *exiling* me.' Fran laughs.

'You daft thing. You know I'm very fond of you – *whatever* happens – may have happened – with you and Will.'

* * *

Saturday morning is grey and dreary, with spots of half-hearted rain. A home-made tarte Tatin is swaddled in place on the passenger seat. At least it would be an undemanding companion.

No fiddling with the radio. No 'Actually, I think maybe you should have turned left back there.' No making her laugh when she was trying to concentrate. No resting a hand on her leg so that she would be aware of his presence at her side, always.

Fran is out in the garden, apparently undeterred by the damp – 'Perfect for planting.'

She hugs Bella.

'You must take some redcurrants when you go. I've a freezer full. I know you'll think of something interesting to do with them. There's only so much redcurrant jelly one person can get through, even if I ate lamb every night.'

Bella works alongside Fran in the garden, now adept at spotting which are weeds and which are not, what to cut back and what to leave. The sound of secateurs reminds her of Will, the way Fran dips in and out of the borders, casually pulling up a weed as she passes, snipping off a faded bloom. Fran avoids talking about him, Bella notices, and speaks instead of her late husband, Hugh.

'I still miss him, y'know? It's over five years ago now. I used to wonder when I'd "get over it" – as if it were some kind of obstacle course. I remember seeing it in my head like a great, craggy rock I'd have to climb. I thought I'd get to the other side, then maybe life would go back to normal. No bloody idea.' She laughs at herself. 'Come in out of this drizzle and let's get some tea.

'I went through all these different feelings. At first, I just could not believe it. Hughie was so alive, do y'see? I kept thinking I saw him. I followed some man in a similar sort of corduroy jacket halfway around Sainsbury's. Daft I know.'

Bella shakes her head. 'It's not daft.'

'And I was so angry with him. Why hadn't he looked after his health better? – he'd already had a minor stroke before – how dare he leave me alone? Then I felt it was all my fault. I should have done something, anything. I was a bad person because I'd let him eat butter. I should have made him take up tennis. When it really sank in, I kept crying in all the most unlikely places. I had to run out of the chemist because I – so stupid – saw that Mycil powder he used to use for his athlete's foot. And I thought how ironic it was when he didn't take enough exercise. Then in the garden, I'd be digging up potatoes for supper and I'd suddenly look down and see that I'd dug enough for two and I'd be off again.'

Bella tops up their mugs.

'But – it did get better.' Fran waves a hand at Bella's eyebrow, twitching into a doubting arch. 'No. I know what you're thinking. It used to make me so angry when people patronized me with all that time's the best healer stuff. But my feelings did shift. I haven't forgotten him, God knows. Things can never go back to being as they were before. Life's different. I'm different. But the pain's not sharp now. I can *enjoy* my memories of him without feeling wretched all the time. And, somewhere along the line, I let myself off the hook.'

There is a silence. Fran gets up and refills the kettle, delves deep into the bread crock for 'something to toast'.

'You've lost someone, too, haven't you?'

The clink of the kettle lid. The striking of a match. The soft hiss of the gas.

'I'm sorry. Perhaps you prefer not to talk about it?'

'I – it's not – I find it hard. I don't. It's so—' She presses her lips tight shut, to hold it in, then, suddenly, her mouth trembles and opens, gaping wide. And Bella is babbling. She is so scared – she couldn't let go of Patrick – she didn't dare – it would be like a betrayal – he needed her to cling on or he'd be really, really gone.

Around her, the kitchen swims into a blur.

And then she'd met Will and she'd felt bad, guilty for loving him so much – then terrified she'd lose him as well. She wouldn't be able to bear it – not Will – she couldn't – she'd be eaten away by the pain of it – cease to exist. And she'd messed things up and driven him away and it was awful. He didn't even know that she loved him because she couldn't say it, she was so afraid. She just knew if she owned it, admitted it, he'd be taken away – she'd be punished – she wouldn't be allowed to be so happy, not for long – just enough to lull her into a false sense of security. She'd get used to him, and life would be rosy, then – BAM – and he'd be hit by a truck or get cancer or flit off to Auckland – and she wouldn't be able to stand it. Only now she'd lost him anyway, but it wasn't so very bad because at least she'd expected it, engineered it – at least she knew where she was this way. Really, it wasn't so very bad. Not so very bad.

And Fran's arms are around her; she is stroking her hair and holding her. She is making comforting, ssshushing sounds into her hair.

'And now I'm getting you all – sno-o-o-t-tty,' Bella wails. 'Ssh, ssh. I never liked this shirt anyway.'

Bella's breaths lurch from her lungs. Her shoulders shake in spasms. Unleashed sobs wrench at her chest. She tries to gulp them down. Tears scrawl mascara in a spidery calligraphy over her cheeks; she wipes her nose with the back of her hand.

'But it's much worse than that – m-much worse.' Fran is still holding her, and Bella looks up at her.

'I've never told anyone. You'll hate me when you know.'

'Hush, hush. I could never hate you.'

Bella is quiet now, even calm. She blows her nose and lets out a long sigh as she remembers. At last, it is time to tell.

* * *

The knowledge has been swirling through her for weeks now, maybe even months if she dare admit it. When had she framed that first thought? Allowed herself to think it? It feels as if it had started deep in her bones, then seeped out, slipping into her bloodstream, making its way to her heart, her head. Now it is like a prickling itch beneath her skin, refusing to be ignored. She can only create the luxury of forgetting when she hurls herself into something else, so she spends long hours at work, gets up early to go swimming, relishing for once the smell of chlorine, climbing up her nostrils, stinging her eyes, scouring her shameful, selfish thoughts. She even begins a tapestry, transferring an old painting she had done of her parents' house onto graph paper as a guide; in the evenings she has licence to concentrate only on the tiny, colour-pencilled squares, sink into her own tiny stitches, a technician hovering over a microscope, on the verge of discovery.

Patrick comments with a laugh, 'Anyone would think you had a lover, Bel. All this staying late at the office.'

'Er... nonsense, darling. Important client, that's all.' She had pretended to be flustered to tease him, as if he had found her out, unearthed her great secret, and he had laughed.

But he hasn't discovered it. Doesn't seem to have a clue. Bella almost wishes she did have a lover, a proper reason, something tangible, someone else she could point to and say, 'See? That's why.' How simple that would be.

As each day passes, she can feel the gap widening between her intentions and her actions. She watches herself moving around the flat, one step behind her false ghost image, sneering at its bright manner, its smiles. Why can't Patrick see it? Surely he will suddenly catch a glimpse of her there, shivering behind that horrible smiling façade?

'Okey-dokey?' Patrick pats her knee, tapping the crossword in the paper with his pencil in unison.

'Yup. Fine,' she answers, feeling like a trained spaniel.

· · ·

She starts to timetable 'Telling Patrick' in her head, then in her diary. Not this weekend because we're going up to his parents. Not in the week because he'll be coming back late from that job in Walthamstow every night. Next weekend? Maybe. Then next weekend comes and they have friends for supper or Patrick seems under the weather or she has a period pain. Maybe she'll do it Tuesday, quickly before it's in the run-up to his birthday or, oh my God, then it'll be Christmas. Maybe it'd be better to wait till after then.

* * *

And so, now it is January 18th and she is standing in a small white room, looking down at Patrick's body spread out before her.

'I'm an impostor,' she tells herself, 'a horrible cheat who didn't deserve him.' But still, through the shock, she knows she is glad she didn't tell him, didn't spoil his last few months; she is glad she never said the words:

'Patrick. I can't do this any more. Be with you. I don't – I don't love you.'

* * *

Fran comes to say good night, tucking her in tightly as if she is a child. Bella pokes her chin over the turned edge of the sheet, comforting as a folded sandwich, and looks around at the rose-patterned wallpaper, with its oddly cheering misaligned joins and irregular edges. The bedside lamp shines on a few bright buttercups, sprawling in a tiny blue jug with sprigs of feathery fennel and daisy-like feverfew. Funny, she thinks, I've never noticed how pretty buttercups are before – how perfect each petal is, how smooth. She drifts into a doze, their yellow heads like tiny suns warming her as she closes her eyes.

Patrick is walking ahead of her, but she is finding it difficult to keep up, his long legs carrying him further from her with each step. Breathless, she reaches him at last and she taps him on the shoulder from behind. He turns round and seems surprised to see her there, annoyed even. Then he lies down on the ground, gesturing with his hand, inviting her to join him.

It is cold here, and the air feels thick and clammy on her skin. She stretches out on the ground beside him. In this milky light, even his face before her is a blur. Behind her, she feels the concrete kerb at her back; beneath her, the sharp stones of his grave. They dig into her skin, her flesh, but she tries not to wince, not to let him see. He doesn't seem to notice them at all. Suddenly, he strikes the headstone with his palm.

'Good solid headboard, eh?' And he laughs.

She starts to smile, trying to join in, to share the joke, but his face is at once serious again. As he takes her hand, she gasps; his skin is cold as stone and loose, like the skin on molten wax. She watches him lift her hand, as if it is a thing apart, and guide it towards the headstone. He makes her finger trace the inscription at the base.

R.I.P.

And he looks at her, then closes his eyes. She traces it again, feeling the grooves in the stone beneath her finger, letting them etch the letters in her mind. It is suddenly clear to her, obvious; even a fool could see it.

Now, she knows what he means, knows what it means. *R.I.P.* Rest in Peace. It is not for the dead, the dead who lie still in the crumbling earth; not for the dead who have no thoughts, no fears, their joys, their pain forgotten.

It is a message for the living.

Early morning. A thin wash of sunlight brushes the room. She opens her eyes and, quietly, begins to weep.

31

She rummages through her sketch-books. Somewhere here, yes. Here. There are several sketches – and her memory.

She begins to paint. It is as she remembers him best, his long form awkwardly folded into an armchair, one leg draped over the side. If only she could capture the way he rotated his foot as he read, first one way, then the other; she could draw it at an angle to suggest it, perhaps. She knows she must paint it all in one sitting, now while he is so clear in her head. She lets his voice wind its way into her ears once more, recalls now his touch with simple fondness, lets the essence of him quicken the sinews of her hands, spilling out onto the paper.

It is good, she realizes, better than she could have hoped. Sometimes, painting was work, work and more work, a battle with the limitations of the paint, the paper or canvas, frustration with the gulf between the image in her head and the insipid translation of it that she set down with her brush. But, occasionally, rare and precious, one came as a gift, flowing from her eyes, her mind, down through her hand, capturing her vision in front of her like a butterfly come to rest.

She phones first, to make sure it will be all right for her to come, saying she won't stay long, she doesn't want to impose, feeling her way through the pauses, wondering if she is welcome. The picture is carefully wrapped, laid on the back seat of the car.

As she raises her hand to the knocker, the door sweeps open. 'Bella!' Joseph, Patrick's father, gathers her close.

'Is that Bella here already?' calls Rose, running through and undoing her apron.

Their delight in seeing her stings her with shame. There is no word of reproach, no veiled hints that she might have visited sooner. Their apparent gratitude that she's bothered to drive all that way to come to see them is more mortifying than any criticism could have been. How could she have been so selfish?

'Come in, come in – and look who's here.'

Sophie, Patrick's young sister, jumps up and throws her arms around Bella.

'Soph! I didn't know you'd be here.'

'We haven't seen you for months. I thought you'd forgotten us.'

'Sophie!' Rose frowns at her. 'Don't be so rude.'

'Oh, Mum. Bel doesn't mind.'

Bella catches a look between Joseph and Rose. 'Oh, Bel! Don't cry. Shit. What have I said now?'

'Language!' says Rose. 'Please excuse her, Bella.'

'No. It's not that. It's not you, Soph, really. It's just me. And you're all being so *nice*.' She takes Joseph's proffered handkerchief.

'I can be horrible if you want,' offers Sophie. 'Mum says I'm horrible most of the time anyway.'

'I do *not*. You can be perfectly pleasant when you can be bothered, Sophie. But it's not trendy or wicked or whatever the thing is now, so you try and make out you're bored by everyone and everything. But now that you're twenty, it's just embarrassing.' Rose sweeps out to the kitchen.

'Wicked? Mum at the cutting edge of street slang as usual.' Sophie makes a naughty-schoolkid face and goofs her teeth at Bella. Bella goofs back. 'Dear God,' prays Sophie, 'send me a new mother.'

'Don't,' says Bella, 'or I'll give you mine. I'm thinking of hiring her out to improve familial harmony – one week with her and you'd appreciate just how lovely Rose is.'

'I brought you something, but I don't know if it's the right thing.'

'No need to bring anything,' says Rose.

'Just a pleasure to see you,' says Joseph. 'Is it your sticky lemon cake?' says Sophie.

Bella goes out to the car to fetch it. What if they hate it? What if they burst into tears? This could be a horrible mistake.

She holds it close to her body.

'I hope it doesn't make it worse. But I did it for you and I want you to have it.'

Bella hands the picture to Joseph. His eyes start to pool above the rims. He nods without speaking. Rose, close beside him on the sofa, clutches his arm. Tears spill down her powdery cheeks, run along the creases around her eyes.

'I didn't mean to upset you. I'm sorry. I thought – I don't know what I thought.'

Rose and Joseph are both shaking their heads.

No – they say – that's not it – they love it – hadn't expected it – there is nothing they could have loved more – nothing better she could possibly have given them – it's just, you see – Joseph looks round for his hankie – it's just so *Patrick*.

Sophie agrees, it is *very* Patrick, look at his foot there, you just know he's winding it round and round like a bloody clockwork toy the way he always did. Won't Alan love it when he sees it?

Alan is not expected until teatime, so Bella stays for tea. When he arrives, he kisses her cheek and holds her arms awkwardly for a few moments. He looks at her half-sideways, the way Patrick used to.

'The folks have missed you, you know.' She nods, abashed.

'The picture. They're really chuffed, you can tell. It was a good thing to do. The right thing. Thank you.'

She had forgotten this feeling, this being part of a family, however briefly. How much easier it was to get on with other people's relatives. Rose has forgotten to defrost the chops she had planned for supper, so Bella insists on making a meal for everyone, spinning a magic *mélange* out of an eclectic collection of fridge foragings. Sophie then begs for zabaglione and the two stand by the stove, swapping rude jokes and taking it in turns to whisk until their arms are stiff. The sweet golden foam is poured into glasses and they all eat in reverent silence, as if honouring some ancient ritual.

Rose won't hear of her driving back all that way at night. Bella must be exhausted. The bed's all made up anyway. They couldn't possibly let her go back so late. Absolutely not.

'But I haven't got my things...'

A clean nightie is presented, a new toothbrush found. She lets herself be fussed over for once.

After breakfast, Joseph walks round the garden with her, impressed by her new-found knowledge as she admires his plants by name. She holds their leaves between her fingers, comforted by the familiar feel of them, letting the names, the scents, roll round her head: thyme, she thinks, lemon balm, rosemary. *Rosmarinus officinalis*. Ah, rosemary.

'I'm glad you came. I don't imagine it's been easy for you either.'

'I'm much better than I was.'

Joseph clears his throat and leans over a plant to pull off a dead leaf. 'You wouldn't ever have married him, would you?'

Bella is silent, then lifts her gaze to meet his.

'It's all right.' He digs his hands down deep into his pockets. 'I think I knew quite a while ago. Rose doesn't. She thinks you were just being young folk, doing the modern thing.'

'I'm sorry.'

'You don't need to be. It's no good cheating on how you feel, is it?'

'S'pose not.'

He folds her in his arms, patting her back. 'Is that why you've kept away?'

She nods into his shoulder.

'I couldn't. I felt such a fraud. I thought you'd hate me.'

He tuts quietly into her hair, shaking his head.

Joseph walks her to her car and calls to the others to come and see her off. 'I hope you find him,' he says to her quietly, 'the one for you.'

32

'That is completely gorgeous, much too nice for you, you old slapper. I want it.' Viv lets the sleeve of the cherry two-piece slither between her fingers. Bella had worried that she would look ridiculously overdressed for her private view, especially when she had arrived and met one of the other artists who is wearing green denims and what Bella mentally catalogues as a mixed-media waistcoat, a garment that might be interesting if it was framed but looks ridiculous on an actual person. Fortunately, Donald MacIntyre is wearing an immaculately pressed suit and a snazzy red and black silk tie and Fiona, the gallery assistant, is in a smart little black dress. Both approve heartily of Bella's outfit, Fiona with a sidelong flare of her nostrils at Mr Wacky Waistcoat.

'You look stunning,' says Viv. 'I thought you'd be wearing an artist's smock. You can't compete with that waistcoat though – what *are* those strange, crunchy-looking bits? Give us a twirl then.'

Bella obliges and the skirt softly swings out around her legs. 'You must have splashed out. That never came from Oxfam.'

'It was Alessandra's. Mum's.'

Viv raises her eyebrows without comment.

'Too glam for me really.' Bella looks down at herself. 'Nonsense. It's very you.'

Nick gives an appreciative whistle and kisses her on the cheek. 'Show us some o' yer art then.' He feigns a nose-wipe-with-sleeve.

She points out her section of the exhibition and the two paintings in the window.

'I thought that looked like Will,' says Viv. 'Not his face exactly but something about the posture, the way he's standing. Shit, you *are* good.

Why've you been footling about all these years when you're a bloody genius, woman? Well, at least you're winding down at Scrotum Design.'

'Ssh.' Bella nods towards Seline.

'Where're the proud parents then?' asks Jane, a friend from London.

'Not here.'

'Oops, sorry, have I put my foot in it?'

'You *did* ask them, Bel, didn't you?' Viv joins in, narrowing her eyes at Bella.

'I did send them an invite.' Bella reaches for another canapé. 'But I forgot to post it till this morning.'

'Forgot, yeah. You meanie. They'd have loved to come. Don't scrunch your nose like that – it makes you look like a pig. Well, more fool you – they might have bought one.'

It should be one of the best evenings of her life. It almost is. She has good friends around her. Her work is on show in the best private gallery in the city and people are praising it. A pleasant, fizzy feeling hovers just beneath her skin. People are showering her with compliments, but she finds it hard to let them sink in. She feels herself discounting them, repelling them like water bouncing off an oilskin. *They're just being polite. They have to say something nice. They've drunk too much wine.* She smiles and nods and says her thank-yous, makes self-deprecating jokes, on guard against feeling too pleased.

But all she can think of is Will. She is glad *his* picture is in the window, facing the street, so she doesn't have to keep catching sight of it as she looks around the room. She keeps thinking how much he would have enjoyed this evening, what he would have said: he'd have been amused by that man over there, inspecting her brushwork at such close range that he is practically wiping his nose on it. She thinks of the way Will's hand would rest on the small of her back for a moment as he passed her, how he would stroke her hair away from her face casually, almost without noticing. He'd have liked Donald MacIntyre with his dry wit and keen intelligence. And they even had canapés and dippy things. Will loved food on sticks. ('Don't you love the word goujons?' he had said. 'Sounds so *chubby,* like your upper arms,' as he bent to chomp on them. 'They are not chubby; they are gently rounded.'

'Chubby, chubby,' he insisted, nibbling away.)

'Sign mine on the back for me some time, will you, Bella?' Seline says. 'You've only initialled it on the front.'

Seline has bought a picture. Spent money – and quite a lot of money – on a painting by Bella, a person she actually knew. How could you take someone's work seriously when you'd argued together, fought over chocolate biscuits, borrowed Tampax from each other?

'But they're so expensive – you mustn't – the gallery sets the prices – and their commission is high – I must do you another one.'

Seline tells her to shut up and stop babbling.

'I love it and I have the perfect spot for it, so let me enjoy it.' She smiles. 'And I also suspect that I have made rather a wise investment.'

She spots Nick writing out a cheque and runs over to try to stop him. Fiona threatens to lock her in the kitchen – 'People are supposed to buy them. That's the point of having an exhibition.' Bella corners Viv.

'You're just doing it because you feel sorry for me, aren't you? Confess.'

'You're right. That's the only reason. We're even going to put it over the fireplace – that's how sorry we are for you. Don't be daft, babe. Nick's never polite, you know that.'

'"s true.' Nick gargles briefly with his wine. 'I can't be arsed. We're just cynical collectors, snapping you up while you're still cheap. Well – not that cheap...'

'Shut up and have one of these mushroom thingies.'

* * *

Work the next day flies by for once, with Anthony returning from lunch with a beret which he plonks on her head – 'You are now officially a bona fide *artiste,* and must wear this at all times'. Back home, she sinks back onto the sofa to relive yesterday evening. The doorbell rings.

It's just a Jehovah's Witness, she tells herself, pausing by the mirror to tweak at her hair, bite her lips to make them more pink. Someone collecting for orphaned gnomes. Viv wanting to know how to sift flour.

She opens the door.

'And what exactly is this, Ms Kreuzer?' Gerald is waving the exhibition invite under her nose.

'Oh, hi, Dads. That's an invite.' Her shoulders drop in disappointment. 'They have them for exhibitions. Just passing by, were you?'

'Most amusing. When did all this happen? And any idea why ours should have got to us so late?'

'Can't imagine. Post, eh? Terrible.' She tuts and shakes her head.

Over her father's shoulder, she sees her mother. Alessandra hovers outside in the street, wondering whether it is safe to venture into the bear's den.

'Hi!' Bella's voice sounds artificially high and bright in her own ears.

She clears her throat 'Er, hi. Hello. Mum. Come in, come in.'

'Thank you, dear.' Alessandra steps cautiously into the hall. 'But the invite was postmarked yesterday. Surely the gallery should send them out much earlier?'

'Mmm.' Bella helps her off with her coat. 'Just an oversight, I suppose.'

'We went to see it,' says Alessandra. 'It was marvellous. We loved it.' Yeah. Right. Course you did.

Gerald is off now: it's fantastic – why hadn't she told them? – she must be over the moon – he is over the moon – they should both have been at the private view – would have been, of course – and the pictures – they were extraordinary – unforgettable – why did they bother having those other people's stuff in there, cluttering up the place – only to be interrupted by Alessandra saying she had thought them beautiful – the colours so rich – the textures so real she wanted to touch them – and they had argued over which one to buy because of course they must have at least one, would have bought one even if she hadn't been their daughter – and the young girl there had been ever so sweet and offered them coffee when they'd said who they were and made a fuss of them – and Alessandra had bought one for Gerald's birthday in advance and would Bella be sure to bring it next time she visited – if she thought she might be visiting – if she had time at some point.

Then there is silence. Gerald coughs.

'We don't want to interrupt you if you're busy.' He looks around the room. 'But we were curious to see the house. Didn't think we should wait for a formal invitation – what with the *post* and all.'

'No sweat.' Abashed, Bella crosses her arms in front of herself, then lets them drop to her sides. 'Tea or coffee?'

'Tea, please,' Gerald says just as Alessandra speaks. 'Coffee would be marvellous.'

Alessandra's gaze meets Bella's. 'Tea's fine.'

'Or coffee,' says Gerald.

Bella shifts a small stack of newspapers from a chair and drops them by the side of the sofa.

'I'd have had a scoot round with the duster if I'd known you were coming.'

Alessandra opens the kitchen drawers and cupboards, like any keen cook. It is small, she agrees, but seems well laid out, very easy to work in, was Bella doing much cooking or was she too busy painting? Looking through the French windows, they exclaim over the garden with its architectural plants dramatically lit up, casting shadows onto the walls. Then they rather obviously try to play down their praise, switching their attention to the drama of the sweeping curtains framing the view outside, how light the house was, what fine details, the fireplace, the cornices, much more spacious than they had imagined.

'Can I poke about in the garden?' Her father stands at the French windows, unable to contain himself any longer. Bella unlocks the doors to let him out.

'Can you see all right? Feel free to weed while you're out there.'

They are alone.

'Do have a look too if you'd like.'

'Maybe in a minute.'

'More coffee?'

'Please.' Alessandra follows her through to the kitchen.

'I'm sorry about last time.' Bella forces herself to look up from her mug. 'I didn't mean – I went a bit overboard. Well, a lot overboard. I was, well, things with Will had— but I don't want to make excuses.'

'I didn't know at the time. I am sorry. I'd have tried to be a bit more...' Alessandra shrugs, Italian-style.

Bella clamps down the thought, 'A bit more... like a different person?'

'It's OK,' she says.

Alessandra seems to be especially fidgety, repinning strands of her hair that are already neatly in place.

'Your father says there's something I ought to tell you. I ought to have told you a long time ago.'

'I'm adopted? I'm the last remaining granddaughter of the lost Czar? I was born a boy? Dads isn't my real father; it was the milkman and that explains why I've got curly hair and can whistle so well.'

Alessandra is silent, waiting for her to finish. 'Sorry,' says Bella.

'It doesn't sound so very big now. Seems silly to have hidden it for so long.'

Alessandra asks if she remembers how, when she was a little girl, she was always asking why she didn't have any brothers or sisters.

'In fact, well I... I did get pregnant again. When you were nearly three. But it didn't feel the same.' She shifts in her seat. 'It was six, nearly seven months, but I couldn't feel the baby moving. And with you – well, you were always kicking me.' Her eyes flick over Bella's face. 'You were very mobile.'

They had examined her again.

'And I was right. She – the baby – was dead.' Alessandra starts to fumble in her handbag. 'Here.' Bella tears her off a sheet of kitchen roll.

'So silly after all this time.' Alessandra shakes her head, impatient with herself. 'And. Well. I'm sure they wouldn't do this now. They couldn't. I hope they don't. But then – they induced me. I had to – you see – go through labour knowing she was already dead.' She seems to subside in her chair, deflated.

'That's horrible.' Bella swallows. 'You shouldn't have had to go through that.'

They had named the baby Susanna. 'Did you try to have another one?' Alessandra shakes her head slowly.

'They said there was no reason why not. Your father was so keen. I could see it in his face, even when he forced himself not to say anything.' She blows her nose on the kitchen roll surprisingly loudly and laughs. 'Not very elegant. No. No, I couldn't. I couldn't face it. In case, you know. Not again.'

She clicks open her powder compact and pats at her cheeks. 'So where's that coffee?'

Bella plunges the cafetière and delves into the cupboard for her biscuit stash. Lays out buttery shortbread on a pretty plate. Alessandra nods appreciatively.

'And were *you* all right?' Bella says quietly.

Alessandra seems to drift off for a moment, staring at her shortbread as if it were fascinating, as if hardly aware of Bella's presence.

'Mmm. Physically. I suppose so. I came home afterwards. From the hospital. We went to pick you up from Mrs Mellors next door and – and you stretched your arms up to me. You were so adorable but so, so – *little,* do you see? You looked so small and I... I couldn't bear it. Gerald always told me I wasn't – wasn't the same after that. With you.'

In her mouth, Bella's biscuit feels like a handful of dry crumbs, flour dust churning into cement. Her throat closes. She turns away and presses a piece of kitchen roll to her lips, discreetly emptying the cloying mass into it; pats her lips, sealing them shut.

'So, shall we join Dad in the garden?' Alessandra rises to her feet. At the French windows, she pauses and lays a hand lightly on Bella's arm.

'I'm glad I've told you.'

'So am I.'

'But still – I'd prefer it if you didn't keep bringing it up. I really can't – you know.' Her head on one side, eyes wide like a child's. 'You do see?'

'Sure.' Bella places her hand on top of Alessandra's and smiles. Alessandra steps out into the garden.

'Well now. Isn't this quite splendid? The lighting! *Magnifico!* Gerald darling, you must be green with envy.'

Bella notices Alessandra peering round the room. She seems to be looking for something. Oh-oh, the lamp. Their house-warming present. Any second now and she would say, 'Was there something wrong with the lamp?' with a studied sweep of the room, implying there was something suspect about Bella's taste. Bella starts to think of a reply. It had got knocked off a side-table by someone and smashed. The wiring was a little loose but was being fixed. She was incorporating it into a still life; it was set up in her studio and mustn't be disturbed. Viv had loved it so much, she'd borrowed it for a week so she could talk Nick into getting one exactly the same.

'These are very elegant, aren't they?' Alessandra gestures to the uplighters on the wall.

'If you're wondering where your lamp is, just say so. The fact is it looked like it belonged in a stately home. It didn't fit in, OK?'

She scans their faces, expecting outrage or that wounded look.

'It's fine.' Gerald is smiling, brows raised in amusement. 'I did give you the receipt in case you wanted to change it.'

She uncrosses her arms and lets her hands fall to her sides.

'It just wasn't quite me. I'm sorry.'

'So what did you get instead?' Alessandra casts around as if she might guess.

Bella's face lights up.

'Here. Come and see.' She tows them upstairs.

They stand in her bedroom, the three of them in a semicircle as if assessing a prize thoroughbred.

'I've never had one before.' Bella suddenly feels embarrassed, like a child showing off her favourite doll while wondering if she were too old for such things.

'I should have thought of it,' says Alessandra. 'Why didn't I think of it?

Everyone should have one.'

Gerald steps forward and poses in front of the full-length cheval mirror, holding his lapels.

'I feel quite the gent seeing myself in this.'

Bella and Alessandra stand behind, flanking him. In the mirror, their eyes meet. A cautious half-smile from Alessandra, like a boy asking a girl out for the first time; the smile returned, then both are eclipsed by Gerald, adopting a certain swagger and beaming fit to bust.

Downstairs again, Alessandra spots the old photographs of herself and Bella on the mantelpiece.

'Oh! That reminds me.' She opens her handbag and starts to search for something with her long, elegant fingers. 'They are lovely, aren't they? You look so sweet in them. I'm so glad you have them up. Gerald-dear, we should have them framed. You'll never guess what I found at the back of my dressing-table drawer. I was having a tidy-up. Wait a minute. Here – here it is.'

She hands Bella a small ring box covered in soft blue velvet. Alessandra nods for her to open it.

'The family jewels?' says Bella.

Inside, lying on a bed of pale pink cotton wool, as if it were a precious stone or a valuable ring, is a shell.

She takes it out and gently probes the inside, at the edge before it starts to curl in on itself; it is touched with pink, and very smooth. She turns the shell over and over in her fingers.

'Beautiful,' she says. 'Where's it from?'

'Don't you remember?' Alessandra is half-smiling, half-frowning. 'I thought you might. You gave it to me when you were only small. From the beach. It was on that day.' She picks up the photograph again. 'Yes, I'm sure it was. I'd just been told I was pregnant – before – yes.' Alessandra nods.

And you've kept it all this time?

Her dreams of those early days. *Warm arms around her. The smell of jasmine and face powder and sea. Rubbing noses.* They were memories.

* * *

The sky is the pure, fierce blue of a child's best summer. It is so blue, it almost hurts to look at it. Still, she tips her head back, trying to swallow the whole sky inside her so that she can have this colour always. She closes her eyes tight shut now to check, her legs carrying her erratically crab-fashion along the beach. Inside her eyelids, the blue stays clear and strong.

'Shall I show you how to build a castle?'

Mummy kneels beside her on the hard sand. She scoops sand into the brand new yellow bucket until there is too much, then shows Bella how to slap it down flat with the red metal spade.

'Now.' She turns the bucket upside down with one deft movement like a conjuror, and sounds a fanfare. *Dah-dah.'*

Daddy comes back, holding three ice creams as carefully as if they were Mummy's best crystal glasses. Strawberry sauce trickles down onto one of his hands, chocolate down the other. He hands them over and licks his fingers. Mummy breaks off the bottom of her cone and shows Bella how to make a mini cornet with it, topping it with a tiny portion of ice-cream and dab of sauce. Then she sucks the broken end of her big cone. Bella watches, fascinated, and copies her, dribbling ice-cream down her chin and getting it all around her mouth.

'You look like a clown.' Daddy laughs and Mummy licks a hankie from her bag and wipes Bella's face.

They add three other sand towers to the first to form the corners of a square, then join between them with walls of sand, patted smooth and firm. A ditch is dug all around the castle. Daddy says it will be a moat and that they can make a channel to it from the sea.

They are several feet from the water, but he digs away, making a narrow trench from the water's edge. When it is nearly at the moat, he stops and hands Bella the spade. She cuts through the last barrier of compacted sand and flicks it up and away, scattering it wide.

The sea rushes through the gap, dividing itself in two where it joins the moat, surging round the ring to meet itself again.

'There. Now no-one can get in.' Daddy stands back to assess their work, stroking his chin. Bella nods seriously and fingers her own chin. 'Unless you want them to, of course.'

'That's beautiful, Bella.' Mummy cups the perfect shell in her palm like a little mouse. It is a curly-wurly shell no bigger than Mummy's thumb. It is almost white, weathered by the salt and the sun. At the opening, it is smooth against her finger, and slightly pink as if reflecting her peachy skin.

'Will you use it to decorate your castle?' Mummy offers it back.

'No.' She shakes her head. She looks at Mummy and not at the shell so she won't be tempted to change her mind. She has decided, ''s for you.' Warm arms around her. The smell of jasmine and face powder and sea. Being squeezed, squee-ee-ee-eezed. Rubbing noses, now. The bright gurgle of sudden giggles.

The click of the camera.

33

Five pictures had been sold at the private view ('An auspicious start' and much nodding from Donald MacIntyre), and her parents had bought one the next day, but there is absolutely no reason whatsoever to imagine that she could have sold any more. They weren't exactly cheap, nor were they pretty-pretty, easy-to-live-with vases of flowers ('Yours won't jump off the walls, but they do get under your skin. People will come back to buy once they've seen them,' pronounced Donald). However, the gallery is hardly out of her way at all. Besides, it is near the better fishmonger, so it makes sense. She rephrases it in her head to prevent probable disappointment: she ought to pick up some fish from the good fishmonger and, while she is passing, she might as well poke her head into the gallery.

There are two of her paintings in the window: one small one, the first she had painted, of the woman holding herself, and a larger one, based on her first drawing of Will, which she had finally worked into a painting. It shocks her afresh to see them there, her own work. It is like entering a clothes shop and suddenly coming across a rail with the contents of your own wardrobe. It is slightly embarrassing in a way; she half-expects people to come up to her and say, 'We *know* you now. We've seen inside your head. It's no use trying to hide.' She looks at the Will painting, as if she is seeing it for the first time. The set of his head on his shoulders there, that is really very Will-ish, better than she'd thought. The stone of the wall beside him – she could almost reach out and stroke it; his face, half in shadow; the light falling behind.

'Hey there,' says Fiona, 'come to check the sales tally?'

'No, no. Just passing by.'

'Uh-huh? Don't be embarrassed. If it were my stuff, I'd be phoning in every half-hour to see if I'd sold anything. Coffee?'

Bella does a tour of the exhibition, checking the red spots. There are eight on her pictures. It doesn't seem like a lot, but she knows that it is good, better than she has a right to expect so early on. Still she tells herself that she can't count the ones bought by Viv, Seline and her parents, so it's really more like five. She surreptitiously counts up the spots for the other three exhibitors. It's not a competition, she tells herself, counting anyway. One artist has sold six, another has three red badges of honour, while the last has none. How awful, but it was hardly unusual. She'd have given Viv the money to buy one if that had happened to her.

Fiona is flicking through the sales book.

'Nine. That's pretty good. Very good in fact. You should do well next time when you have your own show.'

Next time.

'Nine? I only made it eight.'

'Did you count the one in the window?'

Had the little one sold? That would be good, the very first one she had painted.

'No, the bigger one. Actually, I was going to call you anyway. I couldn't see a price for it, but I assume it's the same as the others that size. Chap put a deposit on it yesterday morning. It's my favourite, I think. I love the way you can sort of almost see what the man's thinking, but not quite. It makes me go quite shivery.'

The bigger one? Not the one of Will?

'There must be a mistake. That one's not for sale. I told Donald before it went up but he said he wanted it in the window anyway because it would draw people in.'

'Oh-oh. He didn't tell me.'

Fiona reaches into the window space and lifts the painting. 'See, no sticker.'

'Oh, shoot.' She plucks something from the floor and holds out her finger with a small white sticker on it: NFS.

She cannot apologize enough. Is there any chance Bella would reconsider?

It's only a painting, she tells herself. What's the point of clinging onto it? It'll only make me miserable if I have it hanging about the house. But, but -

But it's all I have of him.

'Well, I really...' she starts to say.

Fiona interrupts her. She will try calling the customer, explain the situation. Maybe he'd buy another one instead and they wouldn't lose the sale altogether. She'll see if there's a daytime phone number for him if Bella doesn't mind waiting.

'Hello. Oh, good morning. It's Fiona at MacIntyre Arts here. Is that Mr Henderson?'

Mr Henderson. Oh my God. Will. '...if you still definitely wanted it?' *Will.*

'...bit of a mix-up...'

Will.

'...any chance you might reconsider...'

Bella waves at Fiona and gestures for a pen, scribbles on the top sheet of the memo pad: LET HIM HAVE IT.

'Er, sorry, Mr Henderson. Apparently it is OK. Yes. Completely my fault. So sorry to have taken up your time.' She laughs. How many times had he made Bella laugh on the phone? 'Yes. Sorry again. Yes. Any time after the 18th. Thank you. 'Bye.'

'Phew,' says Fiona, shaking mock sweat from her brow. 'Nice bloke, but didn't sound keen to let go of the painting. Thank you so much for changing your mind. Donald would have done his dour John Knox face at me for the whole of next week otherwise.'

Bella is just leaving when Fiona asks if she has had a look at her comments as well. Comments? What comments? Fiona hands her the visitors' book. There is the date of the private view, where the guests had signed in. Some had added a brief note:

Viv – Stunning! Should be in the National Gallery.
Nick – Buy now while you still can.
Jane – I may not know much about art but these are fabby.
Seline – Haunting and atmospheric.
Anthony – Beats Vermeer into a cocked hat.

Even her parents, her father's minute writing, detailing his proud views, her mother's exquisite script:

Magnifico! A new diva of the art world.

There are a few others, written by people she doesn't know; real actual people had taken one or two minutes out of their own lifetime to write something about her pictures, things she had created. It is an extraordinary feeling, as if she had trailed through all her life like a ghost, her presence registering no more than a wisp of a breeze, then suddenly she is physical, here, incandescent and alive, and everyone has turned to see her. She scans the comments, wanting to note them down so she will remember them but feels too embarrassed; she blinks her eyes closed at each one, as if photographing them, committing them to the vault: 'Unforgettable and exciting', 'Brooding, mysterious', 'Like a dream, a fantasy', two more 'Atmospherics'.

She flicks forward to yesterday's date. Will Henderson. The feel of the page beneath her fingers, the slightest indentations where he had leant his pen to write. Even his signature makes her want to cry. She moves her finger along the line, tracing his words: I *still love you.*

34

Sunday morning. Normally, this would be pottering day, but today, this morning, now, I have something to do. The walk is not far and the sky is bright and clear. The nearer I get, the more nervous I feel, as if I am about to sit an exam or enter onto a stage, and will suddenly blunder out there, blinking in the bright lights and opening my mouth in goldfish O's because I don't know my lines.

There is no answer when I ring the bell, only the sound of my heart thudding in my ears. I should have phoned first, of course, but what could I say? It seems silly to lug the package home again; perhaps I will leave it in the garden under the pergola and call later.

Through the side gate, along the path. I breathe in the swoony scent of a pink viburnum. I don't see him at first, but I hear the clipping of his secateurs and his breath as he tugs at a stubborn weed. He is there, beyond the garden seat, half-hidden by plants in the far border as if he had grown there. Through the slatted back, I see stripes of Will, rectangles of black jeans and that needlecord shirt that I never really liked; now I want him to wear it always – this is how I will see him when I picture him in my head. He is working with his back turned towards me and I watch for a minute as he dips and leans into the plants, pruning with his secateurs, his movements fluid and precise.

I am tempted to creep up on him, to reach out and touch him, scare him with a lover's certainty, but I am not sure how he will respond, so I call out.

'You've missed a bit.'

He starts slightly and stands up, then slowly turns round, twisting in the way I once drew him, as he does in the painting I have in my arms.

He looks at me and he does not speak and I do not speak.

I walk towards him, then, and hold out the package. He smiles as he realizes what it is and he peels back the paper, looks down at his own image standing before the mural in my garden – the crumbling stone arch, a promise of sunlight glimpsed beyond.

'I wanted to call you so many times,' I say. 'Me too.'

'Me three.'

He reaches out to tuck a strand of my hair back from my face.

'So, are you here just as a courier or have you got time for a proper visit?'

I look at my watch and suck in my breath.

'Hmm, always time for a cup of tea... say about fifty years or so?'

'So, is that like a yes then?'

'That is very like a yes then. A YES of skyscraper dimensions.' I reach up and stroke my fingertip across his eyebrow, pausing at his scar. 'Did I mention that I actually "L"-word you quite a huge amount? Will that be a problem at all?'

'I guess I can handle it.' He smiles and takes me in his arms.

I cup his dear, precious face in my hands and stretch up to kiss him. 'Can we start now?'

MORE FROM CLAIRE CALMAN

We hope you enjoyed reading *Love is a Four Letter Word*. If you did, please leave a review.

If you'd like to gift a copy, this book is also available as an ebook, digital audio download and audiobook CD.

Sign up to Claire Calman's mailing list for news, competitions and updates on future books.

http://bit.ly/ClaireCalmanNewsletter

ABOUT THE AUTHOR

Claire Calman is a writer and broadcaster known for her novels that combine wit and pathos, including the bestseller *Love is a Four-Letter Word*. She has appeared on BBC Radio 4's Woman's Hour and Loose Ends.

 twitter.com/clairecalman

 bookbub.com/authors/claire-calman

ALSO BY CLAIRE CALMAN

Growing Up for Beginners

Lessons for a Sunday Father

Cross My Heart and Hope to Die

ABOUT BOLDWOOD BOOKS

Boldwood Books is a fiction publishing company seeking out the best stories from around the world.

Find out more at www.boldwoodbooks.com

Sign up to the Book and Tonic newsletter for news, offers and competitions from Boldwood Books!

http://www.bit.ly/bookandtonic

We'd love to hear from you, follow us on social media:

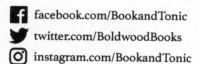

facebook.com/BookandTonic

twitter.com/BoldwoodBooks

instagram.com/BookandTonic